PAY
ME IN
FLESH

PAY ME IN FLESH

K. BENNETT

PINNACLE BOOKS
Kensington Publishing Corp.
www.kensingtonbooks.com

PINNACLE BOOKS are published by

Kensington Publishing Corp.
119 West 40th Street
New York, NY 10018

Copyright © 2011 K. Bennett

All Kensington titles, imprints, and distributed lines are available at special quantity discounts for bulk purchases for sales promotions, premiums, fund-raising, educational, or institutional use. Special book excerpts or customized printings can also be created to fit specific needs. For details, write or phone the office of the Kensington special sales manager: Kensington Publishing Corp., 119 West 40th Street, New York, NY 10018, attn: Special Sales Department; phone 1-800-221-2647.

PINNACLE BOOKS and the Pinnacle logo are Reg. U.S. Pat. & TM Off.

ISBN-13: 978-0-7860-2624-1
ISBN-10: 0-7860-2624-3

First printing: August 2011

10 9 8 7 6 5 4 3 2 1

Printed in the United States of America

PART I

Perhaps there is no life after death . . .
there's just Los Angeles.

—Rick Anderson

CHAPTER 1

"Ms. Caine, I am troubled."

Judge Dixon Darnell leaned back in his chair, put his feet on the desk in his chambers. "I didn't like having to hold you in contempt, but you really left me little choice."

"Would it help if I said sorry?"

"It might."

"Sorry," I said, even though I wasn't. Darnell had refused to let me introduce evidence of a cop's previous altercation with a client just like mine. Then he made me go ahead with the closing arguments. Even though this was a little DUI to him, it was a real case with a real client to me. And I'd talked some junk at the bench about it. Boom. Contempt and three hundred bones.

"I've been watching you closely this whole trial. May I make an observation?"

"You're holding the cards, Judge. Three hundred of them." If I didn't pay the fine, I was going to the clink. "I'm not going to pony up this extortion."

"You seem different," the judge said. "Harder somehow. You appeared in my court, what, a little over a year ago? You were okay then, but now you've got a chip on your shoulder. Have you been going through anything in your personal life?"

Besides being a zombie? Other than being raised from the dead and going on an all-flesh diet? "Not really," I said.

He cleared his throat. Darnell was a big man, in an overfed Teamster sort of way. He was balding on top, his steel wool hair buzzed around the sides. "As you know I am on the committee overseeing the substance abuse section of the Bar."

"There's a lot of substance abuse in a lot of bars."

He didn't smile. "You wouldn't be needing some help in that area, would you?"

"Judge—"

"I mean it, Ms. Caine. I want to help, I do. But you've had your bra in a twist this entire week."

"What did you just say to me?"

"Relax, there's no one who can hear us." He eyed me like an entomologist studying a rare species of Coleoptera. Then he got up and came around to the front of the desk. He parked his ample fundament on the desk edge, his substantial gut at eye-level.

"Would you mind addressing me face to face?" he said.

"What?"

"Stand, please."

I wanted to take a chunk out of him. Wanted to feast on judge breast right then and there, and I was gripping the arms of the chair hard to keep from diving in. Eating a judge in his own chambers would not look good on the old legal record.

I stood, if only to keep my mind off dinner.

Judge Darnell grabbed my shoulders, pulled me to him, and planted his fleshy lips on mine.

I jerked away. "Hey!"

"I can do things for you," he said.

"Judge—"

"If you do things for me."

"I don't work that way."

He pawed at me again. I spun away.

"I can also make life hell," he said.

"Now look, Judge, you don't want to do this."

"Oh, but I do."

"This isn't 1964. What kind of stuff do you think you can pull here?"

"I think you're beautiful," he said. "And dangerous. I'm dangerous, too. Think of what we could do together."

Gack! I did not want to think that, unless it meant him willingly removing his head so I could eat his brain.

"Judge, do you want this story getting out? Because I'm this close."

Darnell sighed deeply. Shook his head. "No one will believe you. I just slapped you with contempt. They'll say you're making this up."

I looked at him and wanted to consume every bit of him above the waist. "You are one sick meal," I said.

"What?"

"*Male.* One sick male."

"Think very carefully about what you say to me."

"Give me a second. Okay. You are one sick male."

"I tried to help you. Just remember that." He punched a button on his desk phone. A moment later the door opened and his courtroom bailiff came in.

"Lockup," Judge Darnell said.

* * *

Practicing law in L.A. is hard. Especially if you're dead.

I was murdered a year ago. The cops don't know who did it. I've been trying to find out ever since.

Then someone brought me back to life. I don't know who that was, either, but I have to find him. Or her. Because if I don't, my soul, wherever it is now, goes to hell. If I'm killed as a zombie, that's what happens, as far as I've been able to determine.

Which is a drag, because now I have to eat flesh to stay alive. Human flesh. Especially brains.

That can be hard on my fellow citizens.

On top of all that I have to make a living.

I defend people accused of crimes.

Like my current client, the pirate musician John "Captain Blarney" Matthews. Who was accused of DUI. And who hadn't paid me yet.

I was busting my hump for him in court, but Darnell was against me all the way. Now I knew why.

Which is how I got jammed in the lockup in the courthouse. Me. In the spot where I usually came to visit my own clients before they came into court.

I was pacing around, fuming, practicing some of my street defense moves, when someone came to the grated window and called my name.

I went to the door and my jaw almost hit the ground. Literally. I put my hand under my chin. Sometimes the old jaw muscles loosen. Undead sinews are not the best in town.

"Aaron! What the—"

"Mallory, this so isn't you," Aaron Argula said.

"Why are you even here?"

"I'm back in town. Working for the DA." Aaron's hair was thick and black, his eyes acetylene blue. I had fallen into those eyes back in law school, in a big way. It didn't hurt that a face to die for sat on top of the broad shoulders of a former defensive back for Cal.

"But I mean what are you doing back here, at the lockup?" I said.

· "I heard out in the hallway the judge held you in contempt," Aaron said. "Still ticking people off, huh?"

When I didn't answer, Aaron said, "What do you say we get out of here and go have a civilized drink?"

"Um, Aaron, you may have noticed I'm incarcerated."

"A perversion of justice soon to be remedied." He turned.

"Hey, where you going?"

"To pay your fine," he said.

"No! I can't have you—"

"It's the least I can do for an old friend," he said, and sped off down the corridor.

Half an hour later we were having martinis at Noé, the bar at the Omni Hotel on Olive Street. I like the classic—Beefeater up with two olives. I can barely taste it on my undead tongue, but it does penetrate the suspended animation of my brain.

It also keeps the Voice at bay on lonely nights. But more of the Voice later.

Aaron's a vodka man. We sat outside, a stone's throw from the orange-and-black control house of Angels Flight.

Aaron slipped a cigar out of the inner pocket of his coat. "You mind?"

"Be my guest," I said. "When did you pick up that habit?"

"Up north, searching for my inner Churchill." He unwrapped the cigar and snipped the end with a little cutter. I had to admire his technique. He lit the cigar with a lighter that shot out its stream of flame. "I can't get over how you look," he said. "You seem, I don't know, healthier somehow."

I almost snorted an olive out my nose. "And so," I said, cutting to the chase, "why'd you dump me?"

That stopped his easy charm. I took a leisurely sip of my martini and let him squirm. Making people squirm on the witness stand is one of the things I do best. I like to practice it in the outside world, too.

Aaron Argula was two years older than my thirty-five years. He was a third year and I was a One-L when we met at USC Law. He was editor-in-chief of the *Law Review*. The year before he'd won the school's Moot Court competition. That's where the entire second year class engages in a mock Supreme Court case, in teams of two. The final round is two teams arguing before three sitting justices—two from California, and one from a federal bench.

The year Aaron won it the federal jurist happened to be Antonin Scalia of the United States Supreme Court.

That was before I got to SC, but they were still talking about it when I did. They said Scalia ripped into Aaron and Aaron ripped right back.

Oh, how I wish I could have been there.

Tall Aaron, with his chiseled features, against the Sicilian-blooded, squat Scalia.

Two sharp minds grinding it out.

Scalia was so impressed he offered Aaron a clerkship after school, which he turned down to work in L.A.

Aaron set his sights on me one day at the law school's cookout just before the Notre Dame game at the Coliseum.

I was toast. Crushed like the Fighting Irish were later in the day. Over burgers and beer, Aaron Argula slipped my heart out of my chest and quietly put it in his back pocket.

When he traded that heart in for another, I was devastated. Almost died when he moved to San Francisco, to join a big firm there. I'd had no serious boyfriend since.

Finally Aaron said, "There's no easy answer. I was a little confused."

"Not too confused for that little tootsie at Scadden, Arps," I said.

"Did you just say *tootsie*?"

"I'm sorry. I meant bimbo."

"Mallory, she was not a bimbo or a tootsie. She also wasn't you."

I was disturbed by my reaction to that. I realized I still wanted him. That ticked me off. It was as if he'd never left.

But he had, and now there was one thing different, and it was bound to put a crimp in our relationship— I wanted to eat him.

Aaron said, "I want to be friends again, maybe see you sometime. Maybe dinner."

"That's not a good idea."

"Why not?"

"It just isn't."

"Give me one reason why."

"Okay. I'm on a special diet. I have to eat at home."

He blinked a couple of times. "You're kidding, right?"

"No."

"You mean you don't go out to eat?"

"Well, sometimes, but I have to pick my spots, and anyway, why would I go out with you again, Aaron? After what you did?"

He sighed. "Can you at least let me explain?"

"No."

"Why not?"

"Because I'm not interested. We had our time, that's over. There's no reason we can't be civil to each other, though."

"Mallory, I must have been nuts."

He gave me a look and I started to feel it, a vibration of desire. But then another one began to well up. One that made me wonder what his lips would taste like if I chewed them off.

"Yes," I said, "you must have been. And now that you're back, I wish you well. Thanks for getting me out of the clink."

I stood.

"Is that it?" he said.

"That's it." It had to be. I had to get away before I made a fool of myself one way or another.

"Mallory, please. Don't go yet."

"I have to," I said. "I just do."

"Can I call you?"

I didn't answer. I walked across the plaza pathway, past Angels Flight and headed down the concrete stairs to Hill Street. I had to get back to my office. I had to think. I was still in trial, still under a contempt citation, still on the bad side of a sexually harassing judge. I couldn't think about Aaron Argula. Not yet anyway.

I knew what it would mean if I did start thinking about him. Complications. They happen a lot more often when you're a zombie.

Because sometimes those you kill can make life really thorny for you. I was about to find that out.

CHAPTER 2

My office is on Broadway, between Third and Fourth, on the second floor of a retrofitted two-story that dates back to World War II. It's just above a tobacco and novelties shop. The tobacco is cheap and the novelties are mostly for laughs.

There's no name on the store, so I just call it the Smoke 'n Joke.

Just inside the doors is a building directory with two names on it—mine and Nikolas Papadoukis, the world's shortest insurance investigator. A glass door with a buzzer alarm system that doesn't work gets you into the hallway where you can take an elevator (with an eighty-five percent success rate) or the stairs to the second floor.

The manager of the building also runs the Smoke 'n Joke. Her name is Lolita Maria Sofia Consuelo Hidalgo. I call her LoGo. She's about seventy years old and was once the hottest singer on this strip of L.A., back in the 1960s when the Million Dollar Theater, half a block away, was the happening Latino venue. She did two shows a night at the Dollar, and opened for Tito Puente in 1968.

LoGo caught me going in.

"Rent," she said, sitting on her stool by the whoopee cushion display.

"Spent," I said.

"Not so funny. You owe two months." LoGo has let herself go. She's three hundred pounds if she's an ounce. If you look real hard you can see, encased in adipose tissue, the torchy vixen from Mexico City who once set hearts aflame downtown.

"Lo, I'm finishing up a case and am bound to get paid."

"I hope. I like you, but the boss, you know, he like to get paid."

"Don't we all."

I took the stairs, unlocked my office door. I went to the window. My view looks out over this distinctly Latino corridor, with its cut-rate retail spots, Mexican food stands, and shadows of history. A hundred years ago this was a place to see and be seen in L.A. Swanks from Bunker Hill and Angeleno Heights would dress up and ride down here—in horse and carriage or that new gas-powered thing—for a high-class night on the town.

Now it's pretty much the low end of commerce in the city, but the price is right for leasing office space.

If I look left out my window I can see the Bradbury Building, the classiest structure left from the golden age of downtown. Its redbrick exterior, officially unveiled in 1893, still looks classic, if you can ignore the Subway sandwich sign stuck on the front.

Continue up Broadway and you pass the *L.A. Times* building, sure to be a dinosaur someday soon, and you eventually get to the Foltz criminal courts building. It was named for the first licensed female attorney in California.

I sometimes wonder if they'll name a building after me someday, the first zombie criminal lawyer in the city. Maybe it'll be a mausoleum.

The phone on my desk rang. I picked up. "Mallory Caine."

"Miss Caine, I need a lawyer right away." An older woman's voice.

"Who am I talking to?"

"My name is Etta Johnson."

"All right," I said. "What's the trouble?"

"It's my granddaughter. I found this number in her book. It says here, in her handwriting, if she ever gets into trouble, this is the number to call."

"What is your granddaughter's name?"

"Traci Ann Johnson."

I lost breath. I knew Traci Ann Johnson from the street. "What happened?"

"The police are here," the woman said. "They say they're going to arrest my Traci Ann."

"What for?"

In a whisper, the woman said, "Murder."

"They haven't arrested her yet?"

"They don't know what to do. I said they can't do anything until I talk to a lawyer. They're just standing around looking at each other right now."

"Let me talk to Traci Ann."

"That just it. She can't come to the phone. That's why I need you to come over here."

"Is she all right?"

Pause. "That all depends on what you mean by all right."

"Well, has she been injured?" I asked.

"Not exactly. I wish you could come down here so I can explain it."

"Suppose you tell me where Traci Ann is." I was

getting a little annoyed by this runaround. I wanted to help Traci Ann, of course, but I didn't want to go driving around L.A. without knowing what I was heading into.

"All right," the woman said. Dropping her voice to barely audible, she added, "She's in her coffin."

There was a tap on my door and Nikolas Papadoukis stuck his head in. He's a shade under four feet tall, has a hook nose, eyebrows like white sand dunes, and knobby hands.

Which would seem to make undercover work pretty exacting.

"Mallory, I must needs your help," Nick said.

I waved him in. I got the address from Etta Johnson and hung up the phone.

"Nick, I have to—"

"Can you lend me twenty until payday?"

"You work for yourself, Nick. You don't have a payday."

"Then until a week Friday?"

I fished in my purse for a twenty. My last. "You need more business, my friend," I said.

He took the twenty from me. "I don't know what to do about that! I am good, but I am not good looking. I am cursed."

"People have overcome worse," I said.

"I only want what's coming to me." He walked to the window and looked out at the city. "There's something going on out there, and I want in."

"What do you mean, something going on?"

"Haven't you noticed? Things are improving. After all these years, we got a mayor and city council doing the right things."

"Yeah? Like what?" I was skeptical about Mayor Brite-Smile. We've had those before.

"Traffic, for one thing. Have you noticed how much better traffic is down here now?"

"You're joking." I usually walk to my office. My loft is only a couple of blocks away. Saves gas and parking.

"Just look around you sometime," he said. "You can feel it."

He seemed to tremble just then, still looking out.

"What's wrong?" I said.

"I don't know. I got scared just then."

"What of, the good traffic?"

He shook his head. "I am a barometer."

"Barometer?"

"I feel things deeply."

"Dandy," I said. "Is it going to rain?"

"This is not a joke," he said, turning back to me. "Hire me."

"Nick—"

"You are a lawyer! You defend the criminals! I can find things out. I am a barometer."

I tried not to laugh. That wouldn't have done his self-esteem much good. "Nick, what experience do you have in criminal investigations?"

"Like I said—"

"You're a barometer—"

"Yes! And I can sneak around. I am a good sneak. To be short, it helps. You could try me? And pay me?"

"I have to go now, Nick."

"You will think at least about it?"

"Sure."

"You are a lovely woman," he said, and bowed.

Etta Johnson lived in a little home south of Wilshire Boulevard, off Western. It was one of those small houses built in the 1920s that stand now by the grace of God and a tenth coat of paint.

I parked my convertible Volkswagen Bug—screaming yellow in color, and I call her Geraldine—at the curb and walked up to the green-and-white clapboard home. Inside were a couple of uniformed officers and a plainclothes detective. I knew him. Richards. He was about my height, six feet, and built like a municipal sprinkler box. Behind him was a younger man, wearing the same slacks, white dress shirt, blue tie, and shield on the belt. Twinsies, only the younger one was in shape.

"Well, there she is," Richards said, giving me a curt nod.

"Nice to see you, Detective," I said.

"Sure. I know how it is."

"And how is it?"

"It's the eternal dance, the forces of good against the forces of defense lawyers."

One of the uniforms guffawed.

Richards said, "This is my partner, Detective Strobert."

Strobert nodded at me. He had a full head of brown hair. His eyes looked green from where I was. I don't trust green eyes.

Etta Johnson came slowly into the living room. She used a walker, which clanked with each labored step. She had bright silver hair done up in curls and wore a housedress the color of summer wheat.

"Don't let them take her," she said. "Don't let them take Traci Ann!"

Richards grimaced. "We got ourselves a situation," he said.

"I just love it when you talk dirty," I said.

"Come with me," Richards said.

"I'm gonna be right behind," Etta said.

Richards rolled his eyes and led me down a small hallway, past a kitchen that smelled like egg salad, to the bedroom at the end.

The room had a dresser with no mirror, and a coffin. And that was it.

"There's your client," Richards said.

So I was supposed to believe that Traci Ann Johnson, a hooker, was inside? I knew Tracie Ann because we worked the streets together, down on Santa Monica.

Oh, yeah, that's what I do to procure. I have an alter ego, Amanda. Streetwalker. More later.

Traci Ann was young, eighteen maybe. She loved to go vampire, dressing in black. Could it have been more than an act?

Who was I to doubt it?

Etta clanked in. "Don't let them take Traci Ann! She'll die!"

"I'm gonna haul this thing downtown, is what I'm gonna do," Richards said. "Find out exactly what's going on here."

"Mind if I have a look?" I asked.

"Be my guest," Richards said.

"This is my house!" Etta said. "I give the permissions! You go ahead and look, Miss Caine."

The casket was cherry red wood, but dull of sheen. It was a one door, not a two door—if that's the right term. I lifted the top and there she was, Traci Ann, eyes closed, hands crossed over her chest.

Her naked chest.

I looked for signs of breathing.

Nothing.

I closed the casket. "Okay. When did this happen?"

"About a year ago," Etta said.

"This crazy woman says her granddaughter's a vampire," Richards said.

"Don't you dare call me crazy in my own house—"

"And I don't know what all the legal ramifications are here, but she insisted you be here and you are. So what now, counselor?"

"Well, Detective, it seems to me you have no authority over this body," I said.

"Like hell," Richards said.

"Watch your language, young man," Etta said.

"That's right," I said. "You're not at the station."

"Spout your case," Richards said.

"You are empowered by the City of Los Angeles to take persons suspected of criminal activity into custody, if and when you have probable cause."

"That's right," Richards said.

"*Persons* being the key phrase. Ms. Johnson, as you can see, is not a person, but a corpse."

Richards scowled. "That's what I'm gonna find out. We're gonna take this thing to the morgue and have the coroner look at it. Vampire my . . . Dockers. I want this body officially declared dead."

"Then you are not placing a person under arrest," I said. "You are attempting to take a corpse into custody."

"So?"

"So what you are proposing is illegal. Because now you're gathering evidence. This casket, with a body inside it, is an item of personal property, under the ownership and control of Mrs. Etta Johnson."

"That's right!" Etta said.

"Thus requiring a warrant," I said. "And I am going to love seeing what you put in your affidavit, and the look on the judge's face when you present it."

For a long moment Richards glared at me. "I'm gonna take the thing anyway," he said, "and sort it all out later."

"You try it, and I'll raise the biggest stink since Rodney King," I said. "The *Times* is going to love it. Tomb Raiding Detective. Aggrieved Grandmother Sues City for Ten Million. Then I'll go down to IA and file a formal complaint, with Mrs. Johnson as a witness. You won't get to hide behind the good faith exception, because you've been advised, by me, that you are breaking the law."

Half of this was bluster, but the other half was sounding pretty darn good. I amaze myself sometimes.

Richards stepped up to my face. "You're wrong if you think you can play me," he said.

"It's your move," I said.

He kept his eyes on mine. I thought for a second he saw something that made him nervous. Or even scared.

"I will be back with a warrant," Richards said. "If the body is not here, I will get an arrest warrant for *you*, for obstruction."

He turned quickly and walked out of the room. I heard him ordering the uniforms and Strobert to leave with him.

When the front door slammed, Etta looked at me and said, "Thank you, Miss Caine."

I said, "I want the whole story. All of it."

"I don't know, Miss Caine. I don't know what happened to my granddaughter. I don't know how. I just know she is what she is."

"Who is she supposed to have murdered?"

"Oh, it was a terrible thing. Maybe you heard about it. A police detective."

I lost breath. "You mean the one a couple nights ago? Where a car was set on fire?"

"Yes! That's the one. They say Traci Ann did it."

But Traci Ann didn't do it.

I did.

CHAPTER 3

It happened this way.

After a day in court, I'd gone back to my loft and slept till about eleven-thirty. That's when I changed into Amanda.

After midnight is when I generally eat.

When I was alive, truly alive, I never would have thought of eating anybody. Not even if I was in the Donner party and hankering for fried chicken.

I did not even like cannibal jokes. You know, where two cannibals are eating a clown, and one says, "Hey, does this taste funny to you?"

Yet now I must eat flesh, especially brain. I must eat brain as surely as I must draw breath. And I hate myself for it.

But in my condition, appetite trumps self-hatred.

So I become Amanda, in purple wig and fishnet stockings. The corner of Santa Monica and Lodi, in Hollywood, is my home base. Lodi's a little street, lined with tall, skinny palms. It stops cold at the boulevard, its rear end pointed at Ralph's Used Appliances. Fitting, because that's what the girls are, isn't it?

A block away is the Hollywood Forever Cemetery.

Also fitting. They got Douglas Fairbanks and Tyrone Power there. Also Valentino and Fay Wray. And Florence Lawrence, who was the first silent screen movie star.

I know this stuff because I read their brochure once, on a slow night.

There's quite a contingent down here after midnight. The trannies prefer the next block west, El Centro, sort of keeping things separate. Like a different section in a cafeteria. If a man is looking for transgendered, he doesn't want to be over with the heteros, and so on.

Dear God, I'm always thinking, what would my Sunday School teachers think of me now?

This night, after I arrived, I heard a voice call my name and knew it was the new girl, Traci Ann. She came out of the streetlamp shadows near the digital film lab. She'd started working the corner a week earlier and usually dressed in tight, bright colors. Tonight, though, she was all in black clothes and makeup.

"What is up?" I said.

"You like my new look?" Traci Ann said.

"You're going bloodsucker?"

"The jacks are into it. They want me to bite." She playfully bared her teeth. I had to admit, in this light, they looked sharp.

"You think that's wise? I mean, who knows what you get doing that."

Traci Ann bobbed her eyebrows at me. "What if it's true?"

"What if what's true?"

"I'm a vampire."

"Right," I said.

"No, really."

"No such thing. You might as well believe in zombies."

"Who says I don't?" Traci Ann asked.

"You be careful now," I said.

"Do I look scared?"

"No."

"'Cause I'm not."

"And that worries me."

"Why do you care so much?" she asked.

"You think I want vampires in my town?" I said.

Traci Ann laughed. "Oops, here they come."

The first car that stopped was a Prius. I leaned in the passenger side window and said, "Nice night."

The guy was a few years older than me. Clean, professional look.

"Yeah," he said. His voice shook like a 4.5 aftershock. He gripped and ungripped the steering wheel.

A first timer. Good. Your experienced johns carry around a superiority complex. You're just meat to them. If you make an out-of-the-ordinary move, like requesting a little drive, you might get an argument.

New guys will drive you just about anywhere you say. I liked the fact he drove a Prius. Prius drivers are a little more intelligent than average. Makes for good brain food.

"So," I said, "where you goin'?"

He looked like he didn't understand the question.

"Goin' out?" I said.

"I . . . think so."

"Okay then." I opened the door and slipped in.

He trembled like a bird on a live wire.

"You all right, honey?" I said.

"I, um, isn't there, um, some transaction?" His hands were still choking the wheel.

"All depends on what you have in mind," I said. "First thing, what school did you go to?"

"Excuse me?"

It's the question I always ask. I want a quality brain. The nutrients last longer, the cholesterol is less harmful. They even taste better, so long as there isn't a lot of drug use or alcoholism involved.

I should do commercials. *For the discriminating zombie, think Harvard or Yale. . . .*

"Where did you go to school?" I said.

"Like college?"

"Yeah."

"Why do you want to—"

"Just tell me."

"Purdue."

"Graduate school?"

"Also Purdue. I have a Masters in English."

My mouth was starting to water.

"You look like a guy I can trust," I said. "I know where we can go to talk about it."

"Go?"

"Drive. We don't want the prying eyes of the law on us now, do we?"

That spooked him. He almost got rear-ended pulling into the street.

"Easy there, slugger," I said. "The night is young."

"I gotta say, I'm new at this."

He chortled. I can take a laugh, a giggle, even a snort. But chortling gets on my nerves.

"Sure, sure. What's your name?"

"You want to know my name?"

We were passing Vine and the night was alive with light—a blue on white Mobile sign, with the red O. A big orange Yoshinoya. A Coors Light billboard with snow-capped mountains.

"Well, why not?" I said. "I'm Amanda."

"Oh." He paused a long time, watching the car ahead of us. "Peter."

"Nice to know you, Pete. Take the next left."

He almost missed it. I guided him to a darkened parking lot off Cole Avenue and had him stop near the cinderblock wall. I've begun transactions here many times. This is the kill zone.

I reached in my purse for Emily, my ice-pick-with-a-hook, when I heard a sniffle.

The guy had his head on the steering wheel.

This was perfect for me. Emily to the back of neck and into the brain. No problem.

But for some reason I heard myself say, "How many kids?" That freaked me out. What was I doing?

He sniffled. Without moving his head he said, "Two."

"What kind?"

"Boy and a girl."

"Under five, I'm guessing."

He gave a facsimile of a nod.

I was hungry. No, *starving*. Feeling weak. And weak is the word for what I did next.

"Go home to your wife and kids," I said. "And don't ever come back."

He pulled his head up and looked at me. "But—"

I took out the ice pick. "Did you hear me?"

His eyes went saucer wide. "Yeah, yeah, please don't . . ."

I got out of the car and pounded my heels back toward the street.

What a lousy zombie I was! I have to eat human flesh. It's survive or go to hell.

Does hell exist, you ask? What if there's only a ten percent chance that it does?

I am not taking even those odds. According to *The Book of the Walking Dead,* translated from the French, this is what is at stake for me.

Plus, I just don't like the idea that somebody did this to me without getting back at him. Or her.

So I am on a search for who has control of my soul. I have to get it back, but until I do I have to eat.

So what am I doing getting feelings of mercy for prime meat in a Prius?

Before I got back to my corner, a muscle car pulled up. A Dodge Charger, fire engine red.

The music system was blasting gangsta.

I leaned in.

He had a blond pompadour, like he was trying out for a 1950s teen movie. Only he was in his forties from the look of him. The effect was a lonely divorced guy in costume hoping to score at a Halloween party.

Only problem, it was July.

"Hi, honey," I said. "What's your sign?"

He smiled. White teeth and dark eyes. "My sign is Benjamin Franklin."

"That's a good sign," I said.

"Hop in," he said. "We'll go running with the shadows of the night."

Pat Benatar now? At least I liked Benatar.

"Where'd you go to school?" I said.

"What?"

"Schooling. How far'd you go?"

"You serious?"

"Humor me."

"Stanford, class of ninety-one."

"Let's ride."

We rode. He tried to put on rap again. I stayed his hand. "Let's listen to the wind," I said.

He smiled again. He was a smiler, this one.

"Take your next left," I said. We were two blocks from where I'd left the crier, but I knew another spot.

"How 'bout we ride some more?" he said.

"No thanks."

"There's another Benjamin in it for you. Two Bens for half an hour."

"Where to?"

"We'll head up to the hills. We'll look at the lights, the stars. Then we'll close our little deal."

"Half an hour?"

He nodded.

"Cool, daddy," I said. Half an hour was about all I could last. I wasn't thrilled about leaving my haunts. But up in the hills would work. There were lots of places to kill up there, and less traffic than on the busier streets below.

At least he drove fast. We tore down Santa Monica, running yellow lights, and took Cahuenga to the freeway.

"Where we going?" I said.

"My dime," he said. "I've got a spot."

"You mean I'm not your first?"

"Funny."

He got off at Barham. Then we headed up into the hills, on the narrow roads above Universal Studios. I hadn't been here in a while.

"So how'd you get into this line of work?" Smiler said.

"Let's not," I said.

"I want to know. Another fifty if you talk."

"You're pretty loose with the money."

"Curious about human nature."

Boy, was he in for a surprise. "You a writer or an actor?" I said.

"How'd you know?" Smiler said.

"If you guess writer or actor in this town, you're going to be right nine times out of ten."

He laughed. "You got that right, pretty lady. But it seems a little untoward to call me just an actor."

"You just said *untoward.*"

"Yeah? So?"

"Maybe you really did go to Stanford," I said.

"I said I did."

"Just checking."

"You sound pretty smart yourself. What are you doing walking the streets?"

"We can all use a little extra money."

He turned up one of those little winding streets off Laurel Canyon. "You've done this before," I said.

"That a problem?"

"Not for me."

"Let me tell you why I do this," Smiler said. "You look like a nice lady, so maybe you need to know. I'm a cop."

"I thought you said you were an actor."

"Writer, actually. You know, all cops and lawyers in L.A. want to write screenplays."

"Sure."

"And what I like to do," he said, "is talk to the girls. Get to know them so I can write about them. Pay for their time. I'm trying to figure out what it is inside that makes them do what they do. What *you* do. Because I know it's not just for the money. You have to have something inside you that is dark and unsettled."

"You do talk like a Stanford man."

He laughed again. We were going up the backbone

of the hills on a long stretch of road without street-lights. It was a clear night and I could see Hollywood sparkling below.

I wished then I had someone to share this with, someone I wasn't going to eat. I wondered if I'd ever be able to share a moment like this with anybody again. The answer was obvious. Not in this lifetime, which might never end.

The cop pulled over to the side and killed the engine. The sound of crickets fill the void. A cool breeze blew through the open windows. The smell of sage was delicate on the wind, soft as a promise.

"You know what I like about you?" he said.

"My sunny personality?"

"Fact that you're thoughtful. That's really going to make it hard for me to kill you."

I didn't flinch. I sort of half expected this. You do this often enough, you're bound to pick up a sex killer. It's part of the risk. Except it holds no fear for me. "And you know what I like about you?" I said. "The fact that you're a thoughtful guy. Only I am not going to feel much of anything, one way or the other, about killing *you*."

His smile went the way of the dodo, replaced by a wolfman look. The one he intended to scare me with. His hand went into his rear pocket and came out with a switchblade knife. He flicked it open in front of my face.

"You're gonna to do exactly what I tell you," he said. "And if you do, I might just let you go."

"You don't have any intention of letting me go, which is a bit of a coincidence, because I don't have any intention of letting you go, either."

His nostrils flared, like tulips opening up. "You see what I have in my hand? Do you know that I am going to shove this in your neck, you don't do what I say?"

"Get serious. You're not going to bloody up the car. If you're a cop, you've heard of DNA."

He snorted. "Car's hot," he said. "I'm gonna do you, then burn it, with you in it."

"You've thought this through. I think you've done this before."

"Shut up! Take your clothes off. Now!"

"Why would I do that if you're going to kill me?"

"I can kill you slow, and I will."

"Listen, blondie, you can't kill me at all. Say, what's your hat size?"

Now he got cockeyed. He put the blade point on my neck. "I'm dead serious."

"You're half right," I said.

"Look in my eyes! You *know* what I can do."

"You look in *my* eyes and tell me why your hand is shaking."

Then he started with the names, the standard epithets sex killers have for their female vics. I yawned. And that's what pushed him over.

He plunged the knife into my throat.

I yawned again.

For a moment he looked perplexed, like a napper suddenly awakened from a dream.

Then he screamed. He started fumbling around. He left the knife sticking out of my throat. He tried to turn and open his door. I removed the knife and jammed it into his side. He screamed again.

Emily and I went to work. I gave the sharp end a push up into his nose and through the cartilage. His eyes bulged. In one second he was paralyzed.

Another shove and it was lights out for him.

But my work was just beginning.

It's not easy to get at a brain. There's a myth floating around that zombies somehow get superhuman jaws and teeth, and can bite through a skull.

Yeah, right.

I get at the brain the way the ancient Egyptians did, by clever use of Emily through the nasal cavity.

Once you get the right traction on a brain you can get most of it. It's a little like fibrous Jell-O, so you have to have the right touch, which I've developed.

Necessity is the mother of deadly skill sets. You don't get quite all of the brain this way (you'd need a cranial saw and good scooping spoon for that), but it's quite enough, thank you.

When I finished I checked the trunk. Sure enough, he had a full gas can there. It didn't take me but two minutes to douse him and the car and set it on fire.

It was dark in the hills, the wind was a whisper. The lights of the city were flickering with life, as if hope were alive.

But it wasn't for me. And it sure wasn't for the cop I ate.

CHAPTER 4

But now Traci Ann, apparently another form of walking dead, was being accused of the very crime I committed.

Which raised a whole lot of troubling questions. Slight conflict of interest maybe? Ya think?

But most important, why Traci Ann? What evidence was there that she had been the one? None, there couldn't be. But I was the only one who knew it.

I told Etta I had to talk to Traci Ann as soon as she came around.

"She only comes out at night," Etta said. She trembled slightly, and I thought for a moment she might faint.

"Can you hang in there for a little while?" I said.

"I think so."

"I'll come back before twilight. I want to be here if the cops come back."

I made sure Etta lay down to rest, then I hopped in my bug and drove.

It's one way to think in L.A. We drive. We are a city of cars, though sometimes those cars don't move. But I find now that getting behind the wheel, with the wind blowing my hair, gives me a sense that I'm alive, even though I'm dead.

I decided to do double duty. As I thought, I pointed the car toward Glendale. Seeing Etta's distress over her daughter reminded me I hadn't seen my own mother in a week. She's a worrier. She thinks I'm not getting enough to eat.

I've not sought to set that record straight anytime soon.

As I headed toward the 101 freeway, passing over Sunset Boulevard, I kept trying to put together a picture of why Traci Ann would be a suspect in the cop killing. I'd gotten the first news feed earlier that morning. It was all over the place. The cop's name was Tom Hennigan. He was indeed a detective, specializing in undercover work.

But the news clips said nothing about his being a sex killer. That little item they missed. Or else someone was hiding the information.

Was Traci Ann being implicated a matter of misidentification by an eyewitness? Maybe somebody saw me getting in the Charger and mistook me for Traci Ann.

But that was unlikely because we looked so different. She wasn't nearly as tall as I was.

Could it be she was being set up by someone?

That didn't make sense, either. Traci Ann was a streetwalker who lived with her mother. There was no reason—at least none that sprang to mind—for anyone to go to such lengths for a frame. She could easily have been picked up and killed in quiet.

Then another thought hit me. Hennigan himself. Maybe he was supposed to pick up Traci Ann and kill her. Maybe he was working for someone. Or maybe he had a connection with her already, and that's why she was a suspect.

Only he picked me up instead. Could he have made a mistake?

These questions couldn't begin to be answered until I got a chance to talk to Traci Ann. Then at least—

Come to me!

I almost lost control of the wheel. It was the Voice.

I could never tell when it was going to hit, and it seemed to love to pick out times when I needed to think. It strikes deep inside my brain. It varies in strength. And I have to fight it back or it gets stronger.

For some reason, it was strong now.

Come to me!

"Get bent!" I said out loud.

I'd started hearing the Voice the moment I was re-upped. And I know enough about real zombie-ism to know that this is the whole *raison d'être*. It's so someone can control the zombie, bend them to their will.

The Voice tried to do that to me from the start, but I fought it. I continue to fight it. And when I find out where it's coming from, I'm going to seriously kick whoever it is right back.

Come! Come!

My head was starting to ache. The Voice sounded angry.

Come!

"No!"

Come, Miss—

"I will not!"

—Uganda.

Uganda? What the—

Come—

"That's it! You're getting the treatment."

No!

"Yes!"

I started humming the theme to *Hawaii Five-O.*
Loudly Nothing gets rid of bad thoughts (or songs
you can't stop thinking about) faster than the *Hawaii
Five-O* theme.

"Bop-bop-bop-bop bah-bahhhh, bop-bop-bop-bop
bahhhh—"

Stop!

"Bop-bop-bop-bop ba-BAHHH, bop-bop-bop-bop
BAHHH . . ."

No response.

"Bop-buh dawdle lawdle lawdle ee-dah . . ."

Nothing. But I kept on humming out loud for a
few miles just in case.

No rest for the wicked, as they say.

No rest indeed, because the next thing that hit me
was a flock of birds. Black birds to be exact. The kind
Stephen King or Alfred Hitchcock would use.

They came out of the sun and swarmed down
around my bug. Not dive bombing me, but making
their presence known.

Just as I got to the Glendale Freeway, my arms
started jerking the wheel. They cut me into the slow
lane. I almost took a motorcyclist out.

This was new. Voice, birds, and a battle for my ex-
tremities.

Now I was mad. I reached into the pit of my head
and screamed at my brain to make my arms obey me.

It felt like I was arm wrestling with an invisible Stal-
lone.

A big black bird, the biggest I've ever seen, cruised
right alongside my bug. I was doing about sixty. How
could a bird go that fast? I gave it a quick glance and
saw it was looking right at me, with big, albino eyes.

Eyes. Eyes like I hadn't seen since the time I was a girl in the trailer park—

WOOONKKK!

A big old Pepsi truck almost clipped me. Or me it, because my arms were wanting to take me to the left.

I fought back. My arms did what they were told. My foot relaxed.

The birds disappeared. They didn't fly away. They literally disappeared.

Breathing fast, I felt myself back in control.

The Voice. The birds. The eyes. My own body.

It was all as obvious as a B actress at the Emmys. Someone, or some*thing*, was issuing me a warning. *We're watching you, and we are in control.*

My head and heart pounded all the way to Glendale.

My mother is Calista Caine. I can best describe her as an ex-hippie who had me rather late in life, leaving what I would describe as a double generation gap. It's like I'm her granddaughter, even though she's only thirty-five years older than me.

I can't relate to her stories of Haight-Ashbury and the Merry Pranksters and the Summer of Love. At least she wasn't at Woodstock. Thank God she wasn't, or I'd have another set of nostalgic stories to sit through.

My memories of life as a girl are all lemon swirls and thick gray smoke, my mother being into the color yellow and the plant marijuana. For most of my childhood I saw that her greatest pleasure in life came not from her daughter bringing home an A from school. Or when I learned to ride a bike for myself—thanks to a neighboring father, not her. No, For Calista Caine in those formative days she was into getting leisurely baked and watching re-runs of *The Andy Griffith Show.*

That was one reason Mom shuttled me off to the local Sunday School when I was eight. It gave her half a Sunday off so she could toss hippie lettuce. It gave me a chance to play with toy arks and start asking questions about a character with whom I've developed a very strained relationship, the Lord God Jehovah.

But in those early, hopeful days I would put on biblical epics for my mother, to show her what I'd learned and to get her to pay attention to me. One Sunday night as she reclined on our beat-up sofa, eyes glazed with half lit euphoria, I regaled her with the taking down of the walls of Jericho. Complete with songs. Yes, I was a nascent Andrew Lloyd Webber, a regular little Hammerstein.

"And they marched, marched, marched!" I sang as I high-stepped around in a circle. I kept checking Mom to see if she was listening. Sometimes her eyes would be open, sometimes closed. I thought she fell asleep once, so I sang louder, "And blew their trumpets loud! Oh, yes! They blew their trumpets loud!"

"Not now, honey," she said.

"Watch out! Watch out! The walls are tumbling down!" I myself fell down in an attempt to symbolize the destruction of the ancient city. As I did, I hit a chair that fell on our dismal little coffee table, which jostled the bong that rested there, which spilled cannabis water on the floor, which caused my mother to scream and, in a very unmellow fashion, grab me by the hair and toss me outside our trailer.

After which she locked the door.

An hour or so later she opened it and I was still crying and she tried to tell me everything was all right. But she smelled like sweet smoke and I knew she wasn't right in the head. I didn't want to have a mom like that, but that was the parental card I was dealt. My father, a biker named Harry Clovis, had hit the road shortly after my birth and died a most unglorious death in Mexico. I eventually realized how much that desertion had messed up my mother, and grew a little more charitable toward her as the years went on.

But only a little.

She now runs a bead shop in Glendale, just off Colorado Street in the eastern part of town. I try to stop in unannounced, to catch her doing that thing she does.

Which she was doing.

"Mom, are you getting wasted again?"

She looked up at me from behind the counter. Her long white hair was held in place by a paisley bandana. She was a symphony of beads and tie-dye and Mary Jane.

"Mallory!" Smoke billowed from her nose. She tried to hide the pipe.

"I see it, Mother." Plus, her eyes were as red as sunrise over Santa Monica.

"I have a medical condition!" Mom said.

"Chronic for the chronic?"

"Well, yes."

"Uh-huh. What is it this month?"

"Honey, that's not fair."

"I don't want you to overcook your brain, Mom."

"Why don't you try some? You won't be so uptight."

Yes, Mother still says *uptight* and sometimes *groovy*. It's best to change the subject.

"How's business?" I asked.

She shrugged. "It is what it is."

"That's very Baba Ram Dass of you, but how is your bottom line? You almost missed your rent last month."

Mom said, "I get by. What about you?"

"I'm fine."

"Don't try to fool your old mother." She stood up quickly and I realized anew that she still refused to wear a bra. The pronounced jiggle and sway that might have been all the rage at an LSD soaked love-in in 1969 was now a couple of polar bears trying to get out of a tent.

She came around from behind the counter and gave me one of her patented we-are-the-world hugs. God love her, she's still a true believer in the oneness of all creation. She has no idea her daughter is undead. That would, as they once said, blow her mind.

"Now let me tell you," Mom said, "that you can have more clients if you'll only use more visualization."

"Mom—"

"How do you think I pay my own rent? I see it coming in, and every time, there's a new or old customer walking through that door."

"Mom—"

She stepped away from me. "You're not eating enough."

"Look—"

"Are you eating enough?"

"Of course."

"Are you sure?"

"I'm sure, Mom."

"Groovy. What brings you out here?" She turned to the counter and started arranging boxes of beads.

"I need a reason to look in on you?"

"You don't need to look in on me, I've told you before." The small box of beads she was fiddling with slipped from her hand and fell to the floor, scattering plastic everywhere.

"Uh-huh," I said.

"Bummer," Mom said.

"Let me get the broom," I said.

"No. I can do it."

"Mom, will you let me help you? Will you let me help you get healthy again?" What a laugh this was, a zombie trying to preach health. But it is what it is.

"I don't need any help."

"Mom, it's no sin to admit you need help."

"I don't believe in sin!"

"I know. You believe in heavy and beautiful, but—"

"Is there anything else? I have to clean up."

"Don't push me away, Mom. You've always . . ."

She stiffened. "You can go now."

"Why, Mom?" Uh-oh. This was about to become one of those soap opera moments. But I was still feeling fragile from the freeway attack, and maybe I just needed her then. Needed a mother I could talk to.

Mom turned her back on me, started toward the back.

"Don't walk away!" I said. "Not this time."

"I don't want to talk about it."

"What's *it?*"

She said nothing.

"Mom, what is—"

"Go away!"

No. Not this time.

My phone went off, jarring me like an electric shock. A call from the court clerk. The jury was ready with its verdict in the Captain Blarney DUI case.

Whatever *it* was, it would have to wait. Again.

I got to the courthouse a little after three. At three-thirty we were all gathered in Darnell's courtroom. Me, my pirate client, and the prosecutor, Norm

Gunsenheiser. As the jury was marched in I figured out they'd probably only been deliberating a little over an hour, considering they had an hour and a half for lunch.

This was not a good sign. The way Darnell had tied my hands, there was no way this quick verdict was going to be anything but guilty.

It was.

Darnell thanked and dismissed the jury. Then he took great glee in doling out a big, fat fine and fees. It didn't matter that I told Captain Blarney this could happen if we went to trial. He wanted to go, and I wanted to try the case. I thought I had a winner with officer prejudice and a questionable blood alcohol test.

But Darnell had seen to it that I couldn't introduce key evidence. So my client got hammered. He's have to play a lot of pirate songs to pay the fine. And me.

Not that I was entirely broken up about this. Blarney was turning out to be a real pain in my tush.

I informed him that there was still an appeal avenue. The judge's not letting in relevant evidence was a big issue. Captain Blarney swore at me in his pirate brogue. The last thing he said to me was, "You're not getting one dime from me."

"Now that's not good business sense, pirate guy," I said.

He swore at me again and walked out of the courtroom. That left Gunsenheiser and me and the bailiff and the clerk. Oh, and Darnell, of course.

"Off the record," Darnell said, "you completely blew that case, Ms. Caine. Don't say anything. I would not want to see you held in contempt again. Once is enough. I have a feeling, Ms. Caine, this isn't the last time I'm going to have trouble with you. Let me just say I hope, for your sake, for the sake of your further legal career, that you will change your attitude toward the court. I do hope I'm making myself clear."

"Oh, yes, Your Honor," I said. "I think you and I have a perfect understanding of each other."

CHAPTER 5

I was back at Etta's place just as the sun was about to set on another day in L.A.

I love the look of burnt orange sky, the silhouettes of palm trees against dying light. It's sad and it's beautiful, the way life is. It's poetry and death. It's a picture of what you want things to be and the way things are.

Sometimes I don't know what to do with it. To laugh or cry. Or some of both.

To call out to a God I can't hear, or keep quiet with an emptiness I can't escape.

Etta was waiting for me inside. She had a plate of Oreos out for me. I forced one down to please her. I didn't tell her that I wanted a different kind of filling between those cookies. I even sipped some milk. Couldn't taste it, but at least it wasn't coming out my nose.

We chatted for a bit, Etta telling me a little about her life. The husband who ran out on her and how she tried to raise a daughter alone. How that daughter went off and had a child, Traci Ann, with a drug dealer father. How that same daughter had died of an overdose a year later. How she'd had thoughts of Traci Ann going to law school someday.

Things didn't quite turn-out the way she'd planned. No one expects to see their granddaughter turn into a vampire.

Finally the sun was down and we heard a creaking from Traci Ann's room.

We went in.

Tracie Ann sat up in the coffin. Etta tenderly put a blanket around her.

"You're the lawyer Amanda knows?" Traci Ann said.

"Yes," I said.

"She said you could understand these things."

"Well, I don't. Not yet. You're a vampire?"

"Do you believe it?"

"You're sleeping in a coffin. But I have to tell you, I've never met a vampire."

"Neither have I," she said. "Except for him, of course."

"Who?"

"The one who made me what I am."

"Okay, Traci Ann, I want you to tell me from the beginning about this whole vampire business. When did it happen to you? How did it happen? Don't leave anything out. I am now your lawyer, and if there is one unbreakable rule about being accused of a crime it's this: never lie to your lawyer. Are you clear about that?"

"Uh-huh."

"Okay then. Talk to me."

"It was about a year ago. Yeah, almost a year ago to this very day."

I sat back. That was about the same time I became a zombie. "Go on."

"I was hooking over on Sixth Street when a big

black car pulls up. I don't even know what kind it was except it was big and fancy and rich. We get some of those kind. Even movie stars sometimes. Anyway, I go to the window and this guy with thick black hair slicked back, and white teeth and looking very, very hot offers me three bills for ten minutes. Now that is a good return on investment, I say to myself. So I get in and off we go. As we're driving, he peels off the bills and hands them to me. We go around the corner and park. The windows are tinted. He leans over and before I can do anything else he sinks his teeth into my neck."

"Just like that?"

"Just like that."

"What happened next?"

"I don't know. I blacked out I guess. When I woke up I knew I was different."

"How so?"

"Well, for one thing, my teeth. I never had good teeth. Now I have great teeth, you know?"

"Go on."

"And then it was like I was under some sort of spell. It's like I would hear a voice in my head, and have to do what it said."

My zombie blood ran cold. She had a Voice, too.

"What sorts of things did this voice tell you to do?" I asked.

"It would tell me to try turning myself into a coyote. Like it was training me or something. Or a bat. Or a fog."

"A fog?"

"Yeah. I never really got the hang of the fog."

"Did you ever figure out where this voice was coming from?"

"Kind of."

"What do you mean *kind of*?"

Her eyes opened a little wider. "Why are you shouting?"

"Was I shouting?"

"Yes."

I knew I was. I tried to dial it down. But knowing that she was hearing a voice, too, was kind of important. As in, maybe this would tell me who turned me into a zombie. Maybe there was someone overseeing this whole thing, vampires and zombies, in an attempt to do . . . what?

"All right, Traci Ann," I said. "I just want to get to the bottom of things. When you say you kind of figured out where the voice was coming from, what did you mean?"

"I mean I tried to follow it once, when I was a coyote. I kept walking around listening to it get louder and softer, and when I figured out the direction where it was getting louder, I kept going. I was up in the Hollywood hills, looking down over the boulevard. And my nose kept going toward the moon, and the voice was louder, and the moon was right over it."

"Right over what?"

"The hotel. The Roosevelt Hotel."

The Roosevelt was right on Hollywood Boulevard, just west of Highland. A storied place. They say Marilyn Monroe and Montgomery Clift still haunt the place.

There was a knock at the front door. Etta went to answer it. I heard her open the door, and then heard Richards's voice say, "Mrs. Johnson, I have a warrant to seize the casket in your house. May we enter please?"

"No!" Etta said.

"I'm sorry," Richards said.

Etta started yelling.

"Stand in the corner," I told Traci Ann. "Cover yourself with the blanket." I closed her door and went to the living room.

Richards was there with two uniformed officers. His partner, Strobert, was behind the uniforms, quietly observing everything with those green eyes of his.

"Good evening," I said.

Richards handed me the warrant. "This should do it," he said.

I looked it over.

"Don't let them," Etta said.

"I'm sorry, Etta," I said. "This is a valid warrant. They can take the casket."

"But—"

"It's better this way," I said. "It's best to cooperate with these fine gentlemen."

"You touch my heart," Richards said. "Take me to it now."

"Follow me, boys," I said.

I went back to Traci Ann's room, the law behind me like ducklings. I opened the door and saw Traci Ann in the far corner, just as I'd told her.

The casket was open in the middle of the room.

"Take it away," I said.

Richards looked at me. "What is this?"

"It's a coffin," I said. "Or a casket. I forget the difference. But this one is suitable for—"

"You know what I mean," Richards said. He looked at Traci Ann. "Traci Ann Johnson?"

Traci Ann said nothing.

"I'm placing you under arrest," Richards said.

"Hold it," I said. "You don't have an arrest warrant.

You have a warrant for one coffin, and that's all you're going to take out of here."

"I warned you not to play me, Ms. Caine."

"The law is not a game, Detective. You came in with a search warrant. You obtained your entrance that way. A home is given the highest form of protection. You cannot—"

"If I may." Detective Strobert stepped into the bedroom.

"Go ahead," Richards said.

Strobert looked at me. "Ms. Caine, I'm sure you're aware of the plain view doctrine which states that police may seize evidence of a crime if they are lawfully in a viewing area?"

"I see where you're going with this," I said. "You're calling my client evidence."

"The doctrine applies to people as well," Strobert said.

"How do you know this?"

"I like to read."

"Is he right, Ms. Caine?" Richards asked.

He was, and I had to admit it. "Well played," I said to Strobert.

"The law is not a game," Strobert said.

I wanted to eat his brain.

"All right," Richards said. "Miss Johnson, we're going to have to place you under arrest now."

"No," Traci Ann said, shuddering in the corner.

"Let me talk to her," I said.

"I won't go, Ms. Caine. They'll kill me!"

"Traci Ann," I said, walking toward her. "I know they're LAPD, but they're not going to kill you."

"You don't know," she said.

"I know enough."

"I can't let them. They'll put me in the sun."

A little problem that had to be addressed, I realized.

"Did you hear that?" I said to Richards.

"This has gone on long enough," Richards said. "No more games, no more pretending to be a vampire. We're arresting her and putting her in—"

He stopped talking. His mouth dropped open.

I looked back at Traci Ann.

She was melting.

Or what looked like melting. Down, down she went toward the floor, the blanket draping her ebbing form, her—body?—pooling, until the blanket covered whatever was there entirely.

No one spoke.

Then, a form under the blanket, rising.

A snout stuck out from the covering.

And charged at Richards.

Snarling.

A coyote.

"*Ahhhh!*" Richards cried and jumped out of the way.

Traci Ann, the coyote version, charged out her bedroom door and past the fright-faced uniforms, who obviously had no idea what to do.

Etta shouted, "Traci Ann!"

I chased after her. In the living room I saw the front door still open.

And coyote Traci Ann was out into the night.

Richards came up behind me. His face was flushed. He was sweating. "What. Just. Happened?"

"You saw it," I said.

"No. I didn't. There is something going on here and you know what it is and you better tell me. I warned you."

"My client turned into a coyote," I said. "You spooked her."

He shook his head. "No. No. No. You can't tell me that."

His partner, Strobert, looked equally perplexed.

"What can I say?" I said. "We all saw the same thing."

Richards's face was returning to his normal state of aggravation with me. "We're going to find out what we just saw." He turned to the uniforms. "Cuff her," he said.

All I ever wanted to do was practice law.

The first time it hit me was watching *Law & Order* when I was around sixteen or so. I loved Claire Kincaid. She had smarts and confidence and looked good, all the things I wanted to be. My mom was living on government aid then, and I didn't want to follow in that line of dependence. I wanted to make money. I wanted to be successful. I also wanted to kick butt in court.

Like Kincaid, I thought that I'd be a prosecutor. Have the law behind me to get the bad guys. But then I was in the high school library one afternoon and found a book about great trials. With pictures and everything. Names from the past that sounded funny, like Sacco and Vanzetti and Bruno Richard Hauptman and Leopold and Loeb.

And then the Scottsboro Boys. A group of black teens accused of raping two white women in the deep South in 1931. Talk about having the deck stacked. I read about the New York lawyer, Sam Lebowitz, and the torturous road of trials and appeals and Supreme Court decisions that said *any* defendant, no matter what color (or, I would recently add, what supernatural state) was entitled to the assistance of counsel.

That, it seemed to me, was what the law should be about. You can have your big corporations and pharmaceutical companies, your divorces and your personal injuries. Where it's at is when the government comes after you for committing a crime.

I knew enough even when I was young to know that most people who got arrested probably did it. But if they didn't get a fair trial, if the government just rolled over them, then someday somebody who didn't do it would get rolled over, sent away, maybe even to Death Row. It happened. We know it happened. With the onset of DNA analysis, many innocent people have been freed, sometimes after decades in prison for a crime they didn't commit.

And they got set free because some lawyer took the case.

You don't often get a completely innocent client in this line of work, but this time I had one. Traci Ann Johnson was innocent. I was the one who had committed the crime.

I bet that never happened to Perry Mason.

I also bet he never had a client turn into a coyote and get himself hauled into jail by a ticked-off cop.

They brought me in through the back of Hollywood Station and cuffed me to a metal rod running along on a wooden bench. A place they normally put public drunks or prostitutes, awaiting booking.

I gave the blue suiters an earful all the way in, to no avail.

As soon as I was planted I smelled wine breath strong enough to sit on. On the other end of the bench was a skinny black man, old and weathered, smiling at me. "Best do what they tell you," he said.

"You got anything to drink?" I said.

He laughed and shook his head and started telling me what they had done with his collection of fine wines. Some of it even made sense.

A few minutes later, Richards came into the holding area and uncuffed me. He ordered me to follow him. I wanted to kick his teeth in. But I was in enough trouble as it was, apparently.

He sat me down in an interview room, closed the door. His face was the same color as the white acoustic tiles lining the walls.

"This is between you and me," he said.

"I'm not in a very you-and-me mood."

"What just happened? What did I just see?"

"What do you think you saw?"

"I want to know exactly what's going on."

"You're the detective. That's your job. My job is to defend my client and keep her alive."

"How did she . . . I can't even believe I'm mouthing these words."

"You want to know how she turned into a coyote, is that it?"

"Yeah, tell me."

"What's in it for me? Or rather, my client?"

"I'm not in a position to make any deals."

"And you've got nothing to hold me on. If you try it, I'm going to be very upset."

Richards started breathing rapidly.

"You okay?" I said.

"Having a little trouble here." He put his head in his hands.

One thing defense lawyers should never feel is

sympathy for a cop. We need all that pent-up animosity in court. But I couldn't help feeling a little sorry for this guy. There he was, longtime protector of his community, and what he just saw was something that could drive a weak man insane.

"My client really and truly is a vampire," I said. "Does that clear things up any?"

"Please, don't do this to me."

"I'm telling you. That's what she is."

"You're telling me your client is one of those things that bites people in the neck? Turns into a bat?"

"Or a coyote. It's called shape-shifting."

"Good grief, what is happening in this city?"

"Why do you say that?" I asked.

"Weird, weird stuff. Some of the homicides, things I've never experienced before. Ms. Caine, can you tell me why you're representing Traci Ann Johnson?"

"Her mother called me."

"Why you?"

"Why not me?"

"There's no other reason?" he asked. "You don't have some sort of insight on what's happening around here?"

I folded my arms. "Maybe," I said.

"What do you mean, maybe?"

"I think the phrase I'm supposed to use at this point is, 'What's it worth to you?'"

He scowled big time. His forehead wrinkles could've held loose change. "It might be worth something. I don't know what yet."

"You know about me?"

"You're a lawyer with an attitude, that's all."

"You know I was shot?"

He shook his head.

"That's right. Over a year ago. Somebody shot me up and I almost died. Did die, in fact, according to the ME. I was pronounced dead at the scene, but I had a little change of plans."

"You almost died?"

"They were zipping up the body bag when I opened my eyes and heard one of the medics yelp like a stuck dog. They got me to the hospital and I was good as new. Except for the holes in my body, of course."

"Who did it?"

"That's just it. There was never an arrest. The case was handled by a guy named Bracamonte."

Richards stiffened. He waited for me to continue.

"I got the feeling Bracamonte wasn't exactly interested in doing his job."

Richards studied me through slitted eyes. His experience must have won out, because he knew exactly what I was thinking. "You saying you think Detective Bracamonte was covering for somebody?"

"I didn't say it, you did."

"Bud Bracamonte was a stand-up guy. Always . . ."

"Always what?" I said.

Richards shook his head as if he didn't want to say anything more.

"What happened to him?" I said.

"What good does it do now?" Richards said. "What good does it do his family?"

"What do you mean?"

"He disappeared six months ago."

"What?"

"That's right."

"Why didn't anybody tell me?"

"Why should anybody tell you?"

I threw up my hands in disgust. "All right, here's what I want from you," I said. "Trading of information. I want to know why my murder—attempted murder—stalled. And I want to know about any leads that weren't followed up. I think Bracamonte buried it. I want to know why."

"You're asking a lot," Richards said. "What do I get out of it?'

"Like I said, shared information."

"This is not exactly legal."

"But it's right," I said. "Now let me go."

CHAPTER 6

I was in Hollywood and I was hungry.

Which is normally a wealth of possibilities, as they say.

But I would have to pick my spot. I walked up Wilcox all the way to Hollywood Boulevard. I needed to work off steam, too. If I wasn't careful I could get caught. I didn't have Emily with me, having kept that little item in Amanda's purse in my loft. So I'd have to improvise. I might not be able to eat brain, so other parts would have to do.

The club scene would be starting up, though it wasn't the weekend peak. Still, there'd be pub crawlers and hipsters, Valley-ites and South Bay-ers, college kids and live-at-home slackers, B-list actors, and rappers in waiting, and just about everything in between.

The music scene would be cranking . . . and I remembered it was Tuesday and my friend Sal would be playing at a club called Créme. Salvatore Estanzio is an eighteen-year-old zombie. He's been on his own since he was eleven, living on the streets. He was re-upped when he was fourteen and I met him one night as Amanda, when we tried to eat each other.

We had a good laugh about that.

Now he's formed a band, Skeen. He describes his music as a collision of alt-punk riffs, juiced trash-blues scraps, percussive schoolyard chants, and forebodingly sentimental antigentrification electro-funk.

I like it.

I headed for Créme. It was half a block north of the boulevard, on Cahuenga. A little hard to find, but they like it that way. You have to go around the side. The doorman there knows me. I asked him if Skeen was on tonight, he said, "Yes," and let me in.

Another band was pounding it out inside. There's a small stage on the right and a long, dark bar on the left. Which is where I saw Sal. He was alone, head bowed over a drink.

I slipped next to him. When he saw me, he didn't give me a friendly greeting. His face was etched with fright.

"Sal, what is it?"

"They're after us," he said. Sal and I have had this conversation before. He's sure that we're doomed, that we're all going to be dead—*stay down dead*, as we call it—before the year is out.

"Sal, just take it easy."

"I can't find Carl."

Carl Gilquist, a zombie plumber who lived on Western.

"What happened?" I asked.

"I don't know! He was supposed to meet me here last night. I've tried to get hold of him, and can't. I'm scared."

"Easy, Sal."

"What should do I do?"

"Stick with your crew, right? Stay with 'em. You playing later?"

"Yeah."

"Stay in the music. Stay with people."

"I don't know . . ."

"You can. I'll see what I can find out. But I've got to eat."

He grabbed my arms. "Mallory, you have to be so careful."

"I know, Sal. I have to find a place around here where I can get in and get out."

He nodded. Sal knew all the best spots around here. "There's a place outside the back of Chest." That was another club, a block or so away. I knew it. Oh, yes, I knew it well. It's where John "Captain Blarney" Matthews played pirate.

Could it just be my lucky night?

"Sal, you take it easy and play," I said.

"Are you going?"

"Don't worry."

"Mallory?"

"Yeah?"

"Don't let anything happen to you. I can't lose you."

There was a small outdoor crowd around the entrance to Chest. I almost walked away right then. What I was contemplating was pretty reckless. But the zombie mind is not always completely rational, especially when one has to eat. In myth, the zombies who eat human flesh and brains are that way because of some virus or apocalyptic event. The truth is much more subtle. Created from the outside through dark magic, it is a side effect of being dead and raised. Only flesh can keep us animated, and it is an instinct that is steel hard and cold.

Instinct drives you past your careful thoughts.

I did remember my sunglasses, and a scarf I had in my purse. It would look a little odd, but do for enough of a disguise that I could make out with it. I also had some nail scissors that would serve me as Emily lite. If I could get a little of his brain matter, it would make this risky plan worth it.

Now to get him out to the back, to the nook Sal told me about. It was where a Dumpster was, and two small retaining walls. A perfect place for what I had to do, if only the one I needed to do it to joined me there.

What was it Captain Blarney couldn't resist? In my initial client interview, he'd tried to come on to me. I quickly disabused him of that notion. But pirates are always into deflowering a wench, and he was no exception. He didn't have a wife or girlfriend, and made no secret of his party habits. A good bit of it blarney, I supposed, but still.

In my purse I had a ten spot on me, and a pen and some scratch paper. I scrawled a note: *Blarney, I want to meet you. Need to meet you. Please. Out back. I love pirates!*

I folded the note a couple of times, then put the ten around it. I walked around to the back door, looking at faces. They were a little hard to read with the shades on, but I'm still a pretty good judge. I finally spotted one I thought would do. He had Westside whitebread written all over him. He was leaning against a wall, smoking. Alone.

"Captain Blarney playing tonight?" I asked.

He gave me a curious look. I did look a little odd. But hey, this was Hollywood.

"Yeah," he said. "He's on right now."

"Really? Oh, man, oh, wow. I really need to talk to him. Could you give him a note for me?"

"I guess so."

"There's a ten in it for you." I held it out to him.

"Cool! I've never been bribed before."

"Technically it's not a bribe. You okay with that anyway?"

"Should I tell him your name?"

"Just give him the note. I'll be waiting."

"Man, I should be in a band."

"I'm sure you do fine on your own. UCLA student?"

"How'd you know?"

"Thanks for delivering the note."

I walked a few yards away to wait. I could see the lit up Capitol Records building peeking through the sky like a giant periscope, watching.

It was twenty minutes later when Blarney finally came out of Chest and looked around. I waited. He saw me, came walking up, showing teeth. I started walking toward the nook.

He said, "Hey!"

I motioned for him to follow.

"Where you going?" he said

"Privacy," I said, using my Amanda, New Jersey, voice.

I kept going, turned the small corner.

"Forget this," he said, stopping where he was.

I pulled my skirt up to my left cheek. "Then forget *this*," I said.

He laughed. And before you could say Jack Sparrow, I faced him in the nook.

"What's your game?" he said.

"No name, sweets," I said. "We have some business to talk about."

"Business?"

I took off the scarf and sunglasses.

He took off his faux charm grin. "You?"

"Your ever-loving attorney."

He gave me an up and down, as if he was seeing me for the first time.

"You stink as a lawyer, but you're pretty hot."

"You're a charmer, you are. You also owe me money."

"For freakin' what?"

"I represented you in court. That doesn't come free."

"You got my license suspended. I got fined!"

"You broke the law, you lost your case."

"*You* lost my case."

"Call it a team effort then. But you still owe me money."

"Dream on."

"Don't make this hard," I said.

"I'm not paying you a dime."

I sighed. "Then you can pay me in flesh."

He blinked a couple of times. His little pirate mind was no doubt trying to figure this whole situation out. Finally, he smiled. "If you want some flesh, I'll give it to you. Because I know you want it."

"Oh, I do, believe me."

He approached me, evil intent in his pirate eyes. He was in character. He was Blackbeard on a pillaging tour of Jamaica. He was full of rum and ready to rumble. I backed up a step, pretending to be a lady in distress. At the same time, I reached behind me and took hold of the nail scissors.

"I'm gonna enjoy this," he said.

I almost felt sorry for him then. Here he was about to meet his doom and the last thing on earth he'd utter was a line of insipid dialogue.

I was back against a wall now. Blarney got within an inch of my face. He licked his lips. I could smell rum and tobacco on his breath. He was slightly larger than I remembered him. He put his hand on my shoulder, softly, but ready to clamp down if I showed any resistance.

When I didn't, he smiled, showed teeth, showed a certain pirate satisfaction at my apparent submission.

I put my left hand on *his* shoulder. "Be gentle," I whispered.

That brought a low, thrusting grunt from the middle of his throat. I could almost feel his pulse pounding in him like angry waves slapping the hull of a ship.

His hand moved down to the collar of my blouse.

Before he tore it, I reached behind his head and grabbed a healthy handful of pirate ponytail.

I yanked his head back. His eyes got as large as doubloons. I think he knew it then, knew that the wench had turned the tables. Knew in his dark pirate heart that the jig was up.

It's times like this, the kill moment, that jerk me around inside. I have to overcome it, I have to, because I must eat, I must stay the living dead, I must until I can find the owner of my soul and get it back.

Even if I wanted to, I could not stop. It's an inner compulsion, a lust.

The scissors worked just fine.

The first entrance through the nose jams the brain, precisely in the area that immediately cripples the victim. I believe, too, there is mercy here, in that the pain is only momentary. Then there is blackout. Then there is death.

Then there is me, pulling out the stuff of my life, the meal of my sustaining.

I was eating there, stuffing my mouth, when the Voice said, *Come!*

It was strong this time, almost knocking me over.

"No!" I said aloud, my words muffled by a mouthful of medulla.

Come! The Voice was clearer now than it had ever been. It was starting to sound like someone really talking, rather than thin whispers in the far reaches of my mind. It sounded like a male voice, but I knew it could also have been a·throaty female voice, too, like that girl in *The Exorcist.*

Or maybe it was a sexless demon of some sort.

"Who are you?" I said.

Silence.

"Who are you?"

Nothing.

"You're pretty chatty when you're not being challenged," I said.

You will know. Come!

"I will not come. I will know now!"

Behind.

"What? Behind what?"

Nothing. But just to be on the safe side, I looked behind me.

It was in shadows, but silhouetted by the dim streetlights behind.

It was large.

And it was holding a sword.

CHAPTER 7

One does not walk around L.A. with a sword unless one intends to use it.

This is called logic.

The big man with the sword took a step toward me. He wore a large hoodie, so I couldn't see his face. I was in the nook, between two buildings. The lifeless body of the pirate troubadour lay behind me. There was nothing to grab to try to protect myself.

A foul stench of a breeze came out of someplace and hit me in the face. Whether it was from him, the dead Blarney, or one of our finer restaurants, I did not know. But it made me think of death.

He swished the sword through the air. It made a sound like a bat wing flapping past your ear.

"The dead must stay dead," the figure said. His voice was low and full of broken glass. Like he'd had his own throat cut once, injuring his larynx.

I put on my New Jersey tough voice. "Look, buddy, you're making a big mistake."

His answer was to swish the sword again.

So I did what any gutsy broad would do in a similar situation. I screamed for help.

We were still in public. And I wasn't afraid for someone to come around. Yes, there was a dead body nearby, but this was Hollywood. Mainly, I hoped to scare the guy off. Of course, he could decide to slice any witnesses, but sometimes you have to take chances. Especially if your own soul is in imminent danger of going straight to hell.

My scream didn't stop him. Instead he flew at me, raising the sword as he did.

I kicked off one of my shoes. If I had to choose, it was going to be bare feet to get me out of here. The shoe went straight at the guy's head and found a sweet spot. He stopped and growled.

One shoe left. And then I'd be without a weapon.

Weapon.

Captain Blarney. Dead Blarney was himself wearing a cutlass. Part of his costume. I hoped it wasn't made out of cardboard.

I kicked the other shoe at the dark figure. This time it got him in the gut. I didn't hesitate. I bent over Blarney and made a grab for the cutlass.

All I got was flesh. A handful of dead pirate booty.

I made another grab, then another, and finally found the handle. I gave it a good pull and the cutlass came out.

Just as my attacker swooped his sword at my neck.

I put my new weapon up, more out of instinct than anything else. In my street fighting class I'd learned the bony forearm move to block a punch. This was the same thing, only with a sword.

The only question was whether it was a real sword, or a toy. It felt heavy enough. When steel clanged and the cutlass vibrated in my hand, I knew I had at least a chance.

If I could take it.

I whipped my own slash at his legs.

The cutlass made purchase on the guy's shin. He screamed like a banshee. I've never heard a banshee, but I imagine the guy wasn't far off.

I didn't sense a deep cut, which told me I wasn't holding a sharp blade. But the guy was temporarily out of commission. He started rubbing his leg.

But he still had me against the nook.

Trapped.

I backed up out of sword range. I didn't want him making me baloney with a quick swipe.

What was I, as a lawyer, able to do?

Talk, of course.

"Look, man, I don't know who you are, but you're slicing up the wrong tree."

"Creature from hell," he said.

"I'm just a working girl," I said.

"Murderess!"

Oh, yeah, Captain Blarney.

"Heart attack," I said. "We need to get him to a doctor."

"Spawn of Satan!" And up went his sword again.

I've had better negotiations.

Trying to think, I put my sword in front of my body, facing upward. I figured it gave me the best chance to keep from losing my head. I wondered what would happen if he got me in the heart or took off one of my legs. I wouldn't bleed to death, but I sure would be hopping around.

As he moved toward me, I took one more step backward. That was all I had.

As he swiped his sword in the air, as if to show me my fate, I listened to the rush of traffic on the street. Where was everybody? Why wasn't anybody out here to see this?

And then, without really planning it, I thought, *Please don't let me die. I'm not ready. I don't want to go to hell.*

At that moment a little dust swirl kicked up between the swordsman and me. I saw a paper bag twirling around. It moved toward the guy and made him stop.

Then, just as quickly, the swirl died down.

And with it went my last hope of getting out unscathed. I would have to fight, like some kind of ninja.

I took a stance I thought a good ninja would take.

A split second later, something fast and flying came out of the darkness above and shot down into my attacker's face.

Which made him scream again. He waved his sword blindly at the flying thing.

An owl?

I didn't stay to find out. I ran.

He swung the sword at my head. I heard the blade whistle past my ear.

There is a myth that zombies are always slow and uncoordinated. Thanks very much, George Romero.

No, we can run if we have to. Even in heels. Especially when a guy with a sword is coming after us.

My salvation, if you want to call it that, would be getting out to the boulevard where people were. Surely the nut wouldn't try anything in public.

Or would he?

And who was he, anyway? The hunter who got Carl?

How did he track me? How did he know where I'd be? How did he know I was who I am?

All that was playing in my mind as I took the wrong turn.

I was heading right through a parking lot with no visible way out on the other side.

A young couple was just emerging from a Lexus in the parking lot.

"LAPD!" I said. "I need your car!"

The guy, looking like some South Bay arm candy, laughed. The girl shook her head.

"I know, that never works," I said. "But watch out for the guy with the sword."

South Bay looked behind him and screamed. The girl screamed.

The guy with the sword screamed.

I was the only one with the decency not to make a girlie noise.

Anyway, it left South Bay momentarily defenseless. He had his keys in his hand. I snatched them.

"Hey!" he cried.

I jumped in the Lexus, closed the door, locked them all.

As a smashing sound radiated through me.

I looked in the mirror. The sword had come down on the trunk. The swordsman, his face obscured by the hoodie, raised it again.

I heard South Bay cry, "Stop!"

Hoodie turned around and South Bay took off running, his girlfriend right behind.

I started the Lexus.

Smash.

The rear window stippled with cracks.

I burned rubber in reverse, turning the wheel sharp left. The bumper hit Hoodie. He went down.

I gunned the Lexus toward the street.

In the mirror, I saw Hoodie rolling on the ground. Hurt.

That told me, at least, he wasn't superhuman. He was a guy with a sword and a way to find me.

I turned right out of the lot and shot toward Hollywood Boulevard. I needed to ditch the car, quick.

And I needed something more, I realized then. I needed to have it out with someone. I couldn't go on like this much longer.

I left the car on Selma, a quiet street between Hollywood and Sunset. It was dark and no one on the sidewalk. I put my scarf and shades back on and walked fast for a few blocks. I came to the little church I'd been to once before, for a wedding. I remembered they advertised being open 24/7.

The front door was open.

I don't know much about Catholics, but they do good churches. This one had alcoves with plaster saints and candles, some burning, others waiting to burn. I raced to the very first alcove and knelt.

"God, why did You do it this way? I want my soul back! You know where it is. You know who took it from me and where it went, and You know I can't die without it or I'm doomed. You say You love us, so why does this happen? Where is my soul? I want it back. I want it inside me. I want to be a person again. I can't take this anymore. Did I do something horrible when I was a girl? Did I think bad thoughts too many times? Have You judged me already? Why did You let me become the living dead? Where are You, God? Why won't You answer my prayers? Can the undead pray? Where is my soul? I want it back!"

A shadow fell over me. I whipped around. My heart, such as it was, pogo sticked into my throat.

"Did I startle you?" a mountainous figure said.

"Who are you?" I said.

"I'm Father Pat," he said. "And hell is not part of this place."

"A priest?"

"That's right." He stepped a little closer. The light from the candles hit his face. It was mostly hair. He had a full beard, dark and bushy. He could have been one of those mountain men who lives with bears in American mythology.

"You are the biggest priest I've ever seen," I said, standing up and leaning on the balustrade.

"Are you a Catholic?"

"Sorry, Father."

He shrugged. "I don't discriminate. Do you know who you were praying to?"

"God," I said.

"And St. Brigid." He nodded at the sculpture. "An Irish nun, known for her compassion. Ready to help anyone, so they say, with anything at all."

"She's got her work cut out for her."

"In the spirit of St. Brigid, can I help you in any way? I couldn't help overhearing your prayer. Something about wanting your soul back."

"You make a habit of eavesdropping on private prayers?"

"I wasn't intending to. But I can assure you that I hold everything I hear in confidence."

I scanned his massive landscape again. "I don't guess anybody's going to argue with you. You ever play football?"

"Matter of fact, yes. Oregon State."

"A Beaver?"

"Defensive tackle."

"Ever play pro?"

He shook his big head. "Things happened."

"Like what?"

"Things."

"I assure you," I said, "that I hold everything I hear in confidence."

He laughed. A big booming laugh. "That's good."

"Yeah, well, nice meeting you—"

"Wait a second," he said. "I really would like to help. I work with street people."

"Is that what you think I am?"

He looked surprised at the question. "I'm pretty sure you're in trouble."

"Why?"

"Pleading to God for your soul was kind of a give-away. But I also have a sense of these things."

For a moment there I felt like telling him everything. Unloading on someone for the very first time since my reanimation. Not only that, a priest, someone with a line to God, and who would not tell.

Or would he? Did priests owe the undead the same consideration as the living? Or would he consider me the spawn of Satan?

"Maybe another time, Father." I started toward the doors.

"Please wait."

I stopped, turned—

—as a dark, robed figure screamed from behind the priest. He was charging at us, holding what looked like a giant crucifix in his hands, upraised for striking.

"Look out!" I heard myself say.

The priest's eyes widened. And widened. And widened some more, until the orbs themselves virtually popped out of his head. They expanded into golf-ball size like in some old cartoon.

The crucifix was in the air, poised for a blow. Closer, closer came the man in the robe, a hood over his head.

On my priest, the buggy eyes were now encased in a red face, the flesh of the padre almost glowing with heat and blood. He parted his lips. His teeth, bared like an animal's, dripped with slobber and foam.

Then he hissed at me. At *me*, not the guy with the crucifix, who was just about to clock him.

From out of the robed figure came a voice, high and keening, shouting in an ear-piercing wail, *"Non semper Saturnalia erunt!"*

The priest with the teeth and golf-ball eyes let out a howl that could have waked the dead. Or in my case, kept me awake for days.

It was a screech from the bowels of hell.

In fact, it was in stereo.

Because the awful noise also came at me from a thing that swooped out of nowhere—a bird or devil bat or some unholy feathered thing—and dove straight for my dome.

I ducked as it buzzed my head.

The screeching bird shot directly at the robed figure, stuck its talons forward into the hood.

"EEEEEAAAAAYYYY!" The robed figure cried out and dropped the crucifix.

Golf-ball Eyes emitted the cursed sound again. So did the flying thing. It was screech city in this little church.

The priest's red cheeks puffed beneath the horrible eyes. His body looked like it might pop, like some Vatican sponsored zeppelin filled with too much demonic gas.

And then he fell in a heap at my feet. His head thudded on the cold tile floor.

The taloned bird wailed, the robed figure screamed one last time, then he, too, hit the floor.

The moment he did, as if he'd flipped some hellish switch, a hot swirling energy spun me around. The wooden pews began to fall forward like dominoes. I caught a look at the statue of St. Brigid just as it exploded into powder.

Another screeching bird swooped in to join the first, and I could make out for the first time the face of an owl. An owl with attitude. Big white irises. Raised ear tufts on either side, like horns. What looked like eyebrows, furrowed down in demonic anger.

The pair were flapping all over the place, screeching and hooting, then dive-bombed me. Sharp little beaks pecked at my shoulders and neck.

That hacked me off.

I went for the one thing that freaked everybody out. The crucifix.

It was lying there on the ground between what looked like two dead priests.

Through another couple of pecks I managed to pick up the heavy icon. Jesus nailed to the thing, his head off to the side.

Wake up and give me a hand, I thought. Maybe I muttered it.

I gripped it down by Jesus' feet and swung it around like I was a hammer thrower at the Olympics.

The screeching got louder, the flapping more intense. The owls kept dodging my weapon, going up and down, hovering and keening.

This little dance could have gone on all night.

I dropped the crucifix to my side, spent. Went down on one knee and cried out, "Please!"

Silence for a moment. Only the flutter of wings, as if they were assessing the situation.

And then they came at me.

Timing is everything, they say. Especially in comedy and demonic owl attacks. I rolled onto my back at the same time I reached across my body with my free hand. With both hands on the crucifix I let the momentum of my body add to the force of my arm swing.

And I landed a perfect shot on one of the birds.

The owl blew up in a spray of blood and feathers.

The other one beat a retreat up to the rafters of the church.

I stood up, feeling as much adrenaline as a zombie has left. I actually felt alive.

I had the crucifix on my shoulder, like a batter at the plate.

The owl had taken refuge somewhere up in the shadows. I couldn't see it or hear it.

I was standing in the middle of a church with a bloody crucifix, two unmoving priests lying at my feet. One crazy owl still poised and waiting.

What does a zombie do in that situation?

I thought back again to Sunday School, and to all those horror movies where a cross came out and scared the bad guys.

What the heck?

I held the crucifix up toward the ceiling and said, "In the name of the Father, Son, and Holy Ghost, I smite thee!"

What do you know? That did it. The owl took off, out the doors and into the night.

A moment later I did the same.

CHAPTER 8

What was I supposed to believe now? Where was God? Why was He silent, except when I was holding up a religious icon?

What was going on? Guys with swords and screech owls in church and vampire clients gone missing?

I needed to get off the street. I needed to get home. I needed to close my door and sink into a chair with a book and pretend I was alive again, really alive. Not some walking thing that people wanted to control or kill.

I got in Geraldine and drove down to Wilshire, then downtown. Felt good when I got back to my 'hood. This area's has been coming back since the days of its decline. We've had a surge of renovation. Lofts in old office buildings and transient hotels. Professionals moving in and walking their dogs at night. Sidewalk seating at restaurants.

A place where a zombie could fit right in. We hope.

This is, after all, the city of hope. That's why people come here.

They come here to find and dream and hustle.

This has always been a city where people chased the elusive vision and the fast buck.

Back in the day they were car salesmen, like Earl "Madman" Muntz, who had a showroom down on 11th and Figueroa. "I want to give these cars away," he'd shout on TV, "but Mrs. Muntz won't let me!"

He was quickly followed by other car pitchers, like Chick Lambert and his dog Storm, Cal Worthington and his dog Spot, and the fast-talking Ralph Williams. "Hi, friends, this is Ralph Williams of Ralph Williams Ford, the largest Ford dealership west of Chicago, in the city of Encino."

If you can talk fast and have something to sell, L.A. is the place for you.

Which is why I wasn't as surprised as I could have been that Aaron Argula was waiting for me in the lobby of my building. Aaron was always selling a little something, even when we were lovers. That's why he was so good in front of juries.

"About time," he said. "What hours do you keep?"

He stood up, tossing the magazine he'd been reading on a table. He wore a long sleeved black shirt and black slacks, looking like a prosperous gunfighter on casual saloon Friday.

"What are you doing in my building?" I said.

"Came to see you. You ran out on me." He smiled that incandescent smile of his. It gave me a momentary jolt.

"I'm a little tired," I said.

"Oh, you need to go to bed? Maybe I can be of—"

"Alone. And have you been drinking?" His eyes had that little sparkle of vodka charm.

"Just a friendly quaff or two around the corner," he said. "There's time for one more."

"Aaron, I really don't think—"

"We have to talk."

"No, we don't."

"I have something to tell you. I thought it would be professional courtesy to deliver the news to you face to face."

"What is it?"

"First a drink," he said, taking my arm.

I pulled it away. "No drink. If you've got something to say to me, say it."

"I just thought you should know I'm prosecuting a case, that's all. The case of a murdered cop named Hennigan and a defendant named Johnson."

My already undead heart flatlined. "You?"

"Me."

"Why?"

"I didn't ask why. I do what I'm assigned. But think of it. You and I, going hammer and tongs in court. We'll be together."

I swallowed hard.

"It's a start at least," he said softly, and that was when I started to melt. He put his hands on my shoulders. I let him. He bent down for a kiss. I let him. His lips touched mine. The back of my neck erupted, sending fire down my spine and into my loins.

Loins! I still had loins. And they still had the blood of desire flowing through them.

I lost myself in the softness of his kiss, the confidence of it, and felt a hunger like I hadn't since I was murdered.

And then I felt another hunger. It came up from inside me like a panther lurching out of a dark cave. I was as powerless to stop it as a kid with a BB gun.

Unable to control myself, I bit his lip.

"Ahh!" He jerked his head back, put his hands to his mouth. I saw red between his fingers.

"Aaron, I'm sorry!"

"Crazy! Ah!" He looked at his hands, cursed, sucked his lip into his mouth so it bled inside.

"Aaron—"

"Whuh wong wih ou?"

"I just, I got carried away in the moment."

"To ite me?"

"Please, I'm just so sorry." I went to him, but he spun away.

He touched his lip a couple of times, checking the blood. It was pretty ghastly. I felt horrible. I also felt like nibbling his earlobes like cocktail weenies.

"Look," he said, getting his clear wording back, "I came to tell you, as a favor. I'm on the case, and also I know where your client is."

"You know where she is?"

"Now I'm thinking twice about telling. I just don't get you."

"Aaron, come on. You have to tell."

"If you wanted to put me off, why didn't you just insult me?"

"I'm sorry, I'm sorry. My client?"

"I want to have dinner with you. I can't believe I'm saying this! I want to see you, Mallory, so if you'll say yes, I'll tell you where she is."

"Okay, Aaron. Yes."

"Deal. They're holding her at Hollywood station. Detective Richards gave that to me. Now I'm giving it to you."

"Thank you, Aaron."

"Don't thank me. Just don't bite me anymore."

"I'll do my best," I said.

"What?"

"Gotta go."

"Animal control picked up a coyote tonight," Richards told me when I got to the station. We were in the lobby, near the ATM machine they have so people can feel safe getting money.

There was no look of safety on Richards's face.

"And the coyote didn't stay a coyote," he said. "And now it, she, is here."

"In a cell?"

"I've got her in a supply closet."

"She's probably scared to death," I said.

"I can't help that. I'm pretty numb myself."

"I want to see her now."

"After you do, will you do something else for me?"

"For you?"

"You'll understand. I know it's late."

"You remember our deal, don't you?"

"Yes, yes. That's all part of it."

"All right then. Where is she?

He led me to the closet, which was in a corridor just past the detective cubicles. Richards unlocked it. I tapped him and opened the door a crack myself. "Traci Ann, it's Mallory. I'm coming in."

I pushed the door open farther. Shelves held things like reams of paper and ink cartridges for printers. At the far end, in a chair and draped in a police blanket, was my client.

"I'll take it from here," I told Richards, and shut the door.

Traci Ann looked up. "Please take me home."

"They're going to arrest you."

"What for?"

"Murder."

Her scared eyes got even larger. "Who?"

"A cop."

She shook her head. "I didn't kill anybody. And especially no cop."

"You've never killed anyone?"

She shook her head. "I suck blood, but that turns them into vampires. Maybe I'm just being technical, but at least they're walking around."

"This cop isn't. His body was burned up."

"No, that's not me."

"I know."

"You believe me?"

"Of course, I do. Now we have to go through the system. But the cops, they're being sticklers. They don't want you turning into an animal or a winged creature and escaping."

Traci Ann took a deep, mournful breath. "I can't escape."

"What's that?"

"I tried. I became *canis latrans,* but he stopped me from running away."

"Who?"

"My master."

"Who you don't know?"

She nodded.

"So let me get this straight. You can shape-shift, but you can't get away?"

"He's holding me back. What's going to happen to me, Mallory?"

"We're going to fight, that's what. We make sure you're taken care of. We make sure you're not convicted of this."

"Can you do that?"

"I can."

"I don't have any money to pay you."

"You know what? I'm used to that."

I wasn't, but in this case I knew I had to pretend.

"Do I have your promise you won't change? Won't try to escape again?"

"I don't think I can anymore, Ms. Caine."

"Call me Mallory."

"He's taken that power from me. I tried to go bat, but couldn't. He *wants* me here. Why?"

I put my hand on her arm. "One step at a time. Okay?"

She put her head in her hands. "I'll try."

"One more thing," I said. "You go into dead mode during daylight hours, right?"

Traci Ann nodded.

"Good," I said. "I've got a friend at the ME's office. Owes me a favor. I'm going to cash it in."

"What kind of favor?"

"Leave it to me, Traci Ann. This is what I do."

Richards was waiting for me outside the closet. "Well?"

"I want her in a single cell."

"But—"

"Don't worry. She won't go coyote again."

"What about something else?"

"No bats, either. You have my word on it."

He scratched under his chin. There was a good deal of stubble on it now. It was past midnight and things were, after all, rather hairy. "Okay," he said. "I'll see to it. Now, I need *you* to see something."

* * *

We took Richards's Crown Vic out of the lot and over to a crime scene on Yucca. The perimeter of a house was yellow taped and two black-and-white patrol cars were parked on the street. A small crowd of the curious, including a couple of kids, milled around.

We ducked under the tape and went to the open door of the modest, 1940s vintage home.

"What is this?" I asked.

"What I want to show you," Richards said. "And I remind you you're a lawyer, an officer of the court, and that you are serving in the capacity of an advisor."

"Fine."

"And that anything I say to you is to be held in confidence."

"I get it."

"Then come with me."

The house was a mess. Somebody had trashed the place. Or there'd been one mama of a fight. Broken glass, overturned furniture and lamps littered the floor. The most curious item was the sofa. It had a couple of gashes on the backrest side, with stuffing popping out of them.

"In here," Richards said from the hallway.

As I walked closer to him, the smell of spoiled meat hit me in the face. I don't care if you're alive or dead, that's not a good smell. I figured it had to be a body and this had to be a homicide, and Richards was out of his element somehow.

I had no idea what my element was supposed to be.

But when I got in the room I found out in a hurry.

His partner, Strobert, was in the room. He gave me a quick nod. Kind of friendly this time, or at least respectful. We weren't adversaries on this one.

At his feet was a dark blue coroner's blanket, covering what was obviously a body.

"Ms. Caine has consented to advise us on this," Richards said to Strobert.

"Appreciated," Strobert said.

Richards closed the door to the room. "This stays here," he said.

"Of course," I said.

"We don't want this leaking out. We want this information under wraps for as long as possible."

"I can do that," I said. "Who is it?"

"We were hoping you could tell us."

"You didn't find ID?"

"We did," Richards said. "But I want you to have a look first. We found your business card in his wallet."

That spiked my curiosity. I didn't know this place. "Let me see," I said.

"One thing," Strobert said. "The head has been severed."

That did it. I reached down and pulled the blanket myself.

And looked into the horrific face of Carl Gilquist, zombie plumber.

I reeled back, put my hand over my mouth. Because Carl had just died the most awful death anyone can suffer.

His mouth was stitched closed with thick, black thread. Rock salt crystals were evident at the corners of his mouth. His eyes were open wide, as if he wanted to scream. And on his forehead the finishing touch: Whoever had killed him had carved a large Z in Carl's forehead with some sharp tool.

I turned away.

"You know him then?" Richards said.

"Yes," I said.

"Client of yours?"

I was about to say, *No, a friend,* but realized that would open up more questions than I wanted to be asked. I nodded.

"Any idea who might have done this to him?"

Oh, I had an idea all right. A guy with a sword. A mad zombie hunter who knew his work well.

"I haven't a clue," I said.

"What about the way it was done. You have an idea about that?'

I tried to swallow. Couldn't.

"Well?" Richards said.

"Well what?" I said.

"Tell me what you know."

"I know he's dead, that's what I know! Why'd you drag me down here to look at this?"

"You're defending a vampire, aren't you? You know about weird stuff. You said you'd help me—"

"A zombie, all right? I think this is how you kill a zombie."

Richards and Strobert exchanged glances.

I said, "That's right. You cut off the head, pour salt in the mouth, and close it up. That's what I've heard, anyway."

"And that does what?" Richards said.

"Isn't it obvious?" I said.

"Why didn't you come out and tell us this at the start?"

"I'm a little stunned, okay?"

"You saying this guy was one of those walking around things who eats brains?"

"I'm telling you what kind of death this looks like, okay? Maybe this is just a murder by some sick joker."

Richards said, "I'm still not satisfied that you're telling me all you know. Why do I have that feeling?"

"It's what cops always think about criminal defense lawyers," I said. "Deal with it."

CHAPTER 9

On Wednesday morning, the mayor of our fine city, Ronaldo Garza, took to the steps of City Hall for a public statement. Garza is a mid-sized Latino, a former city councilman, who won a questionable election against City Councilwoman Rebecca Saltzman. No one was able to prove anything, but the stench of fraud has floated over the mayor's office since then.

Not that you would know it from looking at Garza. With his hundred-watt smile and outgoing ways, he seems every inch the warm-hearted, open-armed city booster Los Angeles always falls in love with. Until it wakes up one day with a knife in its back.

Garza was surrounded by cameras as he spoke. "I want to assure you that the city of Los Angeles is safe. I know that there have been some budgetary constraints and cutbacks, especially with regard to law enforcement. We have all felt those cuts. And now there are fears about some wave of crime, even of things not experienced in our city before. I want you to know that I'm in control and I will get to the bottom of everything. The city is in good hands and nothing has

ever shaken our confidence in ourselves and our ability
to deal with anything that comes our way.

"There have been some reports of violent out-
breaks that seem to make no sense. And I want to tell
you, as a former police officer, crime never make
sense. So do not be alarmed by rumors and second-
and third-hand reports about what's happening in
our city. There are those who would like us to panic.
I assure you that those responsible will be called to
account."

At eleven that morning, in the Foltz criminal courts
building, Traci Ann Johnson was to be arraigned in
Division 30, the felony arraignment court, in front of
Commissioner Norton Roundtree.

Only things didn't exactly go the way the commish
wanted them to.

When he called the case, I came forward to the
podium in front of the PD and DA tables.

"Good morning, Your Honor," I said.

He nodded at me, then said, "Is your client present?"

"Um, there's a little problem here."

"Where is she?"

"I need to explain something, Your Honor."

The commissioner scowled at me. "What is it?"

"There is a little matter of my client's Fifth, Sixth,
and Fourteenth Amendment rights."

"What on earth are you talking about?"

"Interesting phrase, *on earth*."

"Ms. Caine—"

"As you well know, Your Honor, a defendant has
the right to be present in court during trial, to assist

in the defense. To deny presence is a violation of due process, as held in *Hopt v. Utah.*"

"*Hopt v.* who now?"

"*Utah.* United States Supreme Court, 1884."

"Yes, yes, of course. So what's the problem?"

"Well, I'm afraid that my client is only going to be able to appear in court at night."

I thought for a moment the commissioner was going to crawl out of his skin and walk his bones over and slap me. "What is the basis of this request?"

"It's a little complicated, but my client simply cannot, or rather is not, shall we say, awake during the day. And if she were forced to be, she would die."

"What, is she a vampire or something?" The commish laughed. So did the bailiff. So did several other people in the courtroom.

"To be honest, that's exactly what she is."

Roundtree stopped laughing. "Very amusing, Ms. Caine. Stop wasting the court's time and—"

"She is a vampire. She can't come out during the day. And of course, that means her right to a fair trial is compromised as she cannot be present to help with her defense."

Behind me, there was a stirring in the courtroom, a vibe. I didn't have to turn around to know that the media types were getting their fresh meat. Another L.A. trial twist, something like the Night Stalker or Freeway Killer.

"I don't find this funny," Commissioner Roundtree said.

"Your Honor, I am dead serious. So is my client."

A few laughs from the courtroom crowd. I went on. "A county employed medical examiner issued a death certificate on my client two days ago. Here it is."

I took out a copy of the certificate my ME friend had filed. So sweet. I went to the bench and slid it to the commissioner. He snatched it as if he were catching a fly. He put his reading glasses on the edge of his nose and looked at it. Then he looked at Aaron.

"Do you know anything about this?" he said.

Aaron walked up to the bench and took the certificate from the commisioner's hand. He frowned as he read it. "This is the first I've seen of it," he said, shooting me a killer look.

I shot him one right back.

"Shall we have the coroner come in and testify?" I asked.

"This is nuts," the commish said.

I said, "There appear to be only two choices here, Your Honor. You can dismiss this case because my client is officially dead, as the county has determined. There is no further punishment that can be inflicted on her. Or, you can hold the trial at night."

"I can't be hearing this," Roundtree said.

"Oh, and one other minor little matter, Your Honor. As a vampire, my client is going to require a diet of human blood."

No one was laughing now.

"That's my limit," Roundtree said. "I am seriously thinking of holding you in contempt and handing you over for observation."

"Well, that's just dandy," I said. "But you may want to review the Eighth Amendment to the Constitution, which prohibits cruel and unusual punishment, which the Supreme Court has held guarantees a prisoner the right to basic nutrition. And there is no more basic nutrition than that which will keep a prisoner alive."

"Your Honor—" Aaron said.

"I'm not finished. The denial of the right to nutrition while incarcerated also subjects the County of Los Angeles to liability. I'm sure during these economic times that is not exactly going to be looked on with favor by the powers that be. But we have blood banks available that can adequately take care of my client's nutritional needs, and the type of blood does not matter in the least, I am told. There is only a slight difference in flavor."

Roundtree's face began to drain of the very type of blood my client needed.

"I'm sorry, Your Honor, but human blood it must be. Or you can release Miss Johnson O.R. and not have the County have to worry about it."

"I need—I cannot believe I'm saying this—I need to take this under advisement." Commissioner Roundtree pounded his gavel on the bench and got out of there quicker than a bat out of hell, which was fitting under the circumstances.

"What was that all about in there?" Aaron had me cornered in the lobby right outside the courtroom.

"How's that lip healing?" I said. There was an ugly, dark blue bite mark on his lower lip.

"Who cares? I'm talking about what you just did. You're turning this whole thing into a—"

"Please don't tell me you're about to say *circus.*"

"I don't care what you call it, you're being an idiot." He tried to flash his authoritative blue eyes at me.

"Oh, so now you care?" I said.

"Mallory, this isn't about us—"

"I think it is, very much."

"You know what? I don't care what you think. I was

hoping we could oppose each other without it getting personal. That's why I wanted to talk to you. This play for publicity with your client—"

"Open your mind, Aaron. My client is a real vampire."

He rolled his eyes.

"Ask Detective Richards. Has he told you what happened?"

"Okay, some strange stuff, but there's an explanation that doesn't involve Bela Lugosi."

"I don't have to convince you. I only have to convince one commissioner."

"I'm not going to allow you to run around the court playing these games. If need be, I will move for sanctions."

"Do what you want," I said. "But here's a little info for you. I have an innocent client. We don't get many of those in this line of work. But when we do, it makes the case so much easier. And I'm going to tell you another thing, Aaron. I'm not the same person I was when you knew me. Not the same at all."

"I know that," he said.

"What?"

"I saw something in you the other day in court, and even today, though I thought you were acting like a grandstander. I see more confidence in you."

"Oh, so when we were together that's what did it? I wasn't confident enough for you?"

"Can't we just forget the past? Can't we start from here and go where we go?"

"We're not going anywhere except to court. And I intend to beat you like a bongo drum."

He folded his arms. "You've also developed a bit of a mouth."

"Is there anything else you want to tell me?"

"Drop this whole thing. Drop this stupid vampire

idea. I don't know what's wrong with your client. I don't know if there is a medical condition or what, but she's not a vampire and this isn't an HBO series. This is real life and I don't want to be dragged into your little games."

"Do your best in court," I said. "Otherwise you may communicate with me entirely by rumor from now on."

"Mallory."

"What?"

He didn't answer. There was a sudden vulnerability in him. I looked into those deep, liquid eyes, the eyes I had loved so much once. I caught myself. I didn't want to fall into those again.

I mean I did. And didn't.

"Never mind," I said. "Listen, I have to—" I stopped when I saw something dark perched high in the corner of the corridor, just above the men's bathroom. I lost breath.

"What's the matter?" Aaron said.

I was looking at an owl, just as it was up there looking right at me.

I drove Geraldine out to the scene of the crime, as they say. I wanted to look at it in broad daylight, and figure out who could have seen what was going on. The police report, which I got at the arraignment, listed one eyewitness. I wanted to ask her a few questions.

Tareco and Viewpoint streets merge between land developed and undeveloped. Approaching from the Hollywood Freeway side, you get a glimpse of the first few letters of the Hollywood sign on Mount Lee before it sinks behind a hill.

I pulled to a stop at the very spot Hennigan had that night.

The weeds on the right were charred, the fire having consumed the hill below. You could see a bit of the freeway, and then a full-on view of Hollywood.

To my left, high on a ridge, was a mid-century, post-and-beam mansion protected by an iron gate. The jutting lines of the place shot out in aggressive angles. At the very top, looking to the east, was a bronze statue of an owl. An owl with attitude.

I confirmed the address on the police report.

I left my car where it was and walked to the gate. I pressed the button and waited for somebody to answer.

No one did.

I grabbed the gate and pushed. Didn't budge.

I walked back along Tareco, looking up the hillside where the house was perched. A second-story window looked down at the scene. That would have been the only vantage point for the witness. Unless she was outside on the driveway, virtually at the gate itself.

Something was wrong with this picture, I just didn't know what.

I went back to Geraldine and sat on the hood, looking at Hollywood and wondering what it was about murder. Here was one where an innocent party, my client, was being set up.

About fifteen minutes later, a car wound its way up Viewpoint. Not just any car. A big white rich car. Not strange up here where property values were still sky high. A lot of old and new movie money was spread out in these hills.

A moment later the white car nosed its way past me. I saw the hood ornament, a winged B. A Bentley. Oh, my, yes, a fine looking machine. I patted Geraldine's hood so she wouldn't feel bad. She was sincere and didn't put on airs.

And then the gate of the owl house opened. The Bentley headed up the drive.

So I did, too, getting in just before the iron bars clicked shut behind me.

I walked up the curved drive and got to the front of the house just as the driver of the Bentley got out.

He was big and black and wore a cap. An actual chauffeur's hat. He went to the rear door and started to open it, but shot me a look just before he did.

He paused with his hand on the door.

He looked like he was about to say something particularly nasty when somebody tapped on the window of the Bentley. The driver paused a moment and let his eyes burn into mine, then opened the door.

A tall, thin woman emerged, first one leg then the other. She was wearing black high heels and an ankle-length black dress. The driver helped her out with one hand. Her hair was completely white and worn straight. It came down almost to her waist. Her wrinkled face was dominated by two wide eyes with heavy makeup, and a pointed nose that was almost too large for her face. Maybe at one time her face had been full enough to handle it. Now her proboscis seemed the last vestige of a previous life full of health and vitality.

She stared at me. "What do you want?"

"My name is Mallory Caine. I'm a lawyer."

"Is that supposed to impress me? How did you get in?"

"I followed 'Chalmers' here," I said, jerking my thumb at the driver.

Chalmers stiffened.

The tall woman threw back her head and laughed. It was a deep-throated, full-bodied laugh. It would have been creepy if this was a horror movie. But in the middle of the day it was just crazy. Overdone. Theatrical.

"I love funny names," the woman said. "Do you know who I am?"

"You're a witness to a murder. That's all I know."

"How old are you, young lady?"

"What's that have to—"

"Do you know what a DVD is?"

"Um, yeah."

"Then you must know the name Minerva."

"Must I?"

At that she drew herself up to her full height, which must've been about six feet. She raised her arms in a gesture that a witch might have used to call forth all the forces of nature. "Minerva, Mistress of the Night!"

Chalmers took off his hat and, reverently, added, "She's got the movies, you'll get the fright."

I just blinked.

"You will come inside," Minerva said.

Who was I to argue with the Mistress of the Night and her sidekick?

The inside of the house was art deco and dust. A gold, semi-nude statuette with ashtray sat on a massacar ebony round table. A cigarette in a black holder smoldered in the ashtray. The carpet was a 1930s movie palace design. A pink glass-and-iron table lamp gave the chamber a soft hue and the impression of dying light. Heavy burgundy drapes over the windows kept out any light of nature.

A whole wall was taken up with framed photographs, black-and-white shots. They all had in them a younger version of the woman whose house I was in. Her hair was black then. She was always in a shot with somebody else, and I recognized a few of the people. Celebrities from a past era, like Burt Reynolds, and others.

Chalmers said, "Minerva had the best little Saturday movie showcase on local TV. I watched it every week as a kid."

"Yes, yes," Minerva said. "You and thousands of others. Maybe millions."

"You had a TV show?" I said.

"We showed the classics. *House on Haunted Hill, 13 Ghosts, The Pit and the Pendulum.* Oh, those were the days."

"I'm sure they were," I said. "And I would love nothing better than to stroll down Memory Lane with you, but I need to ask you some questions about what you saw on the night of the murder."

She turned to me as if coming out of a dream. "I have told all that to the police."

"I'm the lawyer representing the defendant."

"And I should help you?"

"All I'm looking for is the truth. It might be better to talk about it now than on the witness stand. What I want to know is what you saw that night."

"I miss him," she said.

"Excuse me?"

"I miss him terribly." She was gazing at the wall, with a faraway look.

"I was asking—"

"Don't you?"

"Miss Minerva—"

"Not *Miss*! Minerva, Mistress of the Night."

"About the killing, did you—"

"Vincent Price," she said. "I miss him so."

I closed my eyes. I was starting to believe I was dealing with a nutroll, which raised a few questions. How reliable a witness was she? Could she be manipulated by someone? Might she have imagined the whole thing?

"Minerva, I think Vincent Price was a wonderful actor," I said. "But I—"

"Actor? Actor! You think it was all an act? No one can be that good. He lived what he put on the screen. *The House on Haunted Hill* is the greatest film ever made!"

"I thought it was *Citizen Kane*," I said.

Chalmers said, "Don't joke about *The House on Haunted Hill.*"

"I don't want to joke about anything," I said. "I just want to know—"

"Do you like my house?" Minerva said.

"What? Yes, lovely." Lovely if you were trapped in the 1930s. "Now about the night in question . . ."

"I do not wish to discuss it further," Minerva said.

"May I ask why?"

"Life is so much more than the sum of its parts."

"Excuse me?"

Chalmers said, "Shh. She's pontificating."

I rubbed the bridge of my nose.

Minerva, looking up at some unseen vision, continued. "War is a part. Pain is a part. But so are art and craft and wisdom. All these things I tried to bring to the world through the appreciation of people like Vincent Price."

"Oh, yes, how I loved Vincent Price!" I said. "Underappreciated in his day."

Minerva whipped her head around. "Well said!"

"In fact," I said, "his death was a huge loss to us all."

Minerva's eyes widened. "What makes you think he is dead?"

"Oh. Sorry. Of course, he's not. And if he were standing here in this room, don't you think he'd want you to help me?"

She frowned. "How so?"

"I mean, we're talking about a horrible death. Death by burning up in a car. The sort of thing he would be most interested in, as deaths go. Am I right?"

"Keep going," she said.

"Surely he would want the truth coming out."

"Why?"

"Well, because . . . he's Vincent Price. Need we say more?"

She began to eye me warily, as if not trusting me. Which she shouldn't have, as I'd just laid a big line of horseradish on her. But at least she was listening. And thinking.

Minerva started to open her mouth.

That's when the monster burst in.

CHAPTER 10

It's a funny thing about monsters here in Hollywood. You associate them with big lizards, like Godzilla, or apes like King Kong. Maybe you think of Franken- stein's monster, cobbled together with body parts. Or perhaps killer piranhas with rows of teeth. The shark in *Jaws*.

But in real life, the worst monsters are the ones you can't see. You feel them, and that's a whole lot worse.

This monster was a blackness within the room. It blew in through the French doors and came with a shriek.

Minerva's long white hair blew behind her like snow spray in a windstorm. She opened her mouth and screamed just as loud as the monster.

Chalmers fainted.

The darkness—looking like the form of a woman in a flowing black gown—rushed across the room and picked him up. He cried out. The blackness turned him upside down and tossed him like a duffel bag. He hit the wall and thumped to the floor.

Then it came at me. At least I think it did. It moved to within touching distance. And there it sat. It had no features that I could see. But its malevolence was palpable. It seemed just to be looking at me.

And then, just as quickly as it had come in, it faded. Withdrew is more like it. Until only a motionless Chalmers and a panting Minerva were left with me.

"All right," I said. "Anyone want to explain that?"

"Go," Minerva said. "Leave us. If you stay, there will be more trouble."

"Hey, what just happened here was more than any Vincent Price gag. I—"

"I can call the police, you know." Minerva was regaining her attitude. "You are a trespasser."

"Well, technically I suppose."

"I don't want to speak to you anymore. Go!"

I drove back into Hollywood. To the church where all that shouting and owls hit me the other night. I needed to know what the freak show was all about.

I entered the church and saw a woman in one of the pews, kneeling. The rest of the place was empty, except for a solitary figure at the altar. A spindly looking priest with a shock of white hair. He, too, was kneeling, apparently praying.

My heels clacked along the tile floor, creating an echo. As I walked forward, the priest stood and crossed himself, then turned around. By the time I got to him, he was looking me straight in the eye.

His face was hawklike. It was also dotted with red marks. He was obviously the crazed cleric I had seen the other night, waving a large crucifix. In short, he was the man I had come to see.

He continued to stare at me, wordlessly. I wondered

if he recognized me, but remembered I'd had on a scarf and sunglasses.

"Hello there, Father," I said. Not exactly the most respectful greeting, but what can you do?

"How may I help you?"

"It's not really me, it's a client of mine. I'm a lawyer."

"That is all right. We accept all kinds here."

He was making a joke? Apparently not, because he did not smile.

"Okay," I said. "This client, she was attacked here in this church. Owls and strange doings, she said."

The priest's eyes opened wide. He looked around as if someone might have heard me. He put a finger to his lips and then motioned for me to follow him.

This I did, into a small cell or office, it was hard to tell which. It had a desk and a chair and a crucifix on the wall. And a Bible on top of the desk.

He closed the door. "Where is this client of yours?"

"She's out and about, I expect."

"You must bring her here immediately."

"Why?"

"Her life is in danger. Grave danger."

He had me at *danger*. Grave danger sent a little chill down my undead spine. "Suppose you tell me why that is."

"I must see her."

"Well, I'm here. I am her legal representative. Anything you say to me you are saying to her."

"But—"

"Come on, Father. Give. I want to know what this is all about, and I want to know now."

He ran his bony fingers through the explosion of white hair on his head. He seemed sad for a moment, then walked to the wall behind the desk. He looked at the wall as if you were looking out a window. But there was no window.

"You may want to sit down for this," he said.

"I'm fine," I said.

"You won't be soon enough."

I sat down in the chair.

"Do you believe in demons?" he asked.

"Maybe."

"You should. Because they are real. Are you a Catholic?"

"No."

"Are you anything?"

"Heinz fifty-seven."

"I'm sorry, what?"

"My mother raised me with all sorts of crazy stuff, but none of it stuck."

"Then you have no religion?"

"What does it matter?"

"It matters because we live in a skeptical age. It is very difficult to communicate with skeptics if their minds are closed."

"Try me."

"Demonology, the study of demons, used to be considered a branch of science. But as the Western world has become secularized, this has been deemed a fool's quest. I don't think people will be laughing anytime soon. All of the affairs of life are in one way or another influenced by demons."

"Come on. Everything?"

"Everything. This world is under the dominion of Satan."

"I thought it was under the dominion of God. Isn't that who you work for?"

"There is much you do not know. But back to demons. It is an odd fact, nonetheless, that with the rise of great cities, the influence of demonic activity grows. And what your client underwent the other night is evidence of something happening in this city of ours. Something bigger than has ever happened before."

"Like what?"

He shook his head. "I don't know. The spiritual world is mysterious and comes to us only through periodic revelation. There's so much we don't know. What we do know is that it is real."

"My client says there was some kind of owl involved," I said. "Are you aware of what happened here?"

"I was a witness to it, yes."

"Do you mind telling me what you were doing swinging a big cross at another priest?"

He faced me head on. "How do you know that?"

"My client told me, remember?"

"Oh, yes. For a moment I thought you had seen it yourself."

"Why would that be? Why would I be in this church?"

"Who knows? Perhaps you are being called by God."

It was freaky geeky to hear. I didn't tell him about the Voice that was calling me all the time. "So what about it? What about the birds?"

"I am afraid I cannot tell you very much. The other priest involved has undergone a serious trauma, and this is privileged information, priest to priest."

"What *can* you tell me?"

"I can tell you about Lilith."

The name set me back. I'd heard it before. "Tell me," I said.

"A demoness. The first wife of Adam."

"Adam married a demon?"

"No. From the earth was she created, as Adam himself. Given unto Adam. But she was an adulteress."

"Who could she adult with? There was only the two of them, right?"

"You forget about the serpent."

That little ditty hung in the air for a moment. "You mean, supposedly, she was unfaithful with Satan?"

"And her body taken from her. Her spirit remains. That is what demons are. The disembodied souls of the wicked dead."

This was becoming a mind-blowing little seminar, though I didn't know how much to buy. "What about the bird thing?"

"Ah," the old priest said. He opened the big Bible on the desk and leafed a few pages. Then he ran a spindly finger down until it stopped. "Isaiah the Prophet, Chapter 34, Verse 14. 'The wild beasts of the desert shall also meet with the wild beasts of the island, and the satyr shall cry to his fellow; the screech owl also shall rest there, and find for herself a place of rest.'"

He looked up from the page. "The ancient Hebrew word, *liyliyth*, is translated as screech owl. Her form of passage."

I took in a slow breath. "So what you're telling me here is that we got dive-bombed by Adam's first wife?"

"We?" he asked.

"Journalistic *we*," I said, recovering nicely. "I mean, what we've got here, you're saying, is some kind of demonic activity, involving this Lilith broad."

"Oh, I would not call her a broad. I would not underestimate her power. And that is why I am so concerned with your client. She may be the one Lilith is after."

"What possible reason could there be for that?"

The friar shook his head sadly. "I cannot know. I can only know that it must be something very, very big."

"One more thing, Father, if I may."

"Yes?"

"My client said you shouted something, maybe in Latin. Something to do with Saturn. Do you remember that?"

"Ah," he said.

"Can you share that bit of information with me?"

He looked up, as if trying to draw strength. *"Non semper Saturnalia erunt,"* he said. "'The Saturnalia will not last forever.'"

"Saturnalia?"

"A Roman festival of debauchery," the priest said. "In honor of the god Saturn."

"Why did you say it?"

"Because . . ." he stopped, looking over my shoulder.

I turned around.

The big priest, the one who had freaked out, was standing there. His face was at once peaceful and tormented, as if a vast ocean of horror lay below a placid surface.

"No more," the older priest said, his voice low. "Bring your client to me when you can."

"But wait—"

"We mustn't speak of it. Here, take this to her." He reached in his robe and pulled out a small vial, put it in my hand.

"What is it?" I said.

"Tap water," he said.

"Tap?"

"I blessed this personally, but it's not church sanctioned. I can only tell you it works when the chips are down, and please believe me, the chips are going to be flying very soon."

The big priest said, "Forgive me, Father, for I have sinned."

"Duty calls," the old priest said to me. "You must go."

CHAPTER 11

On a warm Friday evening it was time for the preliminary hearing in the case of the *People of the State of California* versus *Traci Ann Johnson*, for the murder of LAPD Detective Thomas Hennigan.

The courtroom of Judge Jerry Arabian was packed. There are prelims every day in L.A. and no one pays them any mind. But this one was different. This one featured a vampire accused of murdering a cop.

When a defendant enters a plea of not guilty in answer to a felony complaint, the next big step is the prelim. The prosecutor has to establish probable cause to believe the defendant committed the crime charged. If such cause is found, the defendant is "held to answer" and will be bound over for trial.

All the prosecutor has to do is introduce enough evidence to move the judge to bind the defendant over for trial. Unless the defense lawyer can find a way to suppress key evidence, the bind over is virtually pro forma.

My job, then, was to challenge Aaron at every turn, and make him put on more evidence than he wanted.

The more I could get into the official transcript, the better. It would nail his evidence to the wall, so to speak, so he couldn't squiggle out of it later.

They brought Traci Ann into the enclosed box I had requested. She was wearing the modest dress I'd bought for her, and her hands were shackled in front of her body.

She could have turned into a bat to get out of them, but had pledged not to. So far, she was as good as her word.

Judge Arabian called the case. Aaron and I stated our appearances. The judge then warned the gallery to be in order. He knew there were reporters there but also some gawkers. Not your ordinary court watchers, either. Those are usually retirees with not much else to do during the day.

No, there were some vampire fans out there. Goths. About four or five in a group that must have come in together.

Great. All I needed was a vampire glorification brigade.

Then it was time to start. Aaron called an LAPD patrol officer named Kurt Stanley. He and his partner were first on the scene after the fire was reported. Aaron walked him through the events right up to the time the homicide team of Strobert and Richards arrived.

There was nothing to hurt me to that point yet, so I didn't ask him any questions.

Then Aaron called Strobert.

Aaron got his quals on the record, then asked, "Officer Strobert, you were the first on the scene, is that correct?"

"I received the call at 2:13 A.M. and met my partner at the scene at 2:58."

"And you spoke to a patrol officer, is that correct?"

"Yes. Officer Stanley advised us."

"What did Officer Stanley tell you, in general?"

"That he had responded to a call from a driver who saw a vehicle in flames. Officer Stanley arrived at the scene and saw the fire, at which point he called LAFD. He determined there was a body inside, but could not get to it. He then called the station to report a death. The supervisor then notified me and my partner. Officer Stanley told us he also interviewed the witness who reported the fire. The witness said she saw nothing other than what looked like a coyote standing near the vehicle, watching the fire. As soon as the fire department trucks arrived, the coyote ran away. She found that activity very strange."

"Objection," I said. "Now we're getting into third-hand hearsay."

"Goes to state of mind," Aaron said. "Officer Strobert is giving us the foundation for his actions."

"Overruled," Judge Arabian said.

"What did you make of the coyote story?" Aaron asked.

"Nothing at the time," Strobert said.

"Have you subsequently had a chance to review that information?"

"I have."

"Tell us what you've learned."

Uh-oh. I stood up. "May we approach the bench, Your Honor?"

"With the reporter," the judge said.

We gathered at the bench. "I don't know where this is going," I said, "but it sounds like Mr. Argula is about to try to shoehorn in some evidence that requires expert testimony."

"What is your offer of proof, Mr. Argula?" Judge Arabian asked.

"Due to the stance taken by the defense, Your Honor, Detective Strobert has undertaken to investigate those aspects of the case."

"What aspects?"

"Vampirism."

I said, "There is no foundation for this. The detective is not a qualified expert on the subject."

Judge Arabian said, "You have opened the door on this, Ms. Caine. You can't expect to close it to the prosecution. Mr. Argula may continue."

Aaron gave me a smug grin and we all toddled back to our places.

"Detective Strobert," Aaron said. "We were talking about your investigation into the coyote sighting. What did you do with this information?"

"Well, after the arraignment when defense counsel made the claim the defendant was a vampire, I did some research into that area. I read several articles on the subject online."

I said, "What, Wikipedia? Is that going to be admitted into—"

"Ms. Caine!" Judge Arabian said. "Offer a valid objection or do not interrupt Mr. Argula again."

"Then I object on the grounds that there is no foundation, and this testimony is irrelevant and immaterial."

"Overruled. The witness may continue."

Strobert said, "So what I found was that vampires can do what's called shape-shifting. In European countries, a wolf is one of the shapes that is common. A coyote is part of the wolf family."

"All right," Aaron said. "Let's go back to the crime

scene investigation. What, if anything, did you do after you arrived?"

"I consulted with LAFD on the scene, and was told there was a charred body inside the vehicle. While waiting for the coroner team to arrive, I questioned the eyewitness."

"Object to use of the term eyewitness," I said. "There has been no evidence this witness saw the crime committed."

"Overruled."

Aaron said, "And what is the name of the eyewitness?"

"She only gave us one name, Minerva. I believe that is her legal name."

"She was a television personality some time ago, is that correct?"

"That is my understanding."

"After your interview of the witness, what did you do next?"

"I returned to the scene. The MEs were removing the body of the victim, later identified as LAPD Detective Thomas Hennigan. My partner and I were then free to look at the vehicle, with the assistance of an SID unit."

"SID stands for what?"

"Scientific Investigation Division."

"Was anything recovered from the vehicle?"

"Yes. We recovered what appeared to be a necklace. A crucifix."

I sat up like I'd just received a mother goose. I looked over at the box. Traci Ann's face was alive with shock.

Why hadn't Aaron told me about this as required by the rules of discovery?

"Your Honor," I said. "We have not seen the item

just mentioned." I scrambled through the papers on the counsel table. "It was not in the police report, as I recall."

"It is in the amended report," Aaron said.

I looked at him with razor blades. "I never received such a report."

Aaron went to his own table and pulled something out of a folder. "I have a receipt here for the delivery of the amended report to your office. It was received by a Nikolas Papadoukis."

Papadoukis! Some investigator he'd make!

"Let's continue," the judge said. "If I find Ms. Caine needs extra time, I'll give it to her."

Nodding with obvious satisfaction, Aaron picked up a plastic evidence bag from the counsel table and took it to the witness stand. "I am showing you what I have marked as People's Exhibit One for identification. Do you recognize this?"

Strobert looked at it. "Yes. It is the crucifix I recovered from the vehicle."

"Is that your signature on the evidence bag?"

"Yes, it is."

"Were there any markings on the crucifix?"

"Yes."

"What were they?"

"There is an inscription on the back."

"Will you read it to the court, please?"

Strobert read, "'Presented to Traci Ann Johnson by her mother.'"

And now I was ready to kill. S*omebody* had planted evidence to implicate Traci Ann.

And then Aaron announced he had no further questions.

My turn.

"Good morning, Detective Strobert," I said, getting to my feet.

"Good morning," he said.

Neither one of us sounded like we believed it.

"So you're an expert on vampires, are you?"

"I don't pretend to be an expert."

"You've read some articles."

"Yes."

"And feel that qualifies you to talk about how vampires can turn into wolves and such."

"I am telling you what I found out as I investigated the claims made by you."

"The claim that my client is a vampire, correct?"

"Correct."

"You are aware then, are you not, that the one icon a vampire cannot bear to gaze upon is a crucifix, isn't that right?"

Strobert paused. "I don't know that for certain."

"Because you are not an expert, are you?"

"As I said—"

"Detective, if I were to tell you that a vampire cannot look upon a crucifix, indeed cannot touch or handle one, would that make a difference to you?"

"I'd have to think about it."

"Let me ask you this way, as a hypothetical. Assuming that a crucifix cannot be looked upon or handled by a vampire, that would indicate that the crucifix you have just identified was perhaps placed in the vehicle by someone else, wouldn't it?"

His face flushed slightly. His jaw muscles tightened. I liked that. I liked that very much.

"It might," he said.

"In fact, you have no idea how this crucifix got in the car, do you?"

"I have an idea."

"Do you, Detective? Do you have an actual idea?"

"Objection," Aaron said.

"Sustained."

I said, "In point of fact, you do not know how this crucifix got in the vehicle, do you?"

He cleared his throat. "Not at this time."

I looked at him a moment, let him sweat, then waved my hand. "No more for this witness."

Aaron called a deputy medical examiner to the stand. He stated his name as Dr. Cecil Scheppke. Aaron walked him through his creds. He's been doing autopsies for the county for ten years.

"Briefly, Doctor, can you tell us what the cause of death was?"

"Most likely it was the loss of blood due to massive trauma to the neck."

"You say *most likely* because . . . ?"

"The body was severely charred due to the fire, but other indications led me to my conclusion."

"What other indications?"

"Lacerations to the laryngeal cartilage, and a severance of the hyoid bone and cervical spine."

"Which would tell you what?"

"That massive and fatal blood loss was the immediate cause of death, such loss due to severe lacerations to the neck."

"Are these lacerations consistent with someone who has committed suicide?"

"Absolutely not. Someone else caused these injuries."

Aaron said, "Now, Doctor, in your report you indicate something related to the brain matter of the victim, is that correct?"

"Yes."

"Would you please tell the court what you found?"

"Well, it's more a matter of what I didn't find. I did not find a brain."

There were some audible gasps in the courtroom. Not from me, of course. This didn't surprise me in the least, for obvious reasons.

"You're saying that the brain of the victim had been removed?"

"Yes."

"Do you know how it was removed?"

"The most likely explanation is that it was accessed via the vertebrate column, and removed with some sort of sharp instrument."

"The work of a monster, correct?"

"Objection," I said.

"I withdraw the question," Aaron said. "Thank you, Doctor." Aaron turned to me. "Your witness."

I picked up my copy of the autopsy report.

"Doctor," I said, "you indicate massive loss of blood from these injuries, don't you?"

"Yes."

"If someone cut the victim's throat, as you say, the blood would gush out, wouldn't it?"

"Yes, the pumping of the blood would cause that to happen."

"Most likely bleed all over the victim and the perpetrator, correct?"

"Absolutely."

"Which would make the ingestion of blood rather difficult, wouldn't you say?"

"Excuse me, I don't understand the question."

"Ingestion. The putting of the blood of another into one's mouth and drinking it."

"Well, I suppose."

"Come now, Doctor. Is it easier to sip soup through a straw or pour it out on the table and lick it up?"

Someone in the gallery went "Eww!"

I couldn't blame him.

Dr. Scheppke shook his head. "I have no opinion on that."

"Well if a vampire needs to drink blood, cutting the throat would be an awfully inefficient way to do that, correct?"

Aaron objected. "This calls for speculation."

"Sustained," said the judge.

Which meant I had to move on. "Doctor, the removal of the brain is a rather uncharacteristic development, is it not?"

"It is rare, yes."

"Rare? Have you ever autopsied a body where the brain has been removed?"

"I can't say that I have."

"Indeed, it is not an easy process to remove brain matter, is it?"

"I suppose not."

"Unless one is skilled in doing so?"

"I can't answer that."

"But, Doctor, a vampire does not desire brain matter."

Aaron said, "Objection. Argumentative, beyond the scope of direct."

"Sustained," said the judge.

Naturally. But I'd gotten it out on the record.

I put on no witnesses. It's usually pointless at a prelim. I moved that Traci Ann be granted bail, but of course the judge refused. Accused cop killers do not get let out.

We were done, and a tired judge said, "Why wait?

There is ample cause for the defendant to be bound over for trial. Shall we set a date?"

"Just so it's understood," I said, "that the defendant does not and will not waive time. We demand our right to a speedy trial."

"Mr. Argula?" the judge said.

"We're fine with that, Your Honor. The sooner the better."

"You looked incredible in there," Aaron said to me in the hallway.

"Oh?"

"Hot. Smoking, iron-in-the fire hot."

"Good."

"Good?"

"I want to distract you in every way I can," I said.

He smiled, then took my hands in his. "Mallory, do you promise not to bite me again?"

I thought for a moment he was going to kiss me, right there in the corridor. His eyes were alive with primal desire. I felt it, too, but I also thought his eyes would make nice hors d'oeuvres. I didn't have time for this. I couldn't let Aaron distract *me*. Because if he did, I'd lose, and that's the one thing I can't stand.

"Not here," I said.

He smiled and let me go. "All right, let's talk deal."

"We'll take dropping the charges and an apology."

"Are you crazy?"

"Okay, you don't have to apologize," I said.

"Am I wasting my time even talking to you?" he asked.

"She didn't do it."

"You don't know."

"How about if I do know?"

"That would mean you knew that someone else did it and had proof."

I shrugged.

Aaron said, "If you have proof, give it to me."

I put my hands on my hips. "I don't have to give you squat. You have to prove your case, and you can't. You won't."

"You haven't gotten all the discovery yet?"

"You know full well I haven't. You're dragging your cloven hooves."

"You want to insult me?"

"Yes."

"Or," Aaron said softly, "would you rather have my body?"

"For medical experimentation only," I said.

"Why are you doing this to me?"

"What?"

"Treating me like I'm some bug."

"If the thorax fits . . ."

Aaron huffed. "This isn't helping your cause. You're going to see that we have incontrovertible evidence that your client was in that car, that night, and was seen by at least one eyewitness five minutes before the murder inside that very car."

I tried hard not to bite my permanently desensitized tongue. If what he was saying was true, it meant not only that somebody had planted evidence, but someone was being paid or induced to lie.

Maybe that somebody was a detective. Like the one leaning against the wall—Richards. He was glaring at me.

I glared right back.

"I'll see you later, Aaron," I said.

"Where you going?"

"To talk to someone."

Aaron looked around to see who I was talking about. "Won't do you any good," he said.

"I like a challenge," I said.

Richards didn't change his expression when I got to him. "Well, well," he said.

"Cut the small talk," I said. "I want some information."

He shrugged.

"You promised me," I said. "We had a deal. I helped you out on Carl Gilquist. Now I want to know who I can talk to about my mur . . . my attempted murder."

"I said I'd let you know."

"No more stalling. You owe me. And you're going to need me."

He shrugged again. "I'll see what I can do." And off he went down the hallway.

Part of me wanted to charge right after him and take a chunk out of his neck. I was almost tasting his flesh when I felt a tap on my shoulder.

It was Strobert.

"What do you want?" I said.

"I know what's going on," he said.

"Oh, yeah?"

He nodded. "You deserve a break."

"Well thanks so much, Detective. That's a nice thing to say after I grilled your cheese in there."

"I can take it."

I liked that. A cop who didn't hold a grudge against another professional doing her job.

He said, "The name you want is Antoine Thompson."

"Who is that?"

"Maybe a witness to what happened to you."

My dry flesh tingled. "What do you mean *maybe*?"

"You'll have to ask him," Strobert said.

"Why can't you tell me?"

"The actual witness statement is gone from the file. I looked. There's only a summary line stating that the witness was *unhelpful*. I find that hard to believe, because I saw that a statement had been logged in. You don't do that unless there's something in it."

"You saying the statement was lifted?"

"Not saying that. Just saying it isn't there."

"Where can I find this Antoine?"

"He's a gangbanger. Rolling 16s. I've run across him before. I don't advise you see him alone."

"You want to come with me?"

"I wish I could. But you and I can't be seen outside court together. You know that."

Funny, but it almost sounded like he *wanted* to see me outside court. I shook away the thought. I had my hands full with one potential boyfriend I wanted to eat. I couldn't load on anybody else.

"You at least have an address?" I said.

He handed me a slip of paper. "And remember, you didn't hear this from me." He started to walk away

"Hey," I said, stopping him. "Thanks."

He nodded. A little smile.

His green eyes no longer bothered me.

CHAPTER 12

In L.A. you've got a panoply of gangs. Latino gangs, Sueno gangs, Asian, African-American, and neo-Nazi gangs. You've got the occult, the Goths, prison gangs, and motorcycle gangs. Tagger crews and party posses. You have gangs in schools and gangs on the street. And with each one you better look the part or don't go near.

Things being the way they are in this messed-up world, you can get it, sometimes, why they exist. You don't make it as a kid on the streets by walking alone. You get a sense of pride and honor from a gang, instantly. You get people watching your back and you get money in your pocket. You keep alive. If you're lucky.

But you die if you wander into the wrong territory.

Which I was doing right now. It was the morning after the prelim and I was down in South Los Angeles, in the territory of the Rolling 16s. They were one of the oldest and most vicious gangs in the history of the city. They got their start in the early 1960s, right before the Watts riots broke out. Back when white cops took it out on blacks as a matter of routine. The culture under Chief William Parker was one of turning a blind eye to what happened in the African-American community. Not all the apples were bad, but there were enough of them to breed resentment that eventually blew the city apart.

That's when the R-16s came into being. And from there it was all an advance into drugs, counterfeiting, and violence.

Which is why I went down there in the daytime. Most gangbangers sleep during the day. Night is their domain. Best chance I had to get some information from one of them was to catch him getting out of sleep.

Of course, this would make him angry. Maybe even want to kill me. Which didn't frighten me at all.

The address Strobert had given me was for a house with overgrown bougainvillea and chain-link around a spotty front yard. I let myself through the gate and went up to the front door, which was guarded by a wrought-iron screen. I pressed the doorbell. And I knocked a few times.

And waited.

Then I banged some more.

From deep within the house I heard a voice, cursing. The cursing got louder. And then threatening. It got closer to the door, and basically said it better be good or there would be some very painful things done to the body of the person standing outside.

The door swung open. The man was about twenty-five, well muscled. He wore a white T-shirt that stretched across his frame and boxer shorts.

His look told me he was about as shocked to see a young white woman on his doorstep as he would have been at the sight of Mickey Mouse pointing a 9mm.

"Antoine?" I said.

"Who the—"

"Mallory Caine. I'm a lawyer."

"So?"

"Can I talk to you?"

"'Bout what?"

"I'd rather not talk through a wire mesh."

"I don't care what you rather. I don't know you. You come to my house. Pound on my door. Wake me up. Why don't you make a 'pointment?" And then he laughed.

"Well, that's funny," I said. "Because I've got an appointment to kick your butt all over the street, right in front of your homies. How would that look?"

His smile dropped. He called me a few names and peppered me with a few F bombs. Standard stuff.

I waited for him to finish and said, "Feel better now?"

"You ain't scared," he said with an astonished incredulity.

"Should I be?"

He pushed the wrought-iron screen open with his right hand and grabbed my blouse in his left and pulled me inside. I stumbled, but caught myself before I hit the ground.

He slammed the door behind him and stepped up to me. He was a few inches taller, but his brawn suddenly looked as thick as a tank.

"You don't know who you're talkin' to," he said.

"Sure I do. You're Antoine Thompson. I know all about you. I'm not here to bust you down. I'm here to get some information."

"Why you think I got something to give you? Why you think I do it if I had something?"

"Let's just say I'm counting on your good graces."

He laughed again. "Only graces I got ain't good."

"Everybody's got it somewhere in their gut. You just forget about it when all you do is hurt people."

"I don't hurt no people 'cept the ones who got it coming. Call it justice. You a lawyer, you understand that."

"So you have a sense of justice, do you?"

"Sure I do."

"That's why I'm here. Justice. For me."

It looked like he was thinking about it, like I was so totally unexpected to him that he wasn't throwing me out on my ear. Not that I would have let him, of course. I would have given him a lesson in zombie street fighting and the ancient art of kicking a man in the balls.

He suddenly looked a little embarrassed to be standing in front of me in his boxers. He scratched his head and looked around the room. It was messy. There were discarded boxes of pizza, fast food bags, dope seeds, a hash pipe. The place smelled like old party, a sad kind of stench.

"You really a lawyer?" he said

"Got an office and everything."

"You know anybody in the entertainment business?"

"What?"

"You know, movies?"

"I may have a name in my Rolodex. Why?"

He put his finger in the air, indicating for me to wait. He walked out of the room. I heard some scuffling noises, as if he was looking through a drawer. A moment later he came back holding a small stack of bound paper. He handed it to me.

"I wrote a screenplay," he said. "Can you help me get it to the right people?"

* * *

It is a fact, and a law, that if you live in Los Angeles and have opposable thumbs, you have to be working on a screenplay.

But a hardcore banger?

"See," he said, "it's about a kid from the 'hood, he's a musical genius, only he ain't got nobody to tell him how to get out of the life."

"Uh-huh," I said, trying to process this little scene. Although a plan was starting to develop in my mind.

"And then the kid gets shot, see, and a angel comes down and saves him. I see Denzel as the angel. You know Denzel?"

"Not personally, no. But I could have my people call his people."

"Serious?"

"Go on."

"So the kid gets better and starts playin' the one thing he always wanted to play, which is guitar. Blues guitar."

"Okay."

"Then a tidal wave washes over Los Angeles, see, and wipes everything away."

"A tidal wave?"

"'Cause a asteroid hits the earth."

"I can see that," I said.

"This all came to me in a dream."

"I believe that."

"Least I think it was a dream. I was high."

"I believe that, too."

"You do?"

"Sure," I said.

"You don't really," he said. "But I can prove it to you. Look at the last page."

I sighed and flipped to page 110 of Antoine Thompson's screenplay.

"It's the last line," he said. "Read that."

I looked at the last line.

And my mouth dropped open. The hinges of my jaw clicked. I pushed them back in place.

The last line of Antoine's screenplay had a priest saying, *"Non semper Saturnalia erunt."*

"Now, how do I know Latin?" Antoine said. "I found out what them words mean after I wrote 'em. It was in my dream, see. My dream about Los Angeles."

"All right," I said. "Listen to me. I'm going to take this screenplay of yours and do something with it."

He scowled. "Don't you try stealin' it. I got it registered with the Writers Guild."

"Don't worry. I'm going to study this and see if I can get you something. But now you have to give me something. You have to give me a name."

CHAPTER 13

The Men's Central Jail is only a few minutes drive from the courthouse. It's a noodle's toss from Chinatown, a block-style old building that saw its best days maybe never. They really ought to condemn the joint, but there are too many people they have to keep housed here. It's overpacked and undercleaned, a place where only a rat would find solace. Nobody likes working here. It's a cesspool of viruses they don't know anything about.

If a virus were ever to cause zombie-ism, I would bet it starts right here.

I checked in at the front desk. I showed my bar card and said I was here to see Tyrone Mackenzie. They issued me a pass, then buzzed me inside.

I knew my way to the visitor's room. It's just a row of green, round stools in front of Plexiglass separators, with handsets on either side. I gave my pass to one of the guards and sat and waited for Tyrone Mackenzie to show.

How many times had I been in here to talk to clients? How many times seeing the looks of either desperation or defiance? It's a world unto itself, with its own rules and modes of behavior. Sometimes it doesn't make sense.

I had one client who I could have gotten out, but he told me not to. He wanted to stay and do the full 365. I found out later he was assigned to pantry duty and he'd steal hot sauce. Then he charged the Latinos a dollar a pop for some flavor in their otherwise drab grub. They all have bank, and can trade, so my guy was making a pretty good chunk of change. Plus, he wasn't out having to survive on the street.

The interior door opened and a slender, rabbity-looking man in his late twenties came in dressed in jailhouse blues. He scowled at me when the deputy pointed me out. He came over and sat down, picked up his handset.

"What you want?" he said.

"You know who I am?" I said.

"No."

"Mallory Caine."

"So?"

"Lawyer. I got shot in your neighborhood."

His eyes widened and he studied me. "You?"

"That's right."

"You look pretty good, considering."

"Considering I got shot?"

"You walkin' around."

"You saw me get shot that night."

He leaned back a little. "I didn't see nothin'."

"Little Mac, don't play games."

And he jerked forward again. "Don't be callin' me no Little Mac."

"You Big Mac now?"

He smiled. One of his front teeth was capped with turquoise.

"You did see what happened," I said. "Antoine told me."

"Antoine got a big mouth."

"So why don't we go over it again?"

"That all you came for? See ya." He started to get up.

"You want to help your sister, don't you?"

He sat right back down. "What you talkin' about my sister?"

"She was popped for possession."

"What?"

"Antoine told me. You think he has a big mouth now?"

"When this happen?"

"Yesterday. Maybe I can help her."

His eyes narrowed into knife slits. "You tryin' to play me?"

"Like you're a guitar and I'm Stevie Ray Vaughn."

"I don't get played."

"You've got thirty seconds."

"What can you do for my sister?"

"I can get her out, get her a plea deal, get her into diversion."

"How much?"

"I won't charge your family a thing. But your information had better be good."

Big Mac heaved a sigh. He didn't look like a bad kid just then. He just looked lost like the rest of us.

"Listen up," he said. "I can't say nothin'. You can't get nothin' from me. Somebody wanted you dead real bad."

"How do you know?"

"Cops said it was a drive-by, right?"

"It was."

He shook his head. "The car was waitin'."

That was new. That brought me to the edge of the stool. "What are you saying?"

"Just what I said. It was a Escalade with no plates, right? But I seen it waitin' earlier. Those ain't all that rare, know'm sayin'? So I seen it there and I seen you come out of the Robinson place. I was sitting outside, just across the street."

That would have a been a little over a year ago. Back then I was happily working for the public defender's office. I went to visit a client living with his parents in the shadows of Exposition Park. Usually PDs don't have this luxury. There are too many case files.

But I had a real feeling about Maxwell Robinson being innocent. He was eighteen, a gang member no question about it. But he had been continually harassed by a cop who wanted to get him for some reason, and I was sure there was some planting of evidence.

It was a robbery charge, and Maxwell had been bailed out by his older brother, a clerk at a liquor store in Watts. The older brother, Charles, couldn't really afford it, so I figured going down there personally to talk was the least I could do.

Besides, you don't get many innocent clients and you really want to work the case when you do.

So I talked it out, got a lot of good information. I was sure Maxwell was innocent when it was all done. I came out of the Robinson house and headed to my car. It's not the kind of neighborhood anyone wants to walk in at night. Especially a single woman. I got in my car fast and started to drive.

The moment I did, another car started following me. Headlights in my rearview mirror. Tailgating me.

I stepped on the gas and made for the next main drag, Normandie. That's when I heard the first shots.

My rear windshield shattered. Stunned by the noise I jerked my car left and crashed into a car parked at the curb. I heard more shots, then felt a burning in my chest. I looked down and saw blood all over the front of my blouse.

In desperation, thinking more shots were to come, I pushed the door open and stumbled toward the side yard of a house. It was dark, no lights on in the windows. I knew in just a moment people would pour out of their homes to see what the noise was. Somehow I managed to get to the back of this particular house, where I collapsed on a cracked cement driveway.

And that's where I died.

I'll tell you, everything they say about the white light is true. I was standing at the edge of a tunnel. It seemed to go on forever, but at the far end was the brightest light I have ever seen. It was white and warm. It was all encompassing. It was love. And it was drawing me forward, even though I was not conscious of moving my feet or my arms or anything else.

And then something grabbed my ankles.

I got pulled back from the light. I opened my mouth to scream, but no sound came out. I was pulled down into some sort of shrieking darkness, and then I was looking up into a light again. Only this was a single bulb in a room somewhere. I didn't know where. I was lying on the floor on my back.

I felt my chest. I was naked.

And a bandage was over what should've been my chest wound.

Where was I?

And why wasn't I moving?

Get up, I told myself.

Then heard another voice in my mind saying, *Stay down.*

Now I thought I was insane. Or in hell.

Or at the very least in some nightmare.

Get up, I told myself again.

Stay down.

Cursing, and hearing my own voice, I forced myself off the floor.

The voice telling me to stay down began to sound desperate. I wasn't hearing the words so much as sensing them.

And then I started to get mad.

What was I doing naked in a kitchen?

Little Mac's voice crackling on the headset brought me out of the memory flash. "You hear me?" he said

"Say again," I said.

"Come on, listen up! You got in your car, right? The Escalade, it followed you, right? I hear the shots when they came. I don't know, you hear that alla time, you don't even think about it. But this time I think it's you, but that's all. I don't go runnin' to see or nothin'. You keep your own business. And that's all I know. Now you gonna help my sister for reals?"

"Yeah," I said. "For reals. Just one more thing. You see anybody in the Escalade? Can you describe them?"

He shook his head. "Tinted windows, man. There's no way."

"Hey, Mac?"

"Yeah?"

"You're Big Mac for sure. Thanks."

"Hey."

"Yes?"

"Come back and tell me what happens with Yvette, 'kay?"

"I will."

I walked out to Bauchet Street and headed to the lot for my car. My mind was buzzing. Somebody was lying in wait for me that night. It wasn't random what happened. There was somebody gunning for me.

But who could that possibly be? I had no enemies. Not deadly ones, anyway. Could it have been a mistake? Whoever shot thought I was somebody else? Not likely. Not at that hour, in that place.

So there it was. Who would want to kill little ol' me? It was before I was a zombie and everything.

And why had this cop Bracamonte dropped my case? Was he the one who took out the witness statement?

In fact, where the heck was this Bracamonte, anyway?

I wasn't going to have much time to ponder this because when I got to the parking garage Geraldine was gone.

CHAPTER 14

I walked up and down the aisle a couple of times, just to make sure I hadn't gone to the wrong spot.

Nope, it was simply not there.

That's how you assault someone in L.A. You take away their wheels. Their way of getting around. We are too spread out for a practical transit system. You need a car in this town.

Could it have been towed for some reason? No, I'd checked in. I'd shown my bar card.

It had to be stolen.

Fuming, I walked back down toward the jail, thinking what to do. Call up LAPD and CHP and report it, I guess. Which is when my phone bleeped.

It was a blocked number. "Yes?" I said.

"Car trouble?"

"Who is this?"

"Asking if you have car trouble."

It was a man's voice, but muffled in a way that told me he was using the old junior high school trick of putting a handkerchief over the mouthpiece or something like that.

"You took my car?" I said.

"You want it back?"

"All right, what do you want?"

"Listen to me. I will treat your car very gently. It's a lovely yellow. It seems like a good car, well behaved. I don't want it to end up at the bottom of the ocean. And I know you need it. Don't try calling the police. I wouldn't want anything bad to happen to your precious automobile. If you want it, you will follow my directions exactly."

"Look, buddy, you can keep the car. I'm calling the cops. We'll track it down eventually. If you take it to a chop shop, I don't care. I'll buy a new one."

"On what? You can't even make your rent." *Now how does he know that?* "No, all I want is to talk. And to tell you why your client is completely innocent. And how you can prove it."

"That's a pretty loaded statement. How do I know any of this is legit?"

"I'll give you a hint. Police planting evidence. Now if you want to hear about it, you will come to where I am."

"Why go to all this trouble? Why did you have to steal my car? I'm a reasonable—"

"You're not making the rules. Now here is where you are to go, and be sure you are alone. I'll be watching. If you try to pull something, you will never know what I have."

He gave me an address in Marina Del Rey and hung up.

I walked to Broadway and headed toward my office. But when I got to the Bradbury Building at the corner of Third I got an idea, and went inside.

The interior of the Bradbury is still beautiful. There's a skylight, giving the whole place a natural light, like an atrium. It's made up mostly of black, wrought-iron railings, with two elevators of the same look on either side of the lobby. They shot *Blade Runner* here. The place can look like the future or the past, depending on your mood.

Right now it looked like the present to me, because this is where LAPD's Internal Affairs Group is housed.

The public's not supposed to go up the stairs, but I did anyway, up to the third floor where I found the office of a captain I'd crossed rapiers with before. His office door was open. I could see past the front section, through the glass to the outer office, where he sat holding a phone to his ear.

I went in where a woman at a desk asked me what I wanted.

"Captain Ketzler," I said. Garth Ketzler was a thirty-year veteran of the force. He'd been a detective with RHD, Robbery Homicide Division, back when I was with the PD's office. Now he was back in blues and running the Criminal Investigation Division of the IAG. That's the division that investigates bad cops.

"He's on a call right now," the woman said.

"I'll wait."

"You have an appointment?"

"Just a drop in. We're old friends. I'm a lawyer."

"Oh? With the DA's office?"

"No, solo."

Her expression cooled. "Oh."

"No worries, though, I'm friendlier than most defense lawyers. I don't bite unless I'm hungry."

She did not change her expression.

Ketzler saw me through the glass. I gave him a wave. He frowned. Then he finished his call and came to the interior door.

Ketzler was about my height, six feet, with good

rigid lines in his uniform and his face. He was balding slightly, but his hair was neatly combed.

"Mallory Caine," he said.

"Hello, Captain. Sorry to barge in. Can I have a word?"

He looked at his watch. "I've got to be at a meeting with the chief and the mayor in twenty minutes."

"Really? With Hizzoner? Wear your sunglasses."

"Hm?"

"His teeth give off glare."

"Ah. Well, what is it?"

"Can we close the door?"

He nodded. I went into his office. He closed the door and stayed standing. "So?"

"You have a file on an Officer Bracamonte? From Hollywood Division?"

"You know I can't give you information like that."

"And you know I can get a subpoena. I can file a *Pitchess*." A *Pitchess* motion lets the defense get records of a cop's previous bad acts. "I just thought I'd spare everybody the hassle."

"And that's downright neighborly of you, Ms. Caine. I'm sure you're just looking out for all our interests. But anything you were able to get would be redacted. Not much use except what's on the public record."

"So he was being investigated."

"That much you could have found out without barging in here."

"Did I barge? I thought I sashayed. I was really trying to sashay."

"Will there be anything else?"

"I'll tell you what I know," I said. "Feel free to correct me. Bracamonte was the lead investigator on an attempted murder. I happen to be the victim."

"I remember," Ketzler said.

"And there was some monkey business involving a witness statement."

"How do you know that?"

"Am I wrong?"

"I'm asking how you know."

"I got sources, you got sources."

"Then why don't you go back to your sources? We're done here."

"Wait," I said. "Why can't you give me a little break here? This Bracamonte is missing. He flew the coop, as they used to say. Because he knew something heavy was coming down, and you are part of that. Somebody doesn't want my murder—attempted murder—fully investigated. I have a right to know why that is."

He said, "I can't give you anything."

"Just tell me one thing," I said. "Do you know where Bracamonte is? Any idea where I can find him?"

"I'm sorry, Ms. Caine, I really am. But I don't. If you ever find out, let us know."

I walked across Broadway and back to my building. LoGo gave me a look. I smiled. She gave me more of a look.

I went upstairs. As soon as I opened my office door, Nick Papadoukis came out of his office and stepped into mine.

"I am a barometer," he said.

"Oh, yeah? Then why didn't you barometer me the discovery package that you accepted on my behalf?"

"Sorry I am," he said. "But—"

"Nick, if you don't mind—"

"What darkness are you into?"

I looked down at him. He seemed even more troll-like today. "What's that supposed to mean?"

"There was an owl outside your window," he said.

I felt a little zombie shiver. "An owl, you say?"

He nodded.

"So what's your barometer say about that?" I asked.

"Owls are associated with all sorts of things."

"That's your answer?"

"They are nocturnal, and sometimes devilish."

I said, "And aren't they sometimes just birds?"

He shrugged. "I suppose. Mallory, look at this." He pulled a booklet out of his back pocket and showed it to me. It was titled *How to Be a Detective*.

"Nick—"

"I can do it. If you will only give me another chance."

"I told you, Nick, I don't have the funds to hire—"

"First case is free."

I looked at the little gnomelike guy, and wondered how effective it would be for him to follow someone. Wouldn't the subject notice the lawn ornament behind?

"I'll keep it in mind, Nick," I said.

"You will need me someday," he said.

I doubted that.

I waited until eight o'clock, as the instructions specified. When I got there, I saw my car parked in the marina parking lot, as pretty as you please.

I was told it would be there, but that it wouldn't start. Something had been removed, he said. I could pick it up at a specified slip. Just to make sure, I tried to start it with my key. No dice.

I walked out to the docks, looking at the numbers.

A couple of people were having a high time on a boat, laughing it up. So it wasn't like I was alone.

It just felt that way. The sky was dark, the stars obscured by cloud cover. It was a little chilly, though on my skin it feels nice. The salt air does it good. I almost feel human again when I'm by the ocean.

I heard a creak of the boards, looked up. And saw the worst human being without a sword that I could possibly see.

Judge Dixon Darnell said, "Good evening, Ms. Caine."

Every city has its share of corrupt judges. And the powers that be have a way of covering those tracks, unless and until a judge gets to be an embarrassment. Even then, it's hard to get one off the bench, even if they deserve to be thrown out.

In L.A., back in the day, corruption was something of a sport in the justice system. It was the Wild West. Money changed hands. Favors were granted. Winks and nods were made to prosecutors and defenders alike.

Now we are so much more civilized. The rotten apples know how to keep looking like the others in the barrel. They know how to pick their spots.

Like Darnell had picked his.

"I know you are quite surprised to see me," the judge said. He was dressed in white shorts, black socks covering his calves, sandals, and a Hawaiian shirt. The shirt was copious to cover his girth. On his head was a little captain's cap. "But you have to know I'm human, after all."

"You have something for me," I said.

"I surely do," he said, and smiled.

"I mean information, and a car part. Which part, by the way?"

"A nice little drink first, and then you'll get what you want."

Yeah, it was obvious what this guy wanted. He was sure to make a move, offer more threats. I could go along with it far enough to figure out what he had. I could do the vixen thing.

I could also eat him.

That would be risky, though, here on the dock. Still, I had to keep my options open.

"Permission to come aboard granted," Darnell said, giving me a mock salute. He motioned me to step aboard and I did.

"I know what you must think of me," Darnell said. He opened the door to a little lounge, done up in teak and brass.

"Judge," I said, "I try not to think of you. I hope you're okay with that."

"I know I made a blatant attempt to get you to show me a little favor." He closed the door. "But I'm a very direct kind of guy."

"Uh-huh."

"What are you drinking?"

"Nothing for me. I'd like my car part and the information you promised."

"I disconnected one of the battery cables. I'll slip it on for you, no problem."

"That's it?"

"That's it."

"Who stole the car? In fact, how did you even know I was at the jail? Have you had somebody tailing me?"

"I can't reveal that," he said. "I'm sure you understand."

"No, I don't. There's a lot I don't understand. Like why you went to all this trouble to get me here."

"That should be obvious."

"I was hoping it wasn't."

He shrugged. "Let me fix you a drink, come on." He stepped to a liquor cabinet and pulled down a bottle of Jim Beam.

"Let's just end this, shall we?" I said.

He poured the Beam in two glasses, then clinked some ice in them. He returned to where I was standing and held one out.

"Thank you, no," I said.

He put that one down, then sipped his own. And sat himself in a black leather recliner. "If I'm to give you something, something as valuable as I have, you have to give me something."

"Judge—"

"We're not in court, Mallory. Call me Dix."

Gack. This was going to be bad. This was going to be stomach turning. I had to get out of this thing but fast.

"I have to say, Dix, this is also a pretty dopey way of getting what you want. Come on, this isn't the fifties. These aren't grope-the-secretary days."

"I have no choice," he said. "I want you and you must be persuaded."

"Persuade me then. What have you got?"

"No, no. I can't give up my leverage that easily."

"Well, I'm no dope. I have to know you at least have something of value. I'm starting to doubt it."

"What if I gave you a good faith offer of proof?"

"I'll consider it," I said.

"All right then." He took another sip of his drink, then froze. "Did you hear something?"

"Just the beating of my heart, Dix darling."

He scowled. "I'm serious. If you brought someone with you . . ."

"Relax, paranoid boy. What is it you have for me?"

Darnell put his drink down. "You client is being set up to cover someone's behind."

"That much I already know," I said.

"Ah, but did you know that there's a certain person, a certain person of some status in this town, who was seen in the company of your client on two occasions? And that such sighting, should it ever come to light, would be quite damaging to said person of some status?"

I tried not to stay cool. "Who?"

"Now that is the information I choose to withhold at this time." He turned his head. "I could have sworn . . ."

And then the boat lurched as if someone had just jumped on deck.

Darnell bolted out of his chair just as the door crashed open by way of a heavily booted foot.

Which was followed by the other foot, and the rest of the guy.

The guy in the hoodie. And he had his sword.

CHAPTER 15

Have you ever looked into the face of a scary Santa Claus? Maybe one at the mall when you were a kid, with rheumy eyes and a drinker's skin?

Or how about a schizophrenic on the downtown street corner, the one shouting at the voices in his head? Swirling around in a dance of paranoia and making sure everyone around him knows about it?

That is what I was looking at now, because I could see the guy's face in the light. He had a full white beard and wide, crazy eyes. He was like a John Brown, a mad prophet, filled with his own visions of terror and retribution.

And armed with a sword. In this small room on a boat, it gave me very little room to maneuver.

He screamed and charged forward.

I could see Darnell out of the corner of my eye, stock still like a frozen Buddha. Hoodie burst right past him and came for me, bringing the sword down in a vicious arc.

I jumped right.

The sword whacked the little bar top, slicing the thing in half.

I could see my head as a neatly bisected casaba next.

Hoodie withdrew his sword from the wood and shouted, "Devil spawn!"

My legs hit the coffee table as I tried to run for the door. I stumbled, veering right. The boat was still rocking. I couldn't regain my balance. But that saved my zombie life, because hoodie lost equilibrium, too. He made a wild swing at me with the sword, but it missed by a couple of feet.

Which was the only margin for error I had.

Judge Darnell still hadn't moved. Shock does funny things sometimes. Here he was planning a discrete little tryst and now he had a bearded Zorro running around his boat shouting about the devil.

Not that I cared what he thought at the moment.

Thwump! Another swipe with the blade, barely missing my arm and ending in the sofa.

The door. It was my only means of escape. Still reeling, I took a few clumsy steps toward it.

Hoodie moved faster than I thought he could. His heavy boots landed with a chilling thud in the space between the door and me.

"What do you want?" I managed to say.

"Die," he said.

I had to back up now, toward the liquor cabinet. My options were severely limited. In my street fighting class the longest piece of steel we ever prepared for was a knife.

And on the street. Not in a little room on a boat.

Darnell finally moved, toward the door. For a split second we were all aligned, like deadly stars, me in the middle.

That alignment is what ended the life and career of Judge Dixon Darnell.

Because the next swipe of Hoodie's blade was aimed directly at my neck.

I ducked. Hit the floor actually, on my knees.

I heard the dull contact of sword on flesh. I pounced outward and upward, like a scared gazelle, wanting only to get out of the way of another attempt.

At the same time I landed, some four or five feet away, something else landed at my feet.

The head of Judge Darnell. It was severed cleanly at the neck, and there was still a look on his face of complete and utter horror. His mouth was moving, his lips flapping up and down, as if saying, *Mama*, over and over.

One thing the blow had done was stop Hoodie for a moment. He looked down at the torso of his victim. "Oh, no," he said.

That was all the hesitation I needed. I grabbed the coffee table by its end legs and lifted it like a shield. It was lighter than I expected. Or maybe my zombie adrenal glands were pumping power through me.

Whatever it was, I held the table out in front of me and rammed Hoodie's head with it.

I made good contact. The edge of the table whacked his forehead with a satisfying *thunk*.

He fell backwards, stumbling over the legs of the departed jurist.

The back of his head hit the corner of the split bar top. He groaned, rolled once, and stopped moving.

That's when I heard sirens in the distance.

I got out of there. As I passed the boat that had the two people in it, one of them was up on deck. A guy. He had a beer in his hand. "Wuzzup?" he said.

I kept going.

"Hey!"

I got to my car. The sirens were closer. Could be

anything, but I wasn't going to wait to find out. It would be a little hard to explain the headless judge and guy with a sword. Even though I didn't do anything wrong, too many questions would be asked.

I popped open Geraldine and reconnected the battery. At least Darnell had told the truth on that one. The car started right up and I tore out of the lot.

In the rearview mirror I saw the guy with the beer, staggering around, looking at me.

CHAPTER 16

Mornings are the worst.

I don't need much sleep. Not like when I was alive. Remember when they used to say "beauty sleep"? For me, it's the opposite.

It was six o'clock when I woke up. I started the coffee—no one, not even zombies, can exist without coffee—and went to the bathroom for the routine.

My skin will flake and fall off unless I give it the full treatment every day. The only cream I've found that works is made by a young entrepreneur named Paris Richards. Luckily, I defended her brother on a shoplifting rap, and she paid me in part with jars of her skin cream. I've become her best customer.

I put on a layer of cream from head to toe, watching my skin suck it in like a desert floor takes on rain. It takes about fifteen minutes to do the whole ball of wax, as it were.

There's no need for a shower. Water isn't good for undead skin. Kelli's cream keeps me smelling sweet. I do have to wash the hair.

I stopped for a moment and looked at myself in the mirror. I had a body once, a real one. It was a good body. Even though freckles showed up on it more frequently than I would have liked, I was grateful. It was a body I wanted to give to a man I loved, and who loved me. Who'd fight for me, who'd get my back as well as scrub it. I wanted my body to have a baby, maybe two or three.

But now it was a dead thing.

After I dressed, I poured myself a cup of coffee and a glass of water. I downed two shark cartilage capsules, to strengthen my joints and, literally, keep myself together.

You find out about these things by trial and error.

I sat down at my laptop. The news about the headless judge had hit. Oh, man, it was all over. The headline on the *Times* site was SUPERIOR COURT JUDGE SLAIN ON YACHT.

Subhead: *Decapitated body of local judge found on private yacht moored in Marina Del Rey.*

The decapitated body of Judge Dixon Darnell, 48, was found early this morning on a private yacht owned by the judge and moored in Marina Del Rey. A Los Angeles County Medical Examiner, Joyce Peterson, says the severing appears to be the result of a violent swipe of a sharp blade.

Authorities have no theory about a motive . . .

And on it went with one glaring omission. Nothing about the guy with the sword.

Hoodie, it appeared, had gotten out of there before the police arrived.

Great.

I tried scanning some other news in the *Times*. There was a good report about traffic in Hollywood.

The mayor was taking credit for it. A combination of things like traffic light timing and on-the-street traffic control cops was apparently doing the trick.

Especially on club weekend.

When I saw his picture, though, smiling so as to be mistaken for the sun itself, I clicked off and finished my coffee and left.

I got to the office around nine and found a couple of detectives waiting for me in the Smoke 'n Joke. They flashed badges and said they were from the west side and could they talk to me?

About what, I wanted to know.

About let's talk in your office, they said.

There was a tall one named Granger and a shorter one named Smith. The tall one had a hook nose, like a hawk. The short one had a stubby nose, like a balled-up sock. Hawk and Sock, I named them in my mind.

When we got to my office I sat at the desk. Sock went over and looked at some of the things hanging on my wall. Like my law school diploma and a poster of Steven Tyler rocking out.

Hawk said, "You like practicing law up here?"

"Love it," I said. "Thanks for asking. You came a long way for that."

Hawk didn't smile. He sat in one of my client chairs.

"That's not why we're here," he said.

"I kind of figured that," I said. "See, I almost became a detective myself."

"Really?"

"No."

He frowned and drummed the fingers of his right hand on his neatly trousered leg. "Would you mind anwering a few questions?"

"Yes," I said.

"Okay, where—"

"I mean, yes, I'd mind."

That got Sock's attention. He turned around and came over and stood next to Hawk. Hawk said, "You're going to refuse to answer a few questions?"

"That's right," I said. "I don't like answering cop questions unless I know what it's about. And since you didn't tell me up front, that means you want to draw information out of me. I've been in the business too long not to take my own advice. And the advice I always give my clients is, 'Do not talk to the cops.' When they ask me why, I say, because it's true that anything you say to them they'll try to use against you. Yadda yadda yadda."

Hawk took in a long breath. Sock just stared at me. "But that's only if somebody's got something to hide. You don't have anything to hide, do you?"

"I've got lots of things to hide," I said. "I don't like anybody knowing what I eat for breakfast or where I keep my underwear. Also, I was a pretty lousy math student in school. Now don't you dare use any of that."

"Ms. Caine, give us a break here. We're investigating a murder and we think you can give us some help. Not as a suspect."

"Well, that's a relief. Am I a person of interest?"

"You interest me, if that's what you mean."

I snatched a pencil from my pencil holder, which is a small, hollowed out bust of Pancho Villa. I got it at the Smoke 'n Joke some time ago. I like the fact that he was an outlaw. You don't get more outlaw than being a criminal defense lawyer these days.

Which was why I wasn't playing ball with these guys. Long experience showed me it rarely pays off.

I tapped the pencil on my desk a few times, saying nothing.

"So?" Hawk said.

"So?" I said.

"You willing to help us out or not?"

"Not until I know exactly what this is about, and I mean names and places."

Hawk looked at Sock. Sock looked at Hawk. We all looked at each other. A little visual hokey-pokey.

"All right," Hawk said. "A judge was murdered last night. Judge Dixon Darnell. You know him?"

"Judge Darnell? Sure. He held me in contempt of court a couple of weeks ago."

Hawk smiled. "Is that right?"

"Of course, it's right," I said. "And you already knew it. That's why you're here."

That stopped him for a moment, but detectives know how to soldier on. "Well, since we've got that out of the way, how about telling us where you were last night around eight, nine o'clock?"

"How about not?" I said. "Unless you tell me I'm a suspect or put me in custody, at which point I'll consult with a lawyer who's almost as smart as I am and not say anything then, either."

"Why so difficult?"

"General principles," I said. "And why would you even come directly to me? What gives?"

Sock finally took the sock out of his own mouth. "Whyn't you let us ask the questions, Counselor? It'll all go so much faster."

"There's the door, Detective. Go as fast as you want out of it."

I could detect a little steam coming out of the chums, so I said, "Look, fellas. I had a run-in with

Judge Darnell in court. That is not a motive for murder, and especially one as brutal as that."

"Who said anything about how brutal it was?" Hawk asked.

I smiled. "It's all over the news. I do read the news in the morning."

"So why all the game playing, like you didn't know anything?"

"What, the way you did?"

Man, I love it when I can toss irony at cops.

"All right," Hawk said. "Have it your way. A woman fitting your description was seen last night in the vicinity of the judge's boat, where his body was found."

"Oh, really? How detailed a description?"

"Tall. Good shape to her."

"And you think I fit that description? Thanks. Now buy me dinner."

"She was dressed in a nice suit, like a professional."

"What color was the suit?" I asked.

"Unable to say."

"Who was unable to say?"

"Guy who saw her."

"Who was the guy?"

"Am I being cross-examined here?" he said.

"You should be used to that," I said. "Come on, a tall woman? Is that it?"

"Where were you last night at eight?"

"No soap," I said. "And how can you believe I would do something like cut off a judge's head?"

"Maybe you hired somebody to do it," Hawk said.

"And showed up to watch?" I said.

"What a waste of time," Sock said.

Hawk stood up. "I hope you know this isn't scoring you any points."

"I'm very sorry about the judge," I said. And I was, truly, because a perfectly good brain was taken from me. "I hope you catch the guy who did it. And for the record, last night I was with a man. It was some enchanted evening. But that's all I'm going to say."

CHAPTER 17

Midnight on Santa Monica Boulevard.

Amanda, on the make.

Stars above shining, the lights of the cemetery ghostly. I never believed in ghosts, but I never believed in zombies, either.

Tonight, I was starting to believe in a lot of things I hadn't before.

But also to despair. I did not want to be doing this anymore. Eating people. I was hurting inside over it. There was no way out for me. I had to stay alive or I would be forever lost.

God. I wanted to hear from God! I wanted deliverance, but it was not coming.

And it was time to put my Amanda on.

A Crown Vic pulled up and lowered the passenger window. I leaned in. With my shades on, and the dark lighting, I couldn't see his face clearly.

"Evening, sweetheart," I said.

"I want to buy an hour," he said.

"Whatever you want, baby."

"Don't 'baby' me, okay? I'm a cop." He flashed a badge. I felt my undead flesh go colder than normal. I gave him a more careful look from behind my shades. It was him, the cop, the one investigating the murder I had committed while wearing this very disguise— Strobert.

A fine kettle of carp. He would know me in a second if I let down my guard. I have an uncle who grew up in New Jersey and I have a pretty good ear. I used to imitate his accent, and that's what I did now.

"Even if you are a cop, I didn't accept no proposition yet."

"Relax," he said. "I told you I want some time, and I'm going to pay you for it. But not for what you think. Get in."

I had to. If I didn't, there was a good chance he'd run me, and my cover would be completely blown. Not a good thing for a defense lawyer eating brain on the side. And I couldn't exactly let him have it here on the street.

I got in.

"You hungry?" he said.

Oh, yeah I was, but not the way he thought.

"What's this about?" I said.

"Mexican. You like Mexican?"

"I don't like you. I don't like this whole setup. Why don't you just let me out."

"Well, you got no choice. You come along cooperative, we're done in an hour. You want to make trouble we talk down at the station."

"I don't believe this!" I said.

"Sit back and relax," he said.

"Right."

"You look scrawny," he said. "Some food'll do you good."

"What are you, a nurse?"

"Drop it."

I did. I'd put up a tough front, just enough to make me seem real in my role, but now I had to play along and get through this thing.

He took us to a place on Melrose. It had authenticity about it, the kind of Mexican place where you can feel the cooking oil in the air. They knew him there. We got a table in the corner by the window.

"My name's Strobert," he said. "What's yours?"

"What's it matter?"

"I'll tell you. Why don't you take off your shades?"

"Why don't you quit telling me what to do?"

"Hard candy, huh?"

"What of it?"

He put up his hands. "Just doing my job."

"Your job is buying streeters dinner?"

"Every now and then. You know, I got contacts. You don't like the life, I got places can help you."

"What do you care?"

"Just because I carry a badge, I don't care?"

"Cops are cops. You're supposed to be cynical."

He sat back and folded his arms. "You don't sound like a hooker. You sound like you've studied some."

"They got schools everywhere, chum."

"Come on, tell me your name and take off your glasses."

"You're paying for this, right?"

"Right."

"Then order me up a Corona and some fresh guacamole." At least guacamole and beer feel good going down together. "And some chips without salt."

"No salt?"

"I'm sort of on a low sodium diet," I said.

Strobert nodded, called the waiter over and ordered. Then he put his elbows on the table. "I don't want you to be nervous."

"Like having a cop question you doesn't do that?"

"Let's get that out of the way. You work the same corner as Traci Ann Johnson. You know she's charged with the murder of a police officer, don't you?"

"Who again?"

"You know her. We know you do."

"So what? I didn't see her do anything."

"Did you see her get into a red Charger on the night of the twenty-third?"

"I don't check on the other girls."

"You didn't answer my question."

"The answer is no. And here's another thing— there's no way Traci Ann killed any cop."

"Oh, yeah?"

"Take that to the bank."

"That's not going to help her. You need to tell me everything you know about that night."

"I saw nothing of her, okay? Maybe I said hello to her. But she didn't get in any red Charger."

"How do you know?"

"I didn't see it."

"How well do you know her?"

"Just from the street."

He nodded. "She ever come off strange to you?"

"Is this about that vampire thing?" I said.

"Maybe."

"You don't really buy that, do you?"

"I'm just trying to get the facts."

"But come on, a vampire?"

He said, "No, I don't believe it. But like I said, facts."

The waiter arrived with my beer. Strobert had ordered a Coke for himself. We drank. There was a sudden, faraway look in his eyes.

"Why'd you pick this spot?" I asked.

"Does it matter?"

"It does to me. You want me to talk, I want to know."

He looked around at the restaurant and said, "My dad used to bring me down here, to Olvera Street. He'd buy me a toy, then we'd go eat at Philippe's."

"So you grew up here?"

"Northridge."

"You looked sad just then," I said.

He shrugged. "City's changing. I sort of miss the old days."

"Isn't that what everybody says at some point in their lives?" I asked.

Strobert said nothing.

"How'd you get to be a cop?" I said.

"When I got out of the Navy I joined up. I didn't even much think about it. It seemed natural."

"Being a cop isn't natural."

"Neither is being a streetwalker."

I held up my beer. "Well then, cheers. To a couple of unnaturals."

We clinked and drank and I thought how strange it was for a zombie and a cop to be drinking together. But this was L.A., so why not?

The waiter came back with some hot chips and a bowl of fresh guacamole. Strobert offered me a chip. I took one and dipped and ate.

I could barely taste it. On my zombie tongue the flavors of food and drink are like distant train whistles to the ear. It's far away but with just enough pleasure to make you realize how much you miss it.

Strobert picked up a chip and held it over the guac, then stopped. His eyes lasered in on the dip.

"What is it?" I asked.

He didn't answer. He leaned his head closer to the bowl.

"What's wrong?"

Strobert said, "The guacamole."

"What about it?"

"It moved."

I almost laughed, but his face told me this wasn't a laughing matter.

I looked at the guacamole.

And yeah, it was moving. Bubbling, actually, as if it was soup boiling in a pot.

And then an orb formed in the middle of the guacamole, the size of a large marble. A healthy chunk of fresh guacamole, spinning in its own juices?

No. The top half of the orb slipped upward revealing a yellow eyeball underneath.

When I was six or seven I was playing in a trailer park with my friend, Terri Reyburn. She lived with her mom and sister, and I knew they didn't have much money. Her mom worked at a Holiday Inn, in housekeeping, and I'd go over and keep Terri company when her mom was away.

So we were playing hide-and-seek and Terri, who always made me laugh, went off somewhere to hide. When I went to look for her I was checking out the yard in the middle of the complex, looking behind benches and planters and things.

Then I saw the dark man. I saw him even though he wasn't there. What I mean is I saw him in my mind, only it was more than that. It seemed more real than even the things I could see right in front of me. I knew something then. I knew that this man was right outside the complex. I knew he was moving fast. And I knew he was coming for Terri.

I got scared. I called, "Terri!"

No answer.

I closed my eyes and concentrated real hard. I could see the man even better now. He was dark and ugly and gross. I could see he was coming up the alleyway on the east side of the complex. It was like a movie scene in my mind. And then the movie shifted, the camera panned, and I saw Terri squatting behind a Dumpster. She was smiling. She probably heard me call her name and was secretly enjoying the fact that I couldn't find her.

I ran as fast as I could to where the Dumpsters were. Again I called her name, and again there was no answer. I ran all the way to the Dumpster I'd seen in my mind and found Terri exactly where I knew she would be.

She looked up at me and said, "No fair! Somebody told you."

"Come on," I said. "We have to get out of here."

"How come?"

I looked around the Dumpster down the alley. And saw him. The man. He was coming toward us.

I jumped out and shouted, "Help!"

The man stopped. He was about twenty yards away. Close enough that I saw his eyes. They burned yellow. I thought for a second he was going to run right at me, try to choke me or something. Finish me off, then Terri, then throw us both in the Dumpster.

But he got spooked and turned around and ran away.

But that was not the weird thing. The weird thing was what happened next.

It was a clear, sunny afternoon. Not a cloud in the sky.

But right at that moment, as the man was running away, it started to hail. That's right. Big chunks of hail fell right there in the alley, clunking me on the head. The chunks of ice were the size of marbles.

Or eyeballs. Because that's what they turned into. A shower of eyeballs, frosty and hard, and every one of them seemed to look at me.

They bounced on the asphalt.

Terri shouted, "What's happening?"

I grabbed her hand and we ran back to her place. By the time we got there the hail had stopped. But people were coming out of their trailers and chattering about what was going on.

I thought I was crazy. It took me months to get over it. By that time I thought maybe the whole thing had been a dream. Or something I just imagined. But about a year later my mom and I were watching TV and a show came on, one of those crime shows, and it was about a child rapist that had been caught. And they showed his face, and the face was that of the dark man I'd seen in the alley.

Terri Reyburn's family moved away, back to Texas I think it was. We didn't keep in touch, but I would think about her from time to time. Then I saw on Facebook that she was a highly successful surgeon in Texas. She was saving lives right and left.

That was one of the strange things that happened when I was a kid.

Eyeball hail.

The eyeball in the guacamole stared at me.

Then it closed and settled back into the bowl, still.

There was one of those pauses the old playwrights called *pregnant*.

Strobert's face completely blanched. He looked at me and said, "What in the name of everything holy?"

The waiter scurried over, a look of concern on his face.

"There's something. Wrong. With the guacamole," Strobert said.

"*Cómo?*"

"Look." Strobert picked up a spoon and started scooping the guac right onto the table. The green mess spread out.

No eyeball.

Nothing but a smear of avocado and red onion.

"What?" Strobert said to no one.

"I do not understand," the waiter said.

Strobert opened his mouth to speak but nothing came out.

"It's all right, Señor," I said. "My friend just needs some air." I slid out of the booth and took Strobert's arm. He kept looking at the green splotch, even as he allowed himself to stand up.

"What . . . what . . ." Strobert said.

"Come outside," I said. I took out a ten spot from my purse and handed it to the waiter. Then I guided Strobert outside the front doors and into the night.

Outside, Strobert fought to catch his breath. "Did you see what I saw?" he asked. "Tell me you did."

"Bad guacamole," I said. "We ought to report—"

At that he grabbed my shoulders. "There was an eyeball in it! What is going on?"

"Easy." I gently pulled his arms off me. "You've had a shock."

"Ya think?"

I started to feel sorry for him then. I almost wished I could come clean and tell him everything that was going on, at least as far as I knew. But I reminded myself this was my client's adversary at the moment.

"Is this interview over?" I said.

"Huh?"

"I suggest you go home for a while, Detective."

He eyed me. A whole lot of eyeing going on. "You're not telling me something."

"Unless I'm under arrest, I'm leaving."

"No, don't." Almost pleading with me.

"Sorry." I started to walk away.

"Wait," Strobert said. "I'll drive you—"

"I prefer to walk."

CHAPTER 18

And walk I did. Down the mean streets as they say. Down Alameda to the border of Skid Row.

Drug dealers are not always the best source of brains, but they're a step up from the users. They've got to be sharp enough to avoid cops and other dealers. They've got to be survivors.

I was going fishing for one.

It didn't take long to get a nibble.

I was at the corner of San Julian Street and Sixth when I got spotted from across the street.

He was wearing an Oakland Raiders shirt over black jeans and the brightest pair of tennis shoes I'd ever seen. They practically glowed in the dark.

He started to cross toward me as I began south on San Julian, the very heart of the Row. To my right were several street encampments just below the bars of a wrought-iron and razor-wire fence. In the distance you could see the lights of the tallest building in L.A., the U.S. Bank Tower. It was just across town, but might as well have been on the moon. There were two different worlds here, two different landscapes. The way a big city always shakes out, I suppose.

"Hey," Raider said.

I ignored him, walking on. I needed to lure him farther on.

"Nice night," he said. "I got what you need, anything."

I kept going. He got in step alongside me, staying in the street.

"Don't be walking by with no words now," he said. "Just trying to make conversation."

"You don't have what I need," I said.

"Smoke or boot, what you like?"

I walked.

"Smack you up, come on now."

I said, "How much?"

"Now we are talking, you see that? You see how that works?"

He was smiling now and ready to do business.

"Not here," I said.

"Why don't we step into my office?" he said.

"Where?"

"Come with me." He picked up his pace and got up on the sidewalk. We were almost to Seventh when he ducked into an alleyway behind a brick building. The stench of urine and trash and human desperation hit me like a frying pan in the face.

And then we were behind a Dumpster. His office.

"Let's see some money," he said.

We were well protected from the street, from prying eyes.

"Where did you go to school?" I said.

"Huh?"

"School. Or are you a student?"

"What you want to know that for?"

"Informal survey."

"You're a cop!"

"Easy. I'm no cop."

"Mind telling me what you are?"

"No," I said. "I don't mind. I'm a lawyer."

"A junkie lawyer?"

"Is that so strange?"

"Money's the same color," he said. "Show me."

"You're a smart kid, aren't you?" I said.

"I ain't got time for this. You come up with it now, or I take it another way."

"Okay," I said. I reached in my purse and grabbed hold of Emily. She did her work well. Mr. Oakland Raider did not make a sound as he went down and I started to extract what I needed to live on.

I wept as I ate. I wept for the horror that was me.

The next day was a hearing in Traci Ann's case, scheduled for ten o'clock. The reason for the hearing was right outside the courthouse doors—the mob of reporters and photographers and news vans and just plain folks with phone cameras and gawking faces. A contingent of vampire wannabes, dressed up like it was Halloween, crowded in for some action, too. One of them carried a homemade sign that said JUSTICE BITES! FREE TRACI ANN!

I tried to slip though the front doors unnoticed. I hadn't been a high-profile lawyer until now and was hoping I wouldn't be instantly recognized.

I was.

One woman holding an ABC 7 microphone ran over. As soon as she did, a slobbering clutch of reporters started crowding in front of me, throwing out questions.

"Isn't this all for publicity?"

"Isn't this just a diversion?"

"Is this to get attention for your faltering practice?"

"Do you realize people actually believe your client is a vampire?"

I put my hands up and repeated, "No comment! No comment!"

They got physical. I pushed a pudgy camera guy from CBS 2 out of the way. He shouted that I couldn't do that and something about a lawsuit.

I got closer to the doors. Then a reporter, from Fox News I think, shouted, "What do you know about the murder of Judge Darnell?"

How did he know to ask me that? Hawk! He probably leaked it to him, the slime. Putting the pressure on me. I wasn't going to let him get away with it. I ignored the question from the reporter and pushed on.

Finally I was inside. I got through the security line and got on the world's slowest elevator. It spat me out on the tenth floor where I was met with another group of reporters, lying in wait.

More of the same chatter. I kept on pushing and got to the courtroom of Judge Carlotta Hegg, who had been assigned our trial.

Aaron was already inside, and the courtroom was full. A murmur like you see in the movies started up. I had arrived. Elvis was in the building. Nothing was ever going to be quiet for me again, as far as the law was concerned.

"There she is," Aaron said. "Media star."

"Can it," I said, plopping my briefcase on the counsel table.

"Hey, I'm on your side."

"How so?"

"I don't want to see you harassed. If there's any harassing to be done to you, I want to handle that personally." He smiled.

"Save that horseradish for the jury."

"Speaking of which, what do you say we fast track the trial?"

I gave him a look. "You're good with a fast track? Why would you do that?"

"You went speedy trial on me, I'm calling your bluff. Besides, nobody likes the idea of a night trial. The whole system has to put up with it."

"You're the ones who are insisting on prosecuting her. She only comes out at night."

"I still don't know how you're doing that," he said.

"Doing what?"

"Getting her into some sort of suspended animation during the day."

"You think I'm behind that?"

"The whole vampire thing, come on. Clever, but it stinks."

"Aaron, there's something that stinks about this whole case. Traci Ann is innocent. I can say that without reservation. Why is she being framed?"

"I've never heard you talk like this before," Aaron said. "You don't sound rational."

"Forget it. Yeah, let's fast track and get the trial over with." Now I was calling *his* bluff. I was sure he'd back out. Prosecutors never want to go to trial too soon.

But Aaron said, "We'll present it to the judge."

Five minutes later, Judge Carlotta Hegg entered the courtroom. She was a short, rotund woman who looked like a black bean bag chair in her robes. Humorless, she came off as a bit of a New England schoolmarm to me. She liked correcting the lawyers on points of law, even when she wasn't right about it.

She called the case and said, "I note that both counsel are present. Defendant is not present. Ms. Caine, I'll hear from you now."

I stood and said, "Good morning, Your Honor. I'm

here on a motion to exclude media from these proceedings, in the interest of justice. You have discretion to do so, and I am prepared to amend the statement attached to my motion, to include what just happened here today. I could barely get into the courthouse."

Judge Hegg looked at Aaron. "Mr. Argula?"

Aaron said, "While it's true Your Honor has discretion in this matter, it is of course limited by the First Amendment and the U.S. Supreme Court decision in *Press-Enterprise*. It is the burden of the moving party to show that limiting media furthers a compelling governmental interest."

"What greater interest is there than justice?" I said. "The media coverage thus far has been overwhelming and negative. It will impact our ability to select an unbiased jury, or to have the jury free from pressure during the trial."

"Your honor," Aaron said, "*Press-Enterprise* also requires a less-restrictive means test. In this instance, you have the ability to admonish the press as to its behavior in court, complete with warning to exclude. That would certainly be less restrictive than a blanket prohibition of presence."

"I agree, Mr. Argula," the judge said. And then she started to lecture me. "Ms. Caine, the First Amendment to the Constitution is our bedrock freedom. We must never allow its wings to be clipped."

I tried not to roll my eyes.

"Your motion is denied. Next matter, a trial date."

Aaron said, "The People have no objection to a fast track date, Your Honor. I'm sure you, along with everyone else concerned in this matter, would like to get to it as quickly as possible."

"Ms. Caine, are you in agreement?"

"Yes, Your Honor."

"Well then, I see no reason for delay. Shall we say two weeks from today?"

That worked for Aaron's calendar. It also worked for mine, seeing as how it was empty for the rest of my life.

The judge made it official, and we were done. She left the bench and I sat down in the counsel chair. I suddenly felt exhausted. It was an accumulation of everything, I guess. People trying to kill me with swords, eyeballs in guacamole, a Voice in my head. You can fight all that only so long before it starts to get to you. Even zombies can get post-traumatic stress.

Aaron came over and said, "You look beat."

"Not beat," I said. "Not yet, at least."

"Tired, I mean."

"I stayed up a little late last night. Now I have to fight my way out of here."

"No, you don't. I'll take you out the secret passage-way. Come on."

He gathered his case file from the table, and motioned for me to follow him through the door that led to the inner corridor. The deputy DAs and judges don't have to come in through the front, like the public.

We took the interior elevator up to the eighteenth floor, where the district attorney's main office is. Aaron punched the keypad and clicked us in. He took me to his office, which was one of the few with a window.

"Hey, how'd you score this?" I said.

"They like me," he said. "Can you blame them?"

"Oh, brother."

He laughed and closed the door. "Relax a few minutes before we go. Can I get you some coffee?"

"No thanks." I sat in one of the chairs. Aaron took

off his coat and hung it on a hook on the inside of his door. I had to admit he was looking good. The same athletic body. The same ability to look like any clothes he wore were specifically tailored for him, even if he just grabbed them off the rack.

Aaron took a glance out his window. I could see the federal courthouse in the distance. "I love this town," he said.

"What about San Francisco?" I said. "That's where you went when . . . forget it."

Aaron turned back and sat behind his desk. "I'll never forget the first time I saw you, in back of the law school, before the Notre Dame game."

"I remember you walking into my line of vision," I said.

"It was before that. I'd just come down the steps. You were getting a burger handed to you. I saw the burger and then I saw you. From the side. You looked like Renaissance painting."

"Hey! Weren't those nude fat women?"

"Not the saints. You even had a halo. The sun was behind you."

"Were the birds singing?"

"No," he said, "but some cars honked on Exposition Boulevard. Then you turned your head. You saw me. And you smiled. Quickly, then you turned away. And I didn't think. Didn't need to think. I was a Trojan tailback, juking and dancing through the secondary, to get to you before you connected to anybody else."

"Do you remember what you said to me?"

His looked at the floor, smiling sheepishly. "Yes. I'm really sorry, too."

"You should be," I said. "You came up and said, 'Here I am. What were your other two wishes?'"

"Well, what else was I going to say? 'What's your sign?'"

"It would have been better than *that.*"

"True. You didn't take it very well. You said you wished for very big mallet, and a custard pie."

"I wanted to see where you went from there," I said.

"I almost went back inside to kill myself," Aaron said. "Or at least give myself a swirlie in the bathroom."

I laughed. "I wouldn't have let you go. You were too cute."

"At one time."

"Still are. A little harder around the edges maybe."

"Mallory, does a ton of bricks still fall? Because that's what happened to me. It was all over."

"It took *me* longer," I said.

"But you came around," he said.

My heart was starting to pound a little harder now. "Okay, that covers the happy beginning," I said. "What about the bad ending? What was her name, Aaron?"

"Nadine," he said. "But it's not what you think. She was a recruiter for the firm in San Francisco. She wined and dined me a couple of times, but I couldn't let anybody know."

"Yeah, I had to find out from a friend."

"But by that time . . ."

"Yes?"

"Do you recall what happened?"

I did. "Your father," I said.

"He died then, and you know how that shook me up. You know because you tried to help and I just pushed you away."

I nodded. It was starting to get painful again.

"That's when I decided to make the break. To get away from L.A., to get up to San Francisco and start again."

"And break up with me."

He nodded.

"But why? Why didn't you keep it going? I would have understood you needed space and time."

"Really?"

"Well, yeah, maybe outer space for a hundred years, but you get the idea."

"It wasn't just space. Mallory, I was envious of you."

"What?"

"Of your talent, your mind. You didn't know how good you are. I wonder if you even realize it now."

I was too stunned to say anything.

"My dad never thought I was good enough. At anything. He ran me down my whole life. I never wanted anything more than his approval, and I never got it. When he died, it was like the bottom dropped out of everything. Like I could never do anything good enough again, because he was gone." He threw up his hands. "This is all psychobabble. What does it matter?"

"No," I said. "Go on. Finish."

He took in a long breath. "I felt like getting away was the best thing for both of us. I tried to explain it to you."

"I didn't handle that too well, did I?"

"You do pack a mean punch. My shoulder still hurts."

"Conflict Resolution was not my best subject in law school."

Aaron said, "I needed to get alone to prove at least to myself that I could measure up to my dad's expectations. I didn't want to put that on you. And so, that's what happened. It was sudden, I know."

"Real sudden."

"I'm sorry, Mallory."

"Can I ask you one thing?"

"More than one if you like."

"Did you know about my getting shot?"

"Shot? What are you talking about?"

"With a gun, you know? Bang."

Aaron didn't speak for a long moment. "I had . . . I can't believe . . . when did this happen?"

"I'll tell you about it sometime."

"Don't leave me hanging!"

I put on one of my wry smiles. I have a variety of wry smiles. "Leaving people hanging is one of the things I do best."

"Mallory, please. Why didn't I hear about this?"

I shrugged. "There was no reason for you to. It didn't get wide play in the news. The cops wanted it quiet, and so did I."

"I mean, how bad was it?"

"Aaron, another time."

He put his hand on my arm. "I want you back, Mallory. I want you back in my life. I want to go back to what we had and build on it. And I don't want you to bite me."

"No biting?"

"None."

"Well, gee, what kind of relationship is that?"

At least he smiled, which was a relief. Because I honestly didn't know the answer. I didn't know if I could keep from biting him, eating him. But even if I could, what possible love could the two of us share? *Say, honey, just to let you know, I slip out at midnight so I can score some brains. You know, like from people who are*

*still alive? You don't mind that, do you, hon? I mean, we can
still go dancing. . . .*

I was being pulled apart, in five or six or seven directions. Plus, there was a guy out there who wanted
to slice *me* into five or six pieces.

I didn't know how much more of this I could take.
Even a zombie has limits.

But the fun, as they say, was just beginning.

CHAPTER 19

That night I went to see Traci Ann in the special cell they'd made up for her at Lynwood, the women's jail. She was on a gurney, getting a transfusion of blood.

The court order had come through and the system was providing what appeared to be a medically dependent inmate with blood she needed to live. She was dependent all right, but not in the way the matrons here probably thought. But civil rights law is nice and generous when it comes to blood. The government can take it, and it has to give it when there's a need.

In this case there was a need all right. New to the annals of the law, but a need.

"How you doing?" I asked her when I was situated in her cell. She looked a little pale, and a lot distraught.

"I just want this to be over," she said, looking at the IV. "Why do I have to go through this? Why won't he let me die?"

He. The one who controlled her.

"Don't talk about death," I said. "That's not an option. First, we're going to get you acquitted. Then we'll figure out how to set you free."

"Why did this happen, Mallory?"

"Hm?"

"I never believed in vampires, not really. I was into Goth and stuff, but that was all for fun. I never thought I'd end up like this. How can he allow it?"

"Who?"

"God."

"Do you believe in God, Traci Ann?"

"I used to. I want to."

"The crucifix they have, the one they claim they found in the car. Yours. When was the last time you saw it?"

"I don't remember. I know I couldn't look at it after I became . . ." Her voice trailed off and she closed her eyes. "I thought I threw it away. Maybe I didn't."

"Where did you keep it?"

"I don't remember that, either."

"Try."

"I used to have a box of junk, in my closet. But I haven't even opened that closet since I went vamp. I'm tired of being vamp, Mallory."

I almost told her the truth about me then. Two gals just opening up, undead to undead. But I wasn't ready to let the news leak to anyone. And I didn't want her worrying about me, on top of everything else.

No, the best thing for everyone concerned was for me to get ready for trial, to rip Aaron's lungs out (legally speaking, of course), and stay away from men with swords.

There were things watching me, eyeballs appearing, voices voicing, priests warning, and lots of unanswered questions. A zombie could go insane trying to put it all together at the same time she's trying to keep afloat as a lawyer.

CHAPTER 20

The next day, out of the blue, I got a call from Charles Beaumont Manyon.

There are not many legends in the legal profession. Back there in the twentieth century, you had your Clarence Darrow, your Edward Bennett Williams, your Gerry Spence. People who could mesmerize juries and create victories though force of will, superior intelligence, and voices like avenging angels.

You could put your Johnnie Cochrane in there, though you might get moans and groans because he was the O.J. lawyer. But who will ever forget, *If it doesn't fit, you must acquit?*

There's Roy Black, the Florida lawyer, who looks and sounds like a professor, until he takes your case apart in front of a jury.

And then there's the handful that the public doesn't know about but other lawyers do. The big guns, the ones who get the job done day after week after year. The sixtieth-floor crowd, men and women.

But if you had to pick just one lawyer for one cause, the biggest of your life, a lawyer who had not lost a case in twenty-eight years, who had represented some of the richest people and corporations and even countries in the world, then you would, hands down, have to pick Charles Beaumont Manyon.

I knew this even before I met him. When I was in law school, in the course on trial practice, the prof had a veritable man crush on Manyon. He described seeing Manyon in court, and how his voice alone was like a hypnotic drug.

So when he called me and wanted to meet, I was more than a little stunned. What could his eminence want with little ol' criminal lawyer Mallory Caine?

"Ms. Caine. It is a real pleasure."

Charles Beaumont Manyon met me in the reception area. His office was right on the fifty-ninth floor of the tallest building in Los Angeles. His firm took up the entire floor.

Manyon did not look, to me anyway, like the legal legend he was. He should have looked like a Greek god, with a full head of silver hair, dressed in the finest blue pin-striped suit, with a gold tie and matching silk handkerchief.

This was not Charles Beaumont Manyon. He was about five-ten, with bushy brown and thinning hair, and a big walrus moustache. He was a bit chunky and his tan suit was rumpled. And he wore cowboy boots.

He spoke with what might have been an Oklahoma accent. Down home. Pull up a chair kind of thing.

This was the man who controlled juries and commanded courtrooms.

Because Manyon knew that juries don't like to be manipulated by fancy, well-dressed lawyers. If you can give them a folksy tune, a man-on-the-street vibe, you do a lot better. There were trial lawyers who made very good livings being Will Rogers. But it had to be real. You couldn't put on an act.

My assessment of Beaumont right off the bat, then, was that he was truly a country boy lawyer who had come to the city and, by being smarter and more determined than his competition, risen to the very top of the profession.

He smelled heavily of some kind of manly man cologne, too. Did nothing for me.

We shook hands and he took me up the elevator a couple of floors to his office. I could have fit seven of my own in it. There were glass-enclosed bookshelves covering one wall, with what looked like old leather volumes in serried rows. Another wall held framed diplomas and honors and photographs. In the middle of that wall were two pictures, side by side, almost identical in pose. The one on the right showed Manyon shaking hands with George W. Bush. In the one on the left, he was shaking hands with Barack Obama.

In both, the guy he was shaking hands with was looking at him with something like awe.

That should tell you almost all you need to know about Charles Beaumont Manyon.

"Please have a seat," he said.

I did, in a plush chair in front of his massive and immaculate desk. A statuette of a craggy-faced man, scowling, sat on one corner. It appeared to be scowling at me.

"Clarence Darrow," Manyon said. "Greatest lawyer who ever lived."

"Yeah? You'd put him up at the top?"

"No one could hold a jury in his hands like Darrow. Or so they say. And of course you know about the Monkey Trial."

"Sure. Everybody knows about that."

"Not everybody, sad to say. But that's all a bucket of water in yesterday's river. We're here to talk about today."

"And that brings up a good question. Why *are* we here?"

"Do you know much about my little firm here?"

"Little! You guys are a boutique that handles major litigation, criminal or civil, and you like to go to court."

"That's about as good a summary as I've ever heard. Yes, we love to go to court. Not many lawyers do. But that's the battlefield, and we want to be on it. Because of that, we get a lot more done. Folks know when we negotiate, and have to say 'See you in court,' we mean it. We hold feet to the fire, as they say."

"I like holding feet to the fire, too."

"I know you do. That's why I've asked you here. I've heard of your work."

"You have?"

"The word on the street is that you are one tough trial lawyer."

"I try."

"But you only take small cases for some reason."

I shrugged. "There are no small cases when somebody's accused of a crime."

"Well said. And that's why I wanted to see you. I wanted to look you in the eye and talk about your future. Maybe as an associate right here."

"You're looking for an associate?"

"There was a time when Steve Jobs was looking for someone to come in as CEO of Apple. He found a man named Scully, who was running Pepsi at the time. And he told Scully, do you want to sell sugar water the rest of your life, or do you want a chance to change the world? And Scully came."

"As I recall, that didn't work out so well."

Manyon gave a quick nod. "But that is not the point of my story, Ms. Caine. Point is, there's very few opportunities in this life to change the world, and this could be one of 'em for you. It's a matter of saving the city of Los Angeles."

I waited for him to explain.

"There are things happening here that are unprecedented, including your defense of a vampire. That's just the tip of the cow's tail. There's something else happening, below the surface, that threatens to rip right up to the top."

"Something like what?"

"Hard to say just now. I run in some pretty rarified circles, and I can tell you there appears to be unrest. People doing strange things. Not just criminal. I'm talking about normally fine upstanding citizens. I think you might know what I'm talking about."

He didn't explain and was probably looking for me to fill in the blanks. The way a good trial lawyer goes fishing for information from a witness. But I didn't bite. I stayed silent.

Manyon said, "But with unrest comes opportunity. When I was kid, there was a movie called *The Hellstrom Chronicle*. Ever hear of it?"

I shook my head.

"It was about the end of mankind, through whatever means, and that the only thing left would be things like cockroaches. Scared the pants off me when I was young buck. But you know, there are survivors in all walks of life. And in this time, or the times to come, you know who's going to survive? Lawyers."

"You're calling us cockroaches?"

"We've been called worse now, haven't we?" He got out of his chair and looked out the window. "I represent the mayor, Ms. Caine. The city contracts with me to do so. There are a number of issues that he has to deal with, and one of them is to address the sort of thing we see happening. Your vampire client. Other reports of supernatural events. If the mayor is going to succeed in helping the city, he's going to need someone who can navigate those waters with him. I think you could be that someone."

He turned toward me. "Come associate with us. With a chance to make partner in three years. Has to be a good fit, though. You have to be somebody we'd all have full confidence in, who will work like a dog, and will give no quarter in court. Does working for one of the top law firms in the country appeal to you?"

"I never thought along those lines. To tell you the truth—"

"Does two hundred thousand to start sound good to you?"

I almost ate my own head. "Excuse me? I thought you said two hundred thousand."

"I did."

"When do I get to ask for a raise?"

He smiled under that bushy soup strainer of his. "I like a woman with a sense of humor, too. My missus, she'd like you. So how's it sound?"

"Like a lot of lettuce."

"Enough for quite a number of salads, I'd say."

The lure of food wasn't going to motivate me. But the lure of money was. I needed it as much as the next person. I needed to stop worrying about rent. But it would also give me more resources to find out what I needed to find out. Maybe spreading money around would get me to the one who reupped me, and even now was trying to control me.

Because the Voice was saying, *Get out*.

I pushed it back. If it was trying to get me out of here, maybe this had to be a good thing.

"It's a generous offer," I said.

"Why don't you think about it?"

"Why don't you play the *Jeopardy* theme?"

"If that's what it'd take to get someone like you," Manyon said, "I might very well do it."

I stood. "I'll think about it, Mr. Manyon. I really will."

He took my hand. "Thanks for stopping by, Ms. Caine."

Outside, across the street from the Central branch of the library, it was a typical day in L.A. The sun was shining, the birds singing, horns were honking, and another council member was indicted—this time for not living in the district he reps and lying about it for years. It's in keeping with the entrenched pols, whose political outlook runs the gamut from narcissism to lethargy.

I try to think about why I love this city so much. Maybe it's in the very contrasts.

A guy carjacks an old man's car in Silver Lake, while at the very same time a volunteer in a Skid Row mission gives a sack of food to a drug-addled woman and her six-year-old child.

A teenage tagger tries to jump out of the way of an Amtrak train and doesn't make it while a fifty-five-year-old juggler makes children laugh at the Third Street Mall in Santa Monica.

A rich man who bought the Dodgers divorces his wife and the nastiness spills out like an oil slick from a busted derrick.

A movie actor spends $150,000 a year on haircuts and laughs about it. A cafeteria worker spends a buck and a half on a candy bar for her son and thinks it extravagant.

You get the good and the bad, the yin and the yang, the Abbott and the Costello, the living and the dead. It's all here in L.A., from cemeteries to street corners, from the desert to the sea.

It's the only place for me. Which makes it a real bummer when someone's trying to slice your head off.

But when someone else, someone like Charles Beaumont Manyon, is offering you the pot of legal gold at the end of a bright, professional rainbow, you think things might just be going your way for a change.

That's the drama, the heartache, and the dream weaving through my town.

And it never stops.

CHAPTER 21

I went to check on Etta Johnson.

Trials are hard on families, especially if you're convinced your loved one is not guilty. Most of the time they *are* guilty, of course. But in this case Traci Ann truly wasn't, and Etta knew it because she knew her granddaughter.

I wondered if I'd have the guts to come forward with the truth. If it looked like Traci Ann was going to be convicted—in fact, if she *were* convicted—could I spill the beans? At the cost of giving up who I was? Why would I do that for a vampire?

If I did the right thing, would God forgive me? Even if I died a zombie? What if I kept on the way things were?

Crazy, horrible, insane, frightening thoughts. The things I want to do I do not do, and the things I don't want to do, well, those are the things I keep on doing.

Zombie. Undead. Damned.

Etta opened the door, looking fragile and scared.

"What's going to happen to my baby?" she said. Her eyes were like coins buried in dirt. I was worried for her, the way I would have been for my own grand-mother. I only met her once, my mom's mom, and she had that same, sad-eyed look.

"Nothing is going to happen to Traci Ann," I said. "I will make sure of it."

"But how can you?"

"By using the skills I have." So I hoped.

Etta sat down heavily on the sofa. I sat next to her and took her hand.

"She's my own, you know," Etta said. "Her mother, my daughter . . . I can't think of it without crying." She tried to compose herself by taking a breath and putting her hand on her chest. I squeezed her hand. "She got on the drugs real bad after Traci Ann was born. Traci Ann's father was a no-good. He just ran out on Dierdre when he got her pregnant. I tried to warn her about him, but she was just so determined. Strong willed. Like me, I suppose. He went off and got himself shot and killed and . . . I'm sorry to burden you with this."

"No. Please go on." She was telling me my own story.

"Well, Dierdre died of the drugs. I was alone at the time, my husband was gone. So I had this baby, this Traci Ann, to try to take care of. It's hard. It's hard to raise a child in this world if you're all alone. I did my best, Lord knows I did."

"I'm sure He knows," I said, not at all sure about that myself.

"I tried to get her religion, with the church, but she ran from all that. She got to running with the wrong people. How could I stop her? She was so bullheaded, like all of us in this family."

"You said you tried to get her to church?"

Etta nodded.

"The crucifix they found in the Charger, with Traci Ann's name etched on it."

"I gave that to her. When she was confirmed."

"Did she wear it?"

"Once, that I remember. Why would somebody put that in the car? What have they got against Traci Ann?"

I didn't answer. My mind was fixating on that crucifix. It had to get from this house to the car by way of some intermediary. The cops? They searched the place. Did Strobert or Richards pick it up and plant it? No, the search was after the killing. It had to be taken before the cops got there.

The maze was getting crazier. I wondered then, for a moment, if Traci Ann was telling me the whole truth. There are two people you should never lie to, your doctor and your lawyer. Unfortunately, people do both, but they especially lie to their lawyer. If not outright, they puff around the edges. Everybody wants to look good.

"You said Traci Ann was confirmed. That's a Catholic thing."

"Yes. She was thirteen at the time."

"Where was this thing done, or whatever you call it?"

"Just down the street, Our Lady of Sorrows."

"Are you still active there?"

"I am."

"Do they know about Traci Ann?"

"Oh, yes, Father O'Connor knows." Etta sighed. "Do you have family out here?"

"My mom," I said.

"Brothers or sisters?"

"No."

"Father?"

I shook my head.

"Then I want you to know," Etta said, "that you can come to me if you ever need someone to talk to."

"I appreciate that, Etta." And I did. I really did.

CHAPTER 22

It was time to eat, and I was ill prepared. So many things on my mind.

And then, so many things inside me. I did not want to do this anymore.

I drove downtown and parked near Main and Fourth. Got my Amanda gear and got out to walk, toward Alameda. That's a street that runs past Union Station and just keeps on going south. The stretch by the railroad yard, a hundred or so years ago, was the street for prostitution. Lots of cribs for women who sold their bodies.

That's where I went, and walked north.

To my left, Chinatown, with its colorful lights and pagodas. To my right, the darkness of the train tracks. Still trains on them. Imagine that.

Some things never change, like women who sell bodies and trains that move people around.

What's new, I guess, is a woman who doesn't sell flesh, but consumes it.

And hates herself for it.

I turned down Alhambra, a less populated vein of asphalt. I was hungry, stomach growling. But what

I liked was the silence. No Voice, not at the moment at least. No eyeballs. No sense of someone watching me.

And yet . . .

Not completely alone. I couldn't tell if that was good or bad. I figured bad. It's good to figure bad when you're out here.

I stopped for a moment and listened. A train was clattering in from points west. Not the Metro Link, so it probably held product. I didn't know what they moved on trains anymore. Didn't have much curiosity about it. I didn't hit the stores that much anymore, except to buy clothes. The well-dressed zombie lawyer is a must.

When the train was just about dopplered out, I heard something behind me.

I turned.

He was a man of medium height, dressed in dirty, ripped jeans and a dark T-shirt with shreds and holes. No shoes. He moved with a robotic sameness toward me.

I reached in my purse and closed my hand around Emily. It this guy wanted trouble, he'd get it. And while he didn't look that appetizing, his brain might have to do.

"Back off, bub," I said.

But he did not back off. He kept coming, and his form came into the fullness of the streetlight.

His eyes were wide and vacant. No movement in them. He wasn't drunk. He would have had a little nystagmus going on in the eyeballs, the kind of thing cops check for when they pull you over on suspicion of DUI.

He was looking and moving like something I'd

seen in the old movies about zombies. The kind who had no will of their own.

The kind with a voice in their head.

And then I knew. He was a zombie, too.

My first instinct was to call him brother and let him in on our little secret.

But something about the set of his face disturbed me. He was here for a purpose.

He sprang forward and grabbed my throat with his right hand.

The move caught me by surprise. I was momentarily frozen, but that moment was my downfall.

Because his other hand whipped up to my face and shoved a fistful of salt in my mouth.

There are fast-acting poisons that kill a living person within minutes or seconds, depending on how they are administered. Some will paralyze you first and death follows with slow, agonizing inevitability.

Salt in the mouth is a paralyzing agent in a zombie.

I choked and tried to spit it out.

The zombie's hand was on my neck and his other hand was holding my mouth closed.

With my thoughts starting to swirl in a sodium fog, I summoned enough to knee my attacker in his groin. Of course, he felt no pain from that. But it was enough of a blow to weaken his grip.

I pulled away.

He reached for me again.

I tried to push, but already my limbs were not obeying. The salt was rushing through my undead system like a viper's venom.

God, is this what it's come to? Death now, soul death, eternity in pain and separation and suffering?

So many things left undone. Traci Ann, what of Traci Ann? God, she needs me.

Uck.

The Voice. Dim in my soggy thoughts. *Uck?* What did that even mean?

The expression on the zombie's face did not change. His hands were on my neck again.

Duck.

Duck?

Duck!

I simply let go. Let go all effort to stand or resist. And dropped to my knees.

In other words, I ducked.

And when I did, the zombie's hands lost their grip, though they hit under my chin and tilted my head back.

Which allowed me to see what happened next.

A sword flashed in the night light and severed the zombie's head.

Powerless now to move, I could only think: *Gack! Out of the frying pan, into the fire.*

Good-bye, cruel world. I'm sorry I failed you.

And then everything became black as night, deeper than night, a black hole, a falling through into total darkness.

CHAPTER 23

What I saw next:

A pinprick of yellow light in the far, black horizon. As if a ship in a starless Pacific night, from miles away, flashed a signal. A distress signal? Or a searchlight?

Was it looking for me?

And I was in a sea, not liquid but made up of air, or the absence of air. Floating, or held up by some unseen force.

But unable to move. No willing on my part could get so much as a toe twitch.

Was this hell? Was this what they called the outer darkness? Or the second death?

The yellow light got brighter and appeared to be moving. Toward me. Like headlights on a long ribbon of road. Only I was the deer stuck in them, because no amount of will could get me out.

I was afraid. Afraid of the light.

Like it was coming to get me.

It wasn't the white light, the kind I experienced when I died that first time.

No, this was not like that at all. It was full of menace.

Closer and closer it came, and then I saw that there were two lights, two beams of yellow side by side.

Twin beams of death.

But I was already dead. So what were these about?

Torture? Suffering? Punishment? Judgment?

I tried to open my mouth. I wanted to scream. I could not.

Closer still, and then I saw they were eyes. Big, round, malevolent eyes of an . . . owl.

Now I could see the shape of the bird, and its talons upraised, heading directly for my face.

In that way of dreams, I did get my mouth open. No, it was opened for me. Someone or something had opened my mouth, but still I could not scream. . . .

I heard a man's voice say, "Don't fight me."

I felt strong fingers on my jaw, pulling.

I opened my eyes. I was able to open my eyes!

And looked up at a lightbulb, a yellow lightbulb, dangling from a wire on a ceiling.

What? Was I alive? Was I back?

But who was speaking?

I felt something in my mouth, swirling around in it, pushing my cheeks, depressing my tongue.

What was this?

Salt! Whoever this was, was he stuffing salt in my mouth?

But no, I was becoming *more* aware. If I was able to open my eyes, that meant motor function was coming back.

"Steady there," the man said. "I'm cleaning you out."

A voice like broken glass.

Cleaning me out?

He had saved my undead life.

I remembered now, the zombie who had come at

me. His head sliced off. The mad swordsman, Hoodie, he had to be the one who did this.

So why wasn't I headless right now?

"There we are," the man said. "You were almost gone."

I couldn't respond.

His face came into focus, looking down at me.

The face had a white beard. There could be no doubt about it now. It was Hoodie all right.

Which is when I heard the first sound issue from my mouth. *H-e-l-l-l-p.*

What had he brought me here for? Why had he cleaned out my mouth?

Obvious: So he could do the kill himself. Torture.

The slime.

Then he was lifting me up, my limbs dangling like wet spaghetti. Pulling me off the table or slab or whatever it was I was on and dragging me across the room. It was a dismal looking place, what with the yellow lightbulb. Gave the room the feel of old cheese. Smelled like it, too.

Smell. I was getting that back.

Hoodie plopped me in a chair. A rocking chair! My head fell over to the right. Hoodie pushed it back to center.

"Try not to move," he said.

I opened my mouth and said, "I caaaan't . . ."

"Don't talk. I'll do the talking."

Great.

"I don't know what to do with you," he said.

Over his shoulder I could see the back wall. On it was a giant mural. A large, anguished Jesus face. Crown of thorns, blood streaming down.

Oh, don't make me stare at that!

And what did he mean, what to *do* with me?

"You're going to live, if you call this living," he said. "Or not. I can't decide. Why hath God placed me here? What have I done? I have sinned greatly in the eyes of the Lord, but this has been my penance. Now I am Abraham! Why hath God given me this torture?"

My eyes were able to move, and I scanned a portion of the room. Just below the anguished Jesus, leaning against the wall, was the sword.

Just me, him, the sword, and Jesus.

This was not a good situation for me at all.

Hoodie stomped around a bit, looking troubled of soul. He stopped once and faced the Jesus mural and raised his hands, like he was pleading for something.

My arms were hanging straight down on the sides of the chair. I tried moving my fingers. And got a twitch.

My right index finger curled.

I kept trying. My other fingers started to move.

Hoodie kept his eyes on Jesus, so I kept clenching. My hands became weak fists, but at least they were fists.

I turned my head. Yes. I could turn it.

So what? I couldn't just spring up and sprint for the door.

But maybe I could grab the sword.

Hoodie turned around then.

I played possum.

His eyes were wide. "Only silence," he said. "I must choose."

That didn't sound good. This was probably my only chance, my last gasp. If I was going to go down, I was going to go down fighting. With every ounce of my will I sent signals to my legs and arms and rocked myself forward.

I pushed up with my legs and found them wonderfully receptive. I shot forward and put my shoulder into the surprised Hoodie.

He was big, beefy, so it only moved him a step or two. But in that moment I made a long leap toward the wall, reaching for the sword.

And grabbed air.

Fell forward, turned, and landed like an axed birch on the floor.

Hoodie had to step over me to get to the sword, which he did.

I flipped onto my back.

Hoodie had the sword now, and stood over me. He gave a look that was almost mournful. Holding the sword in two hands, he raised it over his head.

Then he brought it down, violent and swift, and embedded the weapon in the hard wood of the floor.

"I can't," he said. Slope shouldered, he ambled to the rocking chair, sat, and bowed his head. "You're a daughter of hell, but I can't. I've failed."

I got myself up to a sitting position.

"Why did it have to be you?" he said. "Oh, the torture!"

My words finally came, thick and slow. "What. Is this. All about?"

"Mallory Caine!"

"How . . . do you know . . . my name?"

"It's in your purse! How else?"

"Why . . . didn't you . . . finish me?"

He shook his head. "To finish you would be to finish myself."

"What are you . . . talking about?"

With a heavy sigh, he said, "I'm Harry Clovis. I'm your father."

CHAPTER 24

There are various colors of emotional wallop. Red is the sudden punch to your gut, the shock to the system that sets your insides aflame. Your first thought is confusion, your eyes marred by the scarlet haze.

Sometimes it's blue, which comes at you slower, like a leopard padding quietly through a forest. By the time it gets to you, it's too late to avoid it. You felt it coming, were mesmerized by its movements at first, then into the jaws of death.

But then there's shock that's bright yellow. An explosion of light that blinds you. That makes you shake your head to clear it, but doesn't go away, that threatens to push out everything from your rational mind until you beg for mercy.

Which I wanted to do right now.

For one extremely long moment, Harry Clovis and I just stared at each other. I couldn't move, this time because of the yellow shock.

There was no way he could be anyone but who he said he was. Who else could have come up with that name? And that he had saved my life, such as it was, was just confirmation he had no reason to lie.

"You? You're my father?"

He nodded slowly.

"Then why did you try to kill me?" My words were sounding normal now. The emotion of the moment loosened my tongue.

"I didn't know it was you at first. My own daughter!"

"But what were you thinking when you came after me with your sword?"

"You are the undead," he said matter-of-factly.

"And how did you know *that*?"

"Oh, daughter, it is so much to know."

"Spill it." I was able to clamber to my feet and regain something that felt like balance.

"I followed you one night. To your office. I saw your name on the sign. Oh, I'm doomed. I have lost my calling."

What was I supposed to call him? Certainly not "Father" or any of its offshoots. He had been no father to me. "Harry, I'm feeling a little weird here."

He raised his head wearily. "I never meant to hurt anyone. It was a strange time back then."

"When you left us? Left Mom?"

"How is your mother?"

"Let's say she's in a bit of a time warp. I think you did a real number on her. Not to mention your only daughter. I *am* your only daughter, right?"

"Maybe. A lot of that time I don't remember."

"Terrific."

"Please, I'm in enough pain as it is."

"Oh, sorry! I'm sure your sword-wielding, head-chopping pain is just too much to bear, you poor thing."

He said nothing. I felt a little bad, but only a little. "Go on," I said.

"Where do I start?"

"Start with you ran out on us!"

"I know."

"What was it? You couldn't take it anymore? You had to go be some biker outlaw, some wild man of the road?"

"I wouldn't have been a good father to you."

"Oh, I can believe that."

He looked at the floor. "It was too much. I was scared."

"Scared? You were scared? Well, welcome to the world, pal."

"I was freaked out. The whole thing freaked me out."

"You had a kid. Me. It happens."

"Not just that. The whole birth scene. I knew it was something heavy. I thought it was something after me. I had to run."

"What are you talking about?"

There was a dawning realization written on his face. "Didn't she tell you about it?"

"Who?"

"Calista. Your mother."

"Tell me about what?"

"The night you were born."

I shook my head. "I was born in a hospital in Las Vegas, is all I know."

He put his head in his hands.

"What is it?" I said. "What's the matter?"

"She never told you," he said.

"Tell me what? Come on, Harry."

With a sigh he looked up. "You weren't born in any hospital in Las Vegas. You were born in the back of a used Ford Maverick, in the desert, about forty miles outside Vegas."

"*What?*"

"I guess I'm not surprised," Harry Clovis said. "You mother was always a sensitive soul, didn't like troubles."

"What kind of troubles are you talking about? So I was born in a car. Why wouldn't she tell me about that? How do you even know this?"

He shook his head.

"Harry, talk to me."

He continued to shake his head.

I went to him and clapped him on the shoulder. "What happened when I was born, Harry? Tell me."

Harry put his hands together and touched his lips, as if he were praying. His eyes were closed. He took a couple of deep breaths before he spoke. "We weren't alone when you were born. We were in the car, but not alone."

"Go on."

"Someone wanted you . . . dead. All of us. Dead."

I heard something moving outside the door. Harry cocked his head. He stood and faced the door, putting his body between it and me.

"What's going on?" I said.

Harry said nothing. He pulled the sword out of the floor. He reached behind as if to check that I was there.

One heartbeat later the door exploded off its hinges.

The room filled with a SWAT team. Two of the black-clad cops held a battering ram, two others had weapons drawn. Behind their Plexiglas masks, they shouted all that cop stuff intended to frighten and freeze you.

It worked.

"Drop your weapon!" one shouted at Harry, pointing a gun at him.

Harry didn't move a muscle.

"Drop. It. Now!"

I put my hand on Harry's shoulder. "You better do it, Harry."

"I failed," he said. Then he tossed his sword on the dusty floor.

In a flash and flurry they had Harry turned around and zip cuffs on him.

One of the SWAT officers, his gun pointed at the floor but ready, came up to me. "Don't move," he said. "Who are you?"

"My name's Mallory Caine. And I'm this man's attorney. Harry, don't say anything."

The SWAT officer lifted his Plexiglas mask. "Turn around, please."

"What?"

"I need to pat you down."

"No," I said. "I told you who I am."

"Ma'am, turn around."

"Don't call me ma'am. Whatever you do, don't call me ma'am."

"Turn around and put your hands on the wall," the SWAT officer said.

Another voice said, "I'll take it from here."

I looked over toward the door.

Strobert walked in, dressed in a regular suit, his detective shield hanging from his coat pocket.

"Did not expect to see you here," he said to me. "You want to explain to me what's going on?"

"No," I said. "I don't. You're the one with some 'splainin' to do."

"What do I do?" the SWAT officer said. "I have to pat her down."

"No, you don't," Strobert said. "She's not carrying anything, except a bad attitude."

"You're right about that, pal," I said. "And it's about to get worse."

CHAPTER 25

Strobert kept his cool. I guess when you've had your butt chewed by street butt chewers—not literally chewing, of course, except in my case—you get used to verbal stings. L.A. cops have a thankless job, even I admit that. They get little respect from the average Joe, little backup from their political higher-ups, are hamstrung by rules and regs, and are still expected to take a bullet if it means protecting the day-to-day life of the city.

You do that for twenty, thirty years, no wonder you carry around some scars.

"What do you say we step into my office for a minute?" Strobert said.

"You want to take me to division?" I said.

"We can talk in my car. I just don't want anyone sticking their nose in."

"You're wasting your time."

"Hey, after you tried to tear me up in court, maybe you owe me a few minutes."

"Nothing personal, Detective," I said. And it wasn't. In fact, I was starting to like him.

We stepped out of what turned out to be a little

shack of a house near the hills of Big Tujunga Canyon. How Harry got me here I had no idea.

Strobert's Crown Vic was parked down at the end of the dirt driveway. He opened the door for me and I got in. He went around and got in behind the wheel. By the interior car light I could see that his face was full of questions.

"Just between us," he said, "off the record. Can you tell me how you got here?"

"Maybe you could tell me how *you* got here, how you found me," I said.

"We do know how to investigate," Strobert said. "Even when it involves a guy with a sword. We know how to stake out and surveil, and we know how to follow. This guy's been on our radar and a tip from a witness got the license plate of his truck. That got us here."

"Why did you break in like that?"

"It was an emergency situation."

"What emergency?"

"You, obviously."

I shook my head. "It wasn't obvious at all now, was it?"

"Now that you say this man is your client. And that's what I want to know. Just how did he hire you?"

"You know I'm not required to tell you any of that."

"I know. I just figured you might." Strobert put his hands on the wheel. It was a gesture that moved me. He was steering a car that was not in motion, the way a five-year-old might imitate his father driving.

I said, "All right, Detective. You'll get this soon enough anyway. The man is my father."

Strobert let go of the wheel. "Your father?"

"Yep."

"Your father runs around L.A. with a sword?"

"I'm not going to confirm or deny anything relating to his activity."

"When did you get in contact with him?"

"I don't think there's anything more to say on this. He's my father and now my client: I need to protect his interests."

Strobert paused a long time before speaking again, as if considered every word carefully. Finally he said, "Ms. Caine, I'm now going to switch gears. I'm going to question you in the capacity of a detective looking into a crime. Basically, the headless man found near the railroad tracks downtown."

"For which you have an alleged eyewitness?"

"Maybe."

"Come on, Detective," I said. "Come out with it. What are you alleging here?"

"You were on the scene when the man—your father, if that's true—"

"It is."

"—and he killed a man by slicing his head off. I want to know exactly what you two were doing down there at that hour."

"This eyewitness, did she describe the woman?"

"Are you saying it wasn't you?"

"What would I be doing by the railroad tracks?" Nothing. Amanda would, but Mallory Caine wouldn't.

"Then how did you wind up here?"

"I told you, I'm not going to get into the dealings with my father."

"Playing it tough, huh?"

"Playing it professional," I said. "Just like you."

"I'm not completely satisfied," Strobert said.

"Wish I could help, but—"

"Maybe you still can," he said. "The identity of the

victim. You'll be informed, but I might as well tell you now."

"Okay."

"Someone you know," Strobert said. "A police officer named Bud Bracamonte."

My zombie heart high-jumped to my throat. "I thought he disappeared."

"We did, too. I want to know how Bud Bracamonte got to be somewhere your father was, and why your father thought it necessary to cut his head off."

CHAPTER 26

They transported my father all the way back to Hollywood and put him in an interview room for me. Strobert said I could have ten minutes.

Harry's face had grown soft and sad. Not the angry looking assassin anymore.

I had no idea how to relate to him. Or what I felt. We had some unfinished business. "Suppose we go back to my birth, Harry."

"Why don't you call me Dad?"

"No."

He sighed. "I'm not proud of a lot of what I did back then. Before the frog."

"The what?"

"Just listen!" His eyes were a little wild now, like when he would wield his sword. "I was a rebel, or thought of myself that way. Motorcycle gangs, you know. Meth trade. Drug dealing. Thumping chumps. Loving fights. I was searching for something I could hang on to, like all living things do, at least living things with a soul."

When he said that I felt a little pull on my heart.

Was I considered a living thing? And where was my soul?

"I met your mother at a truckstop in Amarillo. She was slinging hash. One thing led to another, if you know what I mean."

"I think I can figure it out."

"You came along. You have to know, I didn't run out on you before you were born. I was there."

"Mom never told me that."

"I don't know how much she remembers. Or wants to remember."

"What do *you* remember?"

"Like I told you," he said. "The back of a Maverick. In the desert outside Vegas."

I leaned forward.

Harry said, "It was one of those desert nights when you could see the Milky Way and maybe a space ship or two, if you were really looking."

"In other words, you were high."

"High is a relative term. I was aware, let's put it that way. And so was your mother, as she tried to get you to come out. We were off on a dirt road, too far from civilization to chance trying for town. I want you to know I took off my T-shirt and laid it under your mother's legs, so you could have a smooth place to land."

"Very considerate of you."

"But then they started coming."

"Who?"

He got a faraway look, gazed up at the corner of the cell. "The birds. Black ones. Trying to peck their way in through the windows. It was like that Hitchcock movie. They just kept coming and coming, and cracked a couple of windows, and your mother was screaming and trying to push, and I was half naked wondering what all those birds wanted with us. It was a scene, man."

A scene all right. I tried to picture it in my mind.

"But then, all of a sudden, the pecking stopped. The birds went away. And you came out, as pretty and pink as a little baby rat."

"Thank you."

"But we were not alone. No. There was a watcher."

"A watcher?"

"In the back window. Big ugly face. Yellow eyes. An owl."

My throat went dry.

"I don't know," Harry said, "to this day I don't know why that owl was there. But I thought maybe it was what had saved us from the birds. Got you born. Freaked me out. I was with you for a few weeks, I want you to know. I changed your diaper and I got you up for feedings. I even held you once all night when you had a cold, so you could breathe a little normal."

"Am I supposed to say thank you?"

"Maybe you could say you forgive me."

"I don't know, Harry. What were you doing all these years? How come you never came back?"

"I ended up in Mexico," he said. "In a Mexican prison, matter of fact. Not a place you want to end up. But it was the thing I needed to turn my life around. I had a vision. A vision!"

He took in a deep breath and let it out like steam.

"You okay?" I said.

"One night in my cell, I had a vision of an angel, who told me I would do the work of the Lord. I didn't know what that was, but the angel handed me a sword made of light. I held it in my hand! When the angel left me, the sword left me, too. But right then and there I decided I was going to memorize the entire Bible."

"The whole Bible? You've memorized it?"

"Well, no. I got to Genesis six. Then I got out of prison. I went into the desert and lived for many years off the land. And I sought the Lord. And He answered me."

I waited.

"I was given a task," Harry said. "To know the scriptures, and to hasten His return."

"Um, okay. So how does that get you to L.A. with a sword?"

"The frog," he said.

"The frog again. What is up with that?"

"I don't know if it was really a frog. I was pretty high at the time. I was somewhere south of Ensenada. Sitting by the side of the road. A big frog started talking to me. In Spanish. Maybe it was just a very ugly man, I can't really make that judgment. But he told me I must make my peace with the Lord, and listen for His Voice, and find the parchment."

"What is that?"

Now his eyes got a blazing look. "The lost verses of the Gospel of Mark," he said. "Do you know about it?"

"No. You mean in the Bible?"

"The earliest versions of Mark do not have verses nine through twenty of the sixteenth chapter. Those are the verses where Jesus is saying his followers will manifest signs and wonders, they shall cast out devils, speak with new tongues, take up snakes, and if they drink any deadly thing, it shall not hurt them."

"I know about snake handling," I said. "Mom got involved with a church like that once."

"Verse twenty finishes with, 'And they went forth,

and preached every where, the Lord working with them, and confirming the word with signs following. Amen.'"

"Okay. And?"

"That's what I'm trying to tell you now. Whoever wrote these verses wrote them very early. They may still be an accurate addition to the Scriptures, but there has been talk, ever since the Early Church Fathers, that someone added the 'Amen' and took out the last verse. There was one more verse in the Gospel of Mark. "

"And this is what was on the parchment?"

"Which I found, Mallory. I found it in the keeping of a priest in a chapel on the coast of Ecuador."

"Harry, can I ask you one thing?"

"Yes?"

"Did this priest also sell souvenirs?"

"I was chosen, don't you see?"

"By who? The frog?"

"By the everlasting Lord God Jehovah! He chose me to find the parchment!"

I could not get my mind to believe this wild tale of talking frogs and lost parchments. It was too much like Dan Brown being channeled by William Burroughs. "Whatever," I said. "So you found it. What was on it?"

"Verse twenty-one."

"All right. Give it to me straight."

He leaned toward me. "'And the Adversary sleepeth not, even to the end of the age, until the one who is to come.'"

"I think you were taken in," I said.

"Oh, do you? Then how do you account for my finding you?"

"What does the one have to do with the other?"

"You said it. The one. The one who is to come."

"Who is that? Jesus?"

He shook his head. "I think it means you."

Detective Strobert came in and told me my time was up. I told him I wasn't finished. He said I was, but could see Harry again tomorrow at the Men's Jail on Bauchet Street. That would be his new home while an information was returned against him for murder.

Wonderful. Now I had two clients accused of murder, one of whom was a vampire, and the other who was my father, who had apparently killed a cop who may have been a zombie coming after me.

This would be a tale to tell.

Later, in my loft, I kept hearing my crazy father telling me I was *the one who is to come*. That sounded way too *Matrix* for me. I did not see myself as a Neo, or Nea, or anything else than what I was, a zombie. I was trapped in my skin. I had enough troubles of my own.

I did not want to be part of any prophecy. I just wanted to practice law and find a way out of being a flesh eater.

What was it the Stones sang? You can't always get what you want?

Indeed.

PART II

The American advocate has more liberty of choice, but he is unworthy of the name if he declines a case on the sole ground that it is unpopular. For in the law unpopularity is often the post of Honor.

—Lloyd Paul Stryker

CHAPTER 27

So you want to be a trial lawyer? Then you better understand a few things.

First of all, the jury knows you want to deceive them. They also know you're in it for the money.

They know somebody has hired you. They know it's your job to keep them from seeing unfavorable evidence. Every time you object, they're wondering what you're trying to hide.

So you better get them on your side, and fast.

You better learn the rule of seven. Here's how it works. You give away six things and keep the seventh.

Only the doofus lawyer fights over every point. The way you establish cred with the jury is to give your opponent six minor victories, all the while holding on for the seventh thing, which is a key to your case.

If you don't know how to count, you can't be a trial lawyer.

And you better make the jury believe that you believe in your case. You need to make them forget you are a lawyer who is being paid. They will, if you go about it right.

That means you don't perform. You don't put on

a show. Lawyers who do that are idiots. You better make the jury believe that you believe, and that means you have to find the passionate core you can give your all for.

I happen to believe in the Constitution of the United States. It gives everybody the right to a fair trial before the government can take away your life or liberty. And I'm going to fight you every step of the way on that. I don't care if you say criminals don't deserve it. I don't care if you cry *O.J. Simpson!* all the live-long day. I'm going to fight you if you try to put somebody away without a fair trial. I don't care if you're a senator's son. I don't care if you went to Harvard Law and edited the law review. I don't flipping care if you're a prosecutor with a spotless record who wants to be governor someday.

I'm going to fight you and make you follow the law. And if you don't, I will hammer you. I will stand in front of a jury and make you pay.

Try me.

The trial of Traci Ann Johnson began on a dismal Tuesday night, right after dark, in the courtroom of Judge Carlotta Hegg.

The place was packed with media and onlookers. Anxious voices bounced off the oak-paneled walls. A hundred or so people were out in the hallway, having been turned away at the door by a couple of court security personnel. It didn't matter to most, I'm sure. Just being close to the action was a vibe. This was the story of the year in L.A. The vampire cop-killer trial. The new Night Stalker, they said.

So my first task was to get a jury that would be less than bloodthirsty. Most people think lawyers *pick* a jury. In reality, you *unpick* a jury. You're given a lottery of names, they put people in the box at random. And then you have figure out which jurors you want to kick off.

You do that by asking questions, a process called *voir dire*. That's Old French for *to speak the truth*. You try to uncover potential bias, but what you really want to do is get rid of jurors who you think will hate you or your client.

When you represent a vampire, that comes out to a lot of people.

I had to ask if they could put aside their prejudice against those who, through no fault of their own, had to live on human blood. I got some blank-eyed affirmations. One of the things you do in *voir dire* is train the jury how to think. I had to get them to commit to fairness in the face of this mind-bending fact about my client.

It took two and a half hours, but I got twelve and two alternates I thought we could live with.

Truth be told, Aaron seemed the more comfortable. His was the easier task. I was defending a bloodsucker. But hey, life is pretty dull without challenges, isn't it?

In a jury trial, the prosecution gets the first word and the last word. That may seem unfair, but they do have the burden of proof beyond a reasonable doubt. Not only that, it has to be unanimous with the jury for a conviction.

So I don't care if they spout off first and last. My job is to get in there and plant enough doubts about the case that at least one juror will see my point and vote not guilty.

Of course, I go for all twelve, and I'll get them, too, if you don't watch out.

It's a little harder, though, when cops are planting evidence and the prosecutor is the man you love, who's going along with all the lies. Did Aaron know what was happening, or did he just choose not to find out?

He sure sounded like he believed his case as he opened to the jury.

"Ladies and gentlemen, this is a murder case of the most brutal sort. On the night of July twenty-fourth of this year, Detective Thomas Hennigan was working undercover, attempting to clean up the streets of our city from the blight of prostitution. Street prostitution is one of the most dismal aspects of our civic life, bringing misery to untold numbers of women and—"

"Objection, Your Honor," I said, standing up. "Is this an opening statement or a sermon?"

The judge and Aaron almost issued stereo gasps. Lawyers almost never interrupt the opening statements of their opponents, but this was going too far. It simply wasn't relevant to the facts of the case whether street prostitution was a blight, or what misery it caused, amen and amen.

"Ms. Caine," Judge Carlotta Hegg said, "Mr. Argula hasn't even had a chance to catch his breath. I'll kindly ask you to sit down, and Mr. Argula, I'll ask you to keep to the relevant evidence you intend to present."

Score one for the zombie.

Aaron shot me a glare. We may have been incipient lovers, but in the courtroom we were avowed combatants. I wasn't going to let him walk all over me. He turned back to the jury. "On the night of July 24, Detective Hennigan was working undercover vice on Santa Monica Boulevard. The evidence we present will show that Detective Hennigan participated in a sting to gather evidence of Traci Ann Johnson's prostitution, in an attempt to find out who her pimp was. That in the course of this investigation—"

I was on my feet again, objecting and asking to approach the bench. Hegg did not look pleased. But my look was rock solid back at her. She called us up.

"Ms. Caine," she said, out of the hearing of the jury, "I will not have you interrupting Mr. Argula this way."

"Your Honor," I said, "this is the first I've heard of any sting. Mr. Argula knows I did not receive discovery on that."

"We only just got this information," Aaron said. "The LAPD has been rather slow—"

"Come on!" I said.

"Keep your voice down," Judge Hegg said. "You consented to a fast track, Ms. Caine, so you should have expected this. If you want to bring me evidence that this sting operation was known to the People well before tonight, then go right ahead. If not, you're just going to move on."

Hoist on my own petard, as they say. She was right. Fast tracking makes stuff like this happen.

We went back to our places and Aaron picked up the opening statement. "We will show that the defendant, Traci Ann Johnson, with malice aforethought, did cause the death of Detective Hennigan, whereupon she attempted to cover her crime by setting Detective Hennigan and his vehicle on fire. You will hear from witnesses, police officials, the Los Angeles County coroner, all establishing beyond a reasonable doubt that Traci Ann Johnson is guilty of murder in the first degree."

Aaron went on for another twenty minutes or so, outlining the evidence he was going to present. I took notes on everything he said. One of the things you have to do is hold the prosecutors to their burden, and their promises to the jury about the evidence. I always liked to remind juries of what the prosecutor said in the opening statement, about what he'd produce. Nothing like finding they failed to deliver.

Aaron sat down. Judge Hegg looked at me and said, "You may address the jury, Ms. Caine."

I stood. "I will reserve my opening statement until my case in chief."

I could feel, without seeing, Aaron's shock. Defense lawyers never do this, even though it is allowed. The accepted wisdom is that you need to open right after the prosecutor does, to plant your own account in the jury's collective mind.

I don't do things according to accepted wisdom, just to throw the prosecutors off their game. Even if it's only for a moment. And I don't want them to be able to anticipate anything I might do.

CHAPTER 28

Aaron called Detective Mark Strobert.

I had to admit he looked good. The both of them looked good. Aaron, the dark and deadly trial lawyer. Strobert, the no-nonsense detective.

And both looked delicious. I had to knock that thought out of my head or the jury would see a very strange face on the defense lawyer.

Strobert was sworn and sat in the witness box.

Aaron said, "You are a detective working out of Hollywood division, is that correct?"

"Yes," Strobert said.

"How long have you been an LAPD detective?"

"Four years."

"And in that time, how many murder investigations have you conducted?"

"I've been part of approximately seventy homicide cases, as either primary or secondary."

"And can you tell us what transpired on the night of July twenty-fourth?"

"Yes. I was contacted by the detective supervisor at approximately eleven thirty-five P.M. He said there was a homicide up in the Hollywood Hills, and gave me the address. I phoned my partner, Detective Richards, and we met up at the scene at approximately twelve-fifteen."

"Were you met there by a patrol officer?"

"Yes."

"And what did he tell you?"

"He said that the fire department was on scene, putting out the fire on a Dodge Charger, and that a body was inside the car. He told me he found a witness, a woman who lives in the house adjacent to the crime scene."

"Did you talk to this witness?"

"I did."

"What is her name?"

"Minverva."

"Last name?"

"No last name."

"What did she tell you?"

"Objection," I said. "Hearsay."

"Sustained," Judge Hegg said.

Aaron went on, smooth as a buttered roll. "With the information provided by the eyewitness, what did you do next?"

"My partner and I worked in concert with LAFD and the county medical examiners. Once the senior examiner cleared the body for us, we examined the interior of the car and notified SID to the scene."

"SID is Scientific Investigation Division?"

"Correct."

"Sort of L.A.'s version of CIS?"

"Exactly."

Right, I thought. Nothing like they show on TV. If any of the jurors got a load of what SID actually looked like, they'd be horrified. No Mark Harmon here, no pristine workspace. Ha. But Aaron wanted the jury to think they were all over it.

"What did you recover from the Charger, if anything?"

"We found a charred necklace with a cross, on the floor of the passenger side of the vehicle. We found nothing else recoverable."

Aaron walked to the counsel table and picked up a plastic evidence bag. "Showing you now what has been marked as People's Two for identification, is this the necklace you recovered at the scene?"

Strobert took the bag from Aaron and gave it a quick look. "Yes, it is."

"And were you able to find any inscription on the necklace?"

"Yes. On the back of the cross, on the smooth surface, we found engraved the name of Traci Ann Johnson."

"Thank you." Aaron took the bag and set it back on the counsel table. "Did you subsequently make an arrest?"

"We attempted to make an arrest, but the suspect fled. We were able to effect an arrest subsequently, after another city agency picked the defendant up."

"What agency was that?"

"Animal control."

Murmurs in the courtroom. I usually love murmurs, but only when I cause them.

"What was the reason animal control picked up the defendant?"

Strobert said, "Apparently, they picked up what they thought was a stray coyote." He stopped, swallowed. "But then reported that the animal had somehow turned into a woman, who turned out to be the defendant."

Aaron nodded. It was clear now what his strategy

was. Instead of protesting Traci Ann's vampire status, he was going to lay right into it. Accept it and get the jury all riled up as caretakers of the community. Get those vampires off the streets!

"Your witness," Aaron said to me.

"Good evening, Detective Strobert," I said.

"Evening."

"Have you ever had a case like this one?"

"I'm not sure what you mean. A murder case?"

"No, a vampire murder case."

"I don't make any judgments one way or the other, Counselor. This is a murder of a police officer and I'm treating it like any other case of that kind."

"But you testified on direct that animal control picked up a coyote, and said coyote became Traci Ann Johnson, isn't that right?"

"That's right."

"Have you ever investigated a coyote before?"

"Of course not."

"Never thought about investigating a coyote at all, right?"

"Never."

"You have no expertise on vampires shape-shifting into coyotes then, correct?"

"It makes no difference to me."

He was getting a little testy, which is exactly what I wanted him to be. A testy witness gets careless. And even though Strobert was a vet on the witness stand, this case had to be getting to him. And the events surrounding it—like exploding guacamole. That was my doorway.

"It makes no difference to you what shape or form a suspect takes?"

"Why should it?" he said.

"Are you not aware of the legal concept of duress, Detective?"

He frowned. "Yeah, I'm aware of it. That doesn't mean—"

"Just answer the questions I put to you," I said. "Your answer is yes, you are aware of duress?"

"Yes."

"It means that a person does something under some sort of threat, doesn't it?"

"Yes."

"Are you aware of the concept of *mens rea?*"

Aaron had had enough. "Your Honor, the witness is not testifying as a legal scholar."

I said, "Your Honor, law enforcement is required to have at least a modicum of knowledge about the law. If I may explore Detective Strobert's knowledge a bit?"

"For what purpose?" Judge Hegg said.

"That will be apparent in just a few questions," I said, and gave Strobert a challenging look. He gave me one right back.

"I'll give you a few more questions," Judge Hegg said.

"Detective, you know the term *mens rea?*"

"It's a state of mind for criminal responsibility," he said.

"And if a person does not posses *mens rea,* that person may not be responsible for the crime charged, correct?"

"That's up to a court of law."

"But if a suspect is doing something that is not of their own free will, you would want to know that, wouldn't you? I mean, it might affect how you choose to file a case, am I right?"

"Don't tell me how to do my job, Ms. Caine."

"Your Honor, I would ask you to direct the witness to answer my questions."

Strobert shot me with his look.

"Continue, Ms. Caine," the judge said. "Detective Strobert knows what he's supposed to do."

I looked at him and said, "Does he now? Detective Strobert, who was it who recovered the necklace from the Charger?"

He took a beat before answering. "My partner, Detective Richards, found the necklace."

"Is Detective Richards senior to you?"

"Yes."

"So he was the lead in the investigation?"

"Yes."

"But you are the one who is testifying about it."

"Yes."

"Did you see Detective Richards recover the necklace?"

"No."

"What were you doing at the time?"

"I believe I was talking to one of the patrol officers on the scene."

"And what happened? Did Detective Richards call you over?"

"He said something like, 'Look at this.' I went over to him and he had the necklace by the chain."

"Did Detective Richards show you the inscription on the back?"

"Yes."

I got a copy of Strobert's report from my briefcase. "Detective, do you recognize this?"

"Yes. That's the report I made about the crime scene."

"In this report, you mention recovering a charred necklace, isn't that right?"

"Yes."

"In fact, *charred* is the word you used, right?"

"Yes."

"It's on page three," I said.

"I know," he said.

There's a general rule of cross-examination: Never ask a witness an open-ended question, unless you're absolutely sure you know what the answer will be. But sometimes you have to have a gut instinct about when to break that rule.

I did now. "I'm curious, Detective. With a necklace that was charred and blackened by a fire, how was it you were able to read the inscription on the back?"

There was a flare of doubt in his eyes then, and thinking going on behind those eyes. What was he hiding? Or who was he protecting? Himself? Richards?

"I can only tell you what I saw," Strobert said. "Maybe the smoke only hit one side of it. I'm not an expert."

"No," I said. "You're not."

CHAPTER 29

Next up was the eyewitness, Minerva herself.

I'd seen her in the hallway, all black and flowing, wearing shades even though it was night. She was having her moment on camera, a regular Norma Desmond coming down the spiral staircase.

And that's how she presented herself. I'm sure Aaron was thrilled. Not.

But she was his big witness, the eyes that saw everything. Right. The eyes that lied.

I was ready to upset his applecart from the get-go.

As Minerva came to be sworn, the clerk asked her to raise her right hand.

"I object," I said, as dramatically as possible. It worked, because I got some of those nice murmurs.

Judge Hegg said, "On what grounds?"

"Quite simple, Your Honor. The witness is going to be asked to swear so help her God. But as she does not believe in God, the oath is meaningless."

Minerva cast her princess-of-the-night scowl at me. A little Googling had brought me an interview from some time back when she had discussed her rejection of God. I was ready with a copy should it be required.

But the judge did exactly the right thing, surprise surprise, and asked Minerva if that was so.

"It is," Minerva told the court, "and the cold stones of history lie in the wake of all who claim allegiance to that imaginary despot."

"Please refrain from making speeches," Judge Hegg said. "You will affirm to tell the truth, without reference to God."

"I object to that," I said. "It has no bite, to coin a phrase."

"Overruled." Judge Hegg said. "Ma'am, do you understand that if you do not tell the truth, you can be found guilty of perjury? Do you understand that?"

"Of course!"

"Then sit in the witness box and tell the truth."

With a theatrical flourish, Minerva sat in the witness box. I was of two minds on this. For one thing, I'd let her show a little of her crazy side. But on the other hand, the jury was completely focused on her now and would hang on her every word.

Aaron knew how to guide direct testimony. He began by asking her about how she came to be known as Minerva.

"When I began my show," she said, "one of the most popular of its time, and still in circulation on cable and DVDs, I decided to call myself by a name that had something to do with my calling. I liked Minerva. That's what I chose."

"And is that your legal name now?" Aaron asked.

"It is. Why should anyone need two names? That implies ownership."

"Now, Minerva, you have lived at your current address for how long?"

"Ah, nearly forty years now. I love this city."

"Your house is located at the corner of Tareco and Viewpoint?"

"It is, yes. You've been there."

"For the benefit of the jury, if you please." Aaron tapped his laptop and a map of the crime location flipped up on a screen facing the jury. All the while, Traci Ann just sat there, impassive. Like she didn't really care one way or the other.

"Showing you now a map of the crime scene, is that an accurate rendition of where your home is located?"

"It is."

"And can you tell the jury where on the map your home would be?"

"It is right there at the top, the only house there."

"Indicating for the record the rectangular structure in the top middle of the map."

"So indicated," Judge Hegg said.

"Now can you tell us, Minerva, on the night in question, where you were at approximately twelve-thirty in the morning?"

"In my house, of course!"

"Were you awake?"

"Yes, I was. I was screening a movie, as I do every night at midnight."

"I see—"

"*I Walked With a Zombie* was the film," she added.

"And during the course of that viewing," Aaron said, "did you at some point rise and go—"

"Objection," I said. "Leading the witness."

"Sustained."

"Tell us what you did at some point during the movie," Aaron said.

"I got up to stretch. I get stiff when I am sitting down too long. I walked over to my window and pulled back the curtain and looked down. And that's when I saw her." Minerva pointed right at Traci Ann.

"Let the record show that the witness has identified the defendant," Aaron said.

"It will so reflect," the judge said.

"Now, when you saw her, the defendant, what was she doing?"

"She was pouring something all over the car."

"What was she using?"

"A large container of some kind, like a gas can."

Aaron strode to his counsel table and reached under it and pulled out a red plastic gas container.

"Showing you what has been marked as People's Exhibit Three, is this the container you saw that night?"

Minerva gave it a quick glance. "That's it."

Aaron set the container on top of the table now, so the jury could get a good look at it.

"After you saw the defendant pouring liquid on the car, what did you see next?"

"Why, she lit it on fire!"

"How did she light it on fire?"

"With a match."

"What did she do with the match?"

"She lit it."

"And then?"

"Threw it on the car, of course."

"What, if anything, happened next?"

"She, the defendant, turned into a coyote."

"You mean she transformed into an animal that looked like a coyote to you?"

"I know what a coyote is young man. We get them up in the hills. And that's what happened. She turned into a coyote and started loping away, so I called the fire department and the police."

"And when the police arrived, did they question you?"

"Of course, young man."

"Thank you." Aaron turned to me with a half grin. I wanted to nibble his earlobes.

"Your witness," he said.

CHAPTER 30

I began my cross-examination of Minerva with my usual, sweet, understated, Katie Couric voice. Witnesses expect to be grilled. You have to mix them up by gently drawing out what you need. If you find an opening, you can charge on through.

"Minerva," I said. "You were a very popular television personality in your day, is that correct?"

"It's still my day! You should see the fan mail I get."

"Your specialty was showing horror movies?"

"Horror movies are the greatest art form America has ever produced."

"Like the one you were watching that night?"

"How pitiful your knowledge! Yes, it is one of the great films!"

"All about zombies, is it?"

"As the title states."

"When a film like that comes on, do you watch it carefully? I mean, after seeing it before?"

"I watch every horror film carefully."

"Do you recall, Miss Minerva—"

"Only Minerva!"

"Minerva, excuse me. Do you recall my coming to your home?"

"You broke in, is what you did."

"As I recall, you opened the gate for me."

With narrowed gaze she said, "That is a technicality."

"In fact, you invited me inside, did you not?"

Aaron objected. "What relevance is this line of questioning?"

"Your Honor," I said, "this is going to go directly to credibility."

"I'll give you a little leeway," Judge Hegg said. "But only a little."

"Thank you, Your Honor. I repeat, you did invite me into your home, correct?"

"In a moment of weakness," she said.

"Nevertheless, you recall our conversation inside? With your driver present?"

"I remember it vaguely."

The liar. "What is your driver's name?"

"He's no longer employed by me."

"You let him go?"

"He left me."

"Again I ask, what was his name?"

"Gary was his name, but he liked to be called G Dog."

"I see. Did G Dog give you a reason for leaving your employ?"

"No."

"Might it have had something to do with his being attacked by a dark creature in your living room?"

Aaron shouted, "Objection! May we approach the bench?"

We scampered up to the judge. "We have to stop meeting like this," I said to Aaron.

He said to the judge, "That question was improper

and prejudicial, and Ms. Caine knows it. I want you to admonish her in front of the jury and tell them to disregard the last question."

"Why not whip me with your briefs while you're at it?" I said.

"That's enough," Judge Hegg said. "Ms. Caine, I am going to do exactly as Mr. Argula suggests, and I am warning you, if you ask a clearly improper question again, I will impose sanctions. Do you understand me?"

"I do," I said respectfully, which was hard.

We all returned to our places. The judge looked at the jury. "Ladies and gentlemen, you will disregard the last question of counsel and not give it any weight whatsoever. Continue, Ms. Caine."

I said, "When I was inside your home, with G Dog and you, I noticed your television set up. It looked a bit dated. Is that right?"

"I beg your pardon?" Minerva said.

"The television upon which you watch your movies. It seems to be an old cathode ray tube, as opposed to today's LED or plasma televisions."

"I don't know about all that. I have a television and I'm happy with it."

"I noticed an adapter box on top of the television, with what we would call rabbit ears for reception."

"Someone else set that up for me."

"That would only get you local channels."

"That's all I need. I don't believe in paying for television programs!"

"I see. And I did not notice a tape player."

"Ah-ha! You see I am not so old-fashioned after all. I have a DVD player, like all the kids!"

"Oh, those kids," I said. "So you weren't recording the movie that night?"

"No. It was on Channel 5."

"I see. So you were watching a favorite movie, and right in the middle of it you got up not only to stretch, but also to walk to the window, even though you were not recording and could not pause the movie, is that right?"

She gave a quick couple of blinks. I hoped the jury saw them. I was using the Rule of Probability, an old trial lawyer principle from Louis Nizer. It states that even in simple matters people will act according to basic common sense. Someone watching a beloved movie would not go to a window without a stronger reason than to stretch.

"I often walk around and stretch," Minerva said, though not very convincingly.

I pulled out some notes I'd made during a night of research. I started with what I'd found in the *L.A. Times* database through the L.A. library system. "Your name, before it was Minerva, was Hermione Blodgett?"

Eyes almost popping, Minerva said, "I refuse to recognize that name."

"I just want to make it clear that at some point you legally changed your name to Minerva, correct?"

"Of course! That is my name. I answer to no other."

"Minerva. That is the Roman name for the goddess Athena, is it not?"

She did not answer. She studied me. Looking to see what I had. I think she was surprised I was bringing this all up.

"Is it not?" I repeated.

"Yes," she said.

"Isn't it true that Athena was a warrior goddess?"

"That's not all she is."

"Is?"

"You display your ignorance."

"I beg your pardon," I said. "Help me along. Athena was born out of Zeus's forehead, isn't it so?"

"Yes."

"Didn't she burst out of Zeus's head fully formed and crying out for war?"

"Yes."

"Is it also true that Athena was worshipped in the form of an owl?"

"That is true."

"Could that be why you have a statue of an owl on top of your home?"

"I don't see why that should be so odd."

"I did not say it was odd. I merely asked the question. Do you identify with owls?"

"I like owls."

I placed my notes on the lectern and put my hands behind my back as I stepped out to face Minerva. "Is it not also true that the owl is a representation of the most ancient goddess of all, namely Lilith?"

The moment I said that name, Minerva thrust her hands onto the rail of the witness stand. She pushed herself up and pointed a finger at me. "I know what you're doing! And I will not have it! I will not!"

Judge Hegg pounded her gavel, just like in the movies. "The witness will sit down and be quiet."

Minerva did not sit. "I bow the knee to no one!"

"Except the queen of all goddesses, isn't that right?" I said.

"You know nothing!"

"Quiet!" Judge Hegg said. "Do you hear me?"

Ah, the pleasantness of a prosecution witness imploding on the stand. It almost never happens. Not like in those old TV shows like *Perry Mason*. Not like what Cruise did to Nicholson in *A Few Good Men*.

But here was Minerva and she was going bats. At this point I just paused and played it cool, letting Aaron demand that we approach the bench.

"That's it," Aaron said as soon as we were in chambers. "You warned her. I ask for a mistrial and sanctions."

"I'm not the one who called this nutbag," I said.

"Your Honor, if you please."

Judge Hegg slapped her hand down. "Stop it, you two." She looked at the clock. "I think we're going to call it a night. I will take under advisement the motion for a mistrial, and for sanctions. And I'll tell you, lack of sleep is going to make me very grouchy, Ms. Caine."

When we got back out to the courtroom, waiting for Judge Hegg to come in and adjourn, Aaron said, "Omni. Bar. We need to talk."

There was someone else waiting for me in the hallway. Nick, the world's smallest wannabe investigator. He was waving at me from a seat in the courtroom. I motioned for him to come to the rail.

He had a file in his hand and seemed overly excited. "I found him!" he whispered.

"Found who?"

"Hennigan. I broke into his house."

"What?"

"They didn't tell you everything."

"What are you talking about, Nick?"

He opened the file and showed it to me. It was a page of his scrawled notes, but it had an upside-down pentagram diagram with a circle around it.

"What is this?" I asked.

"Hennigan was a Satan worshipper," Nick said. "They cleaned out his house, but they didn't look under the carpet. Who did? Who do you love? Nick!"

CHAPTER 31

At the Omni, Aaron was stiff and uncomfortable. I was stiff and uncomfortable. The drinks were stiff and uncomfortable. It was almost closing time.

"Tough night in court," I said.

"I don't want to see you become a blight on the legal profession," Aaron said.

"I love it when you talk dirty."

"Don't joke about this, Mallory. I'm really concerned about you."

"Are you? Or are you concerned about losing to me?"

"I'm not going to lose. No matter how many of these crazy stunts you pull."

We were in the corner of the lounge. There was a group of guys at the bar watching a replay of *Sports Center*. Every now and then they would erupt in cheers over some replay. Our server had brought a bowl of spiced peanuts, but I kept looking at the guys at the bar, wondering which one of their brains had the most spice.

"Aaron, is there anything you want to say, of substance, to me?"

"What do you mean by that?"

"Do you want to admit your evidence is tainted? That you know this case is bogus."

"I'm not going to tell you anything like that. Besides, if your client really is a vampire, isn't being locked up the best place for her, for all of us?"

"Interesting ethical conundrum, huh? You owe her a fair trial under the Constitution, but you would skirt the law to get a conviction?"

He took a long sip of his drink, a Manhattan, then said. "I don't care any more. Insults or not. And you know exactly what I'm going to say."

"Case dismissed?"

"You and me. Together."

"Aaron . . ."

He leaned over to kiss me. I looked at his nose. It was appetizing. And that's when I cried. It just happened. Boom. It was embarrassing. I didn't want that to happen, not in front of Aaron. Not in front of anybody. Certainly not in a crowded bar. I grabbed a cocktail napkin and put it on my face.

Aaron said, "What is it, Mallory?"

"It's all so messed up," I said into the napkin. "The world is one pit of a place to have to live your life." He touched my arm. I jerked it away. "Leave me alone why don't you?"

"Mallory, no. Why are you saying that?"

"I'm saying leave me alone, don't you understand English? It'll never work out between us."

"But it can. It can."

"No."

"Why not?"

I looked up from the napkin. "Because I'm becoming a nun."

His eyes almost crossed. "What?"

"I can't be with any man."

"You can't . . . You aren't . . ." He paused, then added, "Not that there's anything wrong with that." Then: "No. You're lying. You're lying to me, Mallory."

"Fine! Just leave it alone, can't you?"

"You love me. I know you love me. I can feel it coming out of you."

"What, like ooze? Am I oozing?"

"Mallory—"

"Listen to me, Aaron." I wadded up the wet cocktail napkin. I was finally not crying, but I dabbed at my eyes. "I'm only going to say this once, because if I have to say it again, I won't be able to do it. I'm no good. I'm no good for you or anyone else. The only ones I'm good for are my clients. Okay? You have to believe me. I have a thing. A bad thing. Inside me. I'm not good inside. Don't ask me any questions. Just know that if you and I were together, it would be bad, for me, but especially for you."

We sat in silence for a long moment. The guys at the bar cheered something. My stomach rumbled. Fortunately, it was too loud in there for Aaron to hear it.

Aaron looked me in the eye and said, "I'm not going to buy into that, Mallory."

"You have no choice!"

He shook his head. "I can't give you up again."

"You sound like a stalker," I said. "You want me to go get a restraining order?"

"You wouldn't do that to me."

"If it's the only way, I would."

"Just tell me you don't love me," he said.

"I don't love you."

"Now say it like you mean it."

"I don't love you."

"Now say it and believe it."

I said nothing. I started crying again. "Damn you," I said. "Why didn't you tell me?"

"Tell you what?"

"About Hennigan. The victim. The cop who worshipped Satan."

"What?"

"Don't act like you didn't know," I said.

Aaron kept a straight face. "This sounds like desperation, Mallory."

"Suppose I can prove it. What'll you do then?"

He shook his head. "It's irrelevant. He could have worshipped Mickey Mouse and it still wouldn't matter."

"But doesn't it matter to you?" I said. "Don't you want to know?"

"And do what?"

"There's more going on here than you know, but you act like you don't want to know."

"I have one job to do," Aaron said. "The evidence is clear. And if you try to muddy the waters with something like this, I'll object on relevance grounds. What do you think Judge Hegg is going to do with that?"

"I'll think of something," I said and got up before he could say another word. I popped out the door to the Angels Flight court. I ran off into the night, cursing the sky, wondering who was up there that could hear me cursing.

I had my Amanda wig in Geraldine's trunk, parked on Hill Street. I grabbed it and went walking, walking alone into the night which is where I belonged. I was crying again, and I hoped that if there was a God, He heard good and loud what He'd done to me, what He had forced me into.

Down Spring Street, past the old plaza, to Cesar Chavez Drive. I put on the wig and the shades, to hide my tears and my face and the windows to my soul.

Gack, where was my soul?

Come now!

The Voice.

"Oh, shut *up*!" I said.

Miss Uganda!

"What does that even mean? No. I don't want to know. I don't want to talk to you. You have no power over me! I will not give in. I will kill you if I can!"

Come!

"Bop-bop-bop-bop bah-bahhhh—"

No!

"—bop-bop-bop-bop bahhhh!"

Silence. Good news. How I hated that Voice.

I ate that night. I think he was a neo-Nazi. He'd pulled a gun on me and shot me in the heart. It felt oddly right to eat him. I was a loathsome thing and if I ate a loathsome thing, then everything balanced out. Somehow, everything had to balance out.

CHAPTER 32

The next day I went to the Men's Central Jail to see my father. He was wearing orange K-10 coveralls. K-10s are the high-security inmates, like gang leaders or guys accused of killing cops with a sword. A deputy shackled his hands to the interview table.

He looked calm, which was something you don't usually see at Central.

"You doing okay?" I asked.

He smiled. "I am not afraid. The Lord will look after me."

"And a good lawyer," I said. "Don't forget that part."

"How is your mother?" he said.

Hadn't expected that one. "She's . . . who she is."

"I'd like to see her again. Does she know I'm back?"

"I don't think she's aware of too much going on, in general."

"Have you thought more about what I told you? About the parchment?"

"Harry, I—"

"Why don't you call me Dad?"

"I don't think so," I said. "I mainly came here to

tell you that we'll be getting ready for a preliminary hearing soon, and I'm going to need to walk you through some things." I kept my voice calm. What he didn't know was that I was feeling strange inside. Defending people accused of crimes is what I do. But when it's your own father, the pressure is on.

True, it was difficult to see him as a father just now. But he had saved my zombie life. I owed him for that.

"What will be, will be," Harry said. "But you must not kill again."

I kept my face passive. "Whatever do you mean?"

"The undead who eat flesh. You must stop."

"Harry, we have enough to think about."

"Thou shalt not kill."

"What is it you were doing with that sword of yours?"

"That was different. That was justice."

"Those little niceties are going to be lost on a jury. Harry, we have a long way to go. I'll be back later."

"Where are you going?"

"To buy a sandwich," I lied.

As I was walking to the parking structure, my phone went off. It was Charles Beaumont Manyon.

"Ms. Caine, did I catch you at a bad time?"

"There are no bad times in the life of a defense lawyer," I said. "Only bad clients."

"Well, we can talk about that at dinner. At which time I'm sure you'll be ready to accept my offer."

I stopped walking then and looked around me at the chain-link and razor wire, at the squat jail building and the police cars. I was in the middle of a concrete jungle and knew that Manyon was calling from a posh office, where every comfort of the modern legal superstar was within reach. As it would be for me if I would only say yes.

But I felt oddly at home here. I knew this place, the hardness, and the despair, and that was what I was here to try to undo for my clients.

"Your offer was very generous," I said. "But I'm afraid I'm going to have to turn you down."

Long pause. I don't think Manyon was used to someone saying no to him.

Finally he said, "You're making a mistake, a huge mistake, Ms. Caine. A mistake of career, of life. You are being offered the world on a gold platter."

"You're right," I said. "No doubt. But I've made big mistakes before. I sat through *Eat, Pray, Love.*"

Manyon did not laugh. He hung up.

That night, in court, Aaron looked uncomfortable around me. He didn't come over and greet me, like he had been, with his smile and swagger. He barely made eye contact. I couldn't blame him. I'd done everything to discourage his advances.

I felt a little sorry about that. I didn't want him to lose his mojo. But I put that aside, because I also didn't want to lose this case.

Judge Hegg called Aaron and me into her chambers. She was going to let us both know what was what on Aaron's motions for a mistrial.

"I hope you two have calmed down," she said. "Is everything all right between you?"

We looked at each other, knowing it wasn't all right.

"I am not going to declare a mistrial," she said. "There's too much invested to go through this again. I'm not going to lay sanctions on Ms. Caine, though

I was very close. I want to get this over with. Ms. Caine, are you through with the cross-examination of this Minerva character?"

"I don't see any point in continuing it," I said.

"Mr. Argula, are you going to have any re-direct?"

"I have to, Your Honor, after what Ms. Caine did. And I am going to ask Your Honor to keep a tight leash on her."

"Hey!" I said.

"I agree," Judge Hegg said.

"Make sure it goes both ways," I said.

I was feeling confident when we got back into court. After Minerva's meltdown, I felt like I could sow enough reasonable doubt to get a hung jury, if not an outright acquittal. All I had to do was hang on and not make any blunders.

Minerva, looking delicate and suspicious, took the stand once again. She eyed me with contempt just before Aaron started his questioning. The full courtroom seemed to crackle with anticipation. I'm sure everyone was hoping for another exciting incident out of the vampire trial.

If possible, I was going to give it to them.

"Minerva," Aaron said, "last night Ms. Caine asked you some questions that got you upset, is that fair to say?"

"Yes," she said coolly, no doubt because Aaron had coached her well.

"Would you mind explaining to the jury what it was that caused you distress?"

Minerva swiveled to face the jurors. "I was rather offended that Ms. Caine would imply I worship a goddess named Lilith. I do not worship anyone. I am an atheist. I rely on my intellect and my will. I have spent my career this way, and I did not want to have it implied that I am in any way associated with goddess worship. I regret that I allowed my emotions to run away with me."

"Thank you," Aaron said. "Your Honor, that is all I have of this witness."

"Re-cross, Ms. Caine?" the judge said.

Most trial lawyers make a big mistake. They think you have to take advantage of every opportunity for cross-examination, even if it's just a few questions. Like they have to flap their gums or lose them.

Wrong. When you've got what you wanted, and no harm has been done, let the witness go.

"No questions," I said.

The judge told Minerva she could step down. "Mr. Argula, how many more witnesses are you going to call?"

"Your Honor," Aaron said. "The People rest."

Shocker. I was sure Aaron was going to call at least a couple more witnesses. But now he was making a play, tossing the ball in my court.

I still had the opportunity to address the jury. I had reserved my opening statement until now.

Judge Hegg said, "Ms. Caine, are you ready to proceed with your case in chief?"

"I am, Your Honor," I said. "I am prepared to make my opening statement."

"Why don't we take a ten-minute recess, and then you may do so."

The jury filed out of the courtroom, then the judge.

Traci Ann was taken to the holding cell, where I joined her for a few minutes. I was going to tell her that I would make my opening, then call no witnesses. That we had enough to establish reasonable doubt.

But then I got the shock of my legal life.

"You *what?*" I said, giving Traci Ann the nastiest, you-must-be-crazy look I could come up with.

"I want to take the stand," she said again, as cold as refrigerated herring.

After a breath to compose myself, I spoke in calm notes. "Traci Ann, let me explain something to you. When handed a case like ours, where the prosecution's own witnesses have imploded—"

"One witness," Traci Ann said.

"A key witness. They have a weak case. They're not going to convince twelve people beyond a reasonable doubt. And when you get a case like that, the worst thing, the absolute worst, is for the defendant to get on the stand and testify. Because it can only make things worse, not better. A skilled prosecutor, and Mr. Argula is that, can tie you up in little knots."

"Even if I'm not guilty?"

"Especially if you're not guilty, because he'll take your confidence and make it seem like arrogance. He'll take your story and chop it up into little pieces, and set those pieces in front of the jury like bird feed. They'll gobble it up, and you'll be the one who suffers."

"But I can look the jury in the face and tell them I didn't do it."

"And they'll look back at you and think, 'What a skilled little liar she is.' But if you just let me take the case and argue it, the way I can, I'll sow so many seeds of doubt, they'll never convict."

What I wasn't telling her, what I couldn't tell her, was that if the jury came back with a verdict of guilty, that wasn't going to be the end of it. Because then I'd have to step up and tell the truth, the whole truth and nothing but the truth. I would have to confess, and then it would be all over. My life, my unlife, my practice of law, my soul. Because they'd stick me in the can and I doubt they'd honor my request for human flesh and brains.

I would die of starvation, and that would be that.

"I have the right to testify, don't I?" she said. "Isn't that in the Constitution?"

"Actually, the Constitution says you have the right not to be a witness against yourself, and that's what you'll be doing if you take the stand."

"I thought I could if I wanted to."

"You do have that right, but I'm strongly advising you against it."

"I don't have to take your advice, do I?"

Checkmate. "Don't do this, Traci Ann."

"I am going to," she said. "I want to. Tell the judge."

"At least tell *me* what you're going to say."

"Just let me talk," she said.

Something was very wrong here. But I was powerless to stop her.

CHAPTER 33

We gathered back in the courtroom. It was 9:36 P.M.

I decided to forgo my opening statement altogether. Everything was going to hinge on what Traci Ann said, and I had no way to know what it was.

Hell broke loose exactly two minutes later.

"I call as my next witness Ms. Traci Ann Johnson." I heard the voices of the gallery behind me. It was a wave of surprise sweeping over them. No one anticipated this. Not the press, not the court watchers, who knew what went on better than most people.

The sudden electricity of anticipation was palpable. The vampire was taking the stand. The bloodsucker was going to tell her story! Oh, to be in on this!

I, of course, was terrified.

Traci Ann hadn't told me, or even hinted at, what she was going to say. What facts she was going to testify to. What alibi she supposedly had. I highly doubted she had one that could be verified. Not in her line of work.

And if it could not be corroborated, the jury wouldn't buy it. A witness is always assumed to be self-serving, especially a defendant testifying on her own behalf.

I could almost hear the derision in Aaron's closing argument.

Traci Ann got up from her chair and walked to the witness stand, where she faced the clerk.

Just before the oath Aaron said, "I will object to the oath as well, Your Honor. This witness is a self-described vampire. She obviously does not believe in God."

"Yes, I do!" Traci Ann said. "I pray that He'll save me every day!"

Judge Hegg looked momentarily flummoxed. Who could blame her?

"Do you want to take her on *voir dire* for that?" the judge said to Aaron.

I gave Aaron a look that said, *Don't even think about going there.*

Remarkably, Aaron decided not to pick that particular nit. "No need, Your Honor. We will take the witness at her word."

And so Traci Ann Johnson was given the oath, and answered, "I do."

It was the last thing she would say that night.

A guy from the gallery screamed and jumped the banister.

He flashed by me on the right, between the podium and the jury box.

I saw his face as if it were in close up. The side of his face actually. He was mid twenties, Caucasian but tanned. Rough two days' growth of beard. Dressed nicely, slacks and sport coat over open-collared shirt.

But that was the only thing normal about him.

He was foaming at the mouth. Thick, white gob at the corner, and more where that came from.

And in his right hand, coming up in attack formation, a thick, pointed wooden stake.

The next tick of time had him past me, coattails flying. The jurors' faces were in various aspects of shock and fright.

My feet seemed buried in sand as I attempted to follow the man who I knew was trying to kill my client.

The bailiff was flat bottomed, on the other side of the courtroom, seated at his desk, and on the phone.

Which he dropped as he tried to rise.

Traci Ann was trapped in the box, with nowhere to go. But her face advertised everything. She knew what was coming and was powerless to do anything about it.

And just like in those movie moments, where the guy shouts, "Noooo," and they slow down the sound, I shouted, "Noooo," and they slowed down the sound.

The man with the stake leaped like a predatory animal. He virtually flew over the rail and thrust forward with the stake.

Which was buried deep in Traci Ann's chest.

By now people were screaming, several of the jurors, and me. My scream was feral and angry and wanting to taste death—his.

The bailiff was on his feet now. Drawing his weapon, though that wasn't going to do any good. He wouldn't shoot in a crowded courtroom. He didn't look like he knew what to do anyway, so he shouted, "Don't move!"

The guy turned around in front of the witness box. Still foaming. Teeth bared, he growled. Actually growled.

The poor bailiff, who would no doubt be haunted by this forever, charged to within three feet of the attacker and pointed his gun straght at him.

"On the ground! Now!"

The guy's lips stretched farther over his teeth, into a wicked smile.

"Now!" the bailiff shouted.

And the guy did get closer to the ground. Only he did it by turning into a wolf.

I saw all this from behind the bailiff. The wolf had his shirt on, but with a vicious turn came out of his pants and shoes. Then he jumped at the bailiff and clamped down with big, bad incisors on the short arm of the law. The bailiff cried out in pain, dropping his gun to the floor.

Blood spurted from between the wolf's teeth.

That was it. I had nothing to fear, deathwise, from a stupid wolf.

I threw myself at the fur bag, wrapping my left arm around his neck, and with my right hand clawed his eyes.

An angry growl of pain issued from the lupus. But it loosened his jaw, which was my intent. He released the bailiff and turned his attentions to me.

Have you ever wrestled a wolf? They have no body fat to speak of, at least the ones who shape-shift in courtrooms. He had muscles as taut and hard as the rocks of Chatsworth Canyon.

He began to snap at me, but couldn't get his jaws far enough for purchase on my skin.

And then he spoke, in wolfish tones. "Release me or die," he said.

"Bite me," I said.

He tried again, missed.

This only redoubled his effort to get away. His paws pushed hard against the floor. He began to slip from my grasp.

Desperation kicked in. Enough of this! Enough with the forces of darkness, or whatever they were, coming after me or my client. I was going to go into this heart of darkness and chew it up and spit it out. Once and for all.

As he was almost free, I gripped one of his back legs. And then, with all the strength I could muster, I bit him. Bit into the meaty and tendony back of his wolf leg.

He howled so loudly it rattled the windows. At least I think it did. Bitter-tasting blood dripped down my chin.

And then he was free. But hobbled. He began to limp toward the attorney gate at the bar, to charge through it.

Of course, the people in the courtroom were screaming and running and jostling to get out. Which was not good, because the doors of the courtroom were open and the wolf could get away.

I scrambled to my feet. Just as the wolf pushed through the gate, I dove over it and landed on its back. I was able to get both arms around his neck and pull into a classic, street fighting headlock.

This is for you, Traci Ann, I told myself. This is for you, Mallory Caine. This is for whatever there is left in me that thinks there's a sliver of good left in the world. This is for my life, if I have any, for my soul if anybody's watching. This is—

Zap!

I popped off wolfie like exploding popcorn. On the floor, on my back, I looked up at another bailiff.

Must have come in when all the commotion broke out. He was holding a Taser in his hand. Had he tased me? No, it was wolfie, lying there on the floor now. Motionless.

And slowly transforming back into human form.

"Mallory!" Aaron's voice. It came to me through my fuzzy, electrified brain.

"Who's Mallory?" I said.

"Are you all right?" He knelt by me. I could feel his hand stroke my cheek. "What on earth . . . blood . . ."

"Traci Ann," I said.

"They're looking after her."

"No!"

"No what?"

"Get me up."

"Just wait—"

"Get me up!" I started the process and Aaron helped me finish it. I looked at the witness stand and it was empty.

"She doesn't need medical," I said. "She needs a priest."

Aaron said, "She got stabbed in the chest, Mallory."

"She's a vampire, remember? Where is she?"

"They went down the back elevator I think."

"Who?"

"Two guys. I think one said he was a doctor."

Fresh electricity, this time in my blood, shot through me.

"And you let them? Come on!" I started for the back of the courtroom. "Come with me, Aaron!"

I charged out the rear courtroom door. I banked left, past the open door of Judge Hegg's chambers. I saw her sitting on the floor with her hands wrapped around her knees, hyperventilating.

I kept heading down the hall, toward the judges' elevator. I picked up a scent, the stench of sulfur and Old Spice. I looked behind me once. Aaron was there.

One more turn and there they were. Two men dragging Traci Ann, who looked unconscious.

Both men turned their heads toward me, bared their teeth, and hissed.

Okay, now what? Were they going to turn into wolves, too? What powers did they possess? Who was I to stop them?

But Traci Ann needed me. Because I was convinced that if they got her out of the building, she would be destroyed, if she wasn't already, and her soul sent to hell. I'm kind of obsessed with that.

"What are they doing?" Aaron said behind me.

"Trying to get her out of the building. We're not going to let them."

The two men hissed again. Which reminded me of something. Once, back in the crazy days of my mother's church hopping, she'd gone to a snake handling cult for a while. I went with her. One crazy, snake handling reverend held up snakes one by one, called them the devil, and said whenever they hissed he would ask their name. He said a demon had to give his name if you asked directly. So he kept asking the snakes their names, and they would hiss, but then the reverend would translate that into some name or other and tell everybody what it was. And then he would say, "I send you away to the name above all names." Then the snakes would stop hissing.

I totally didn't get any of that and was glad when Mom switched over to worshipping at Arthur Murray dance studio for a while.

But what the heck? I had nothing else. "Are you two demons?" I asked loudly.

They hissed. It sounded like air coming out of a bike tire. But that was the wrong question. "What is your name?" I said with as much Katherine Hepburn authority as I could.

Now they didn't hiss. They got stiff and their faces showed fear.

The one on the left, the younger of the two, looking a bit like George Clooney in his prime, said something that sounded like *I am Margaret.*

"Margaret?"

"Marduk!"

"Got it." I looked at the other one, a thin older man. "What is your name?"

"I am Nebo."

Whatever, I thought, and wound up for the big fastball. "Okay, Marduk and Nebo, I send you away to the name—"

Both of them screamed. It sent icicles into my pelvis.

"—above all names!"

The result was instantaneous. Both bodies went down. Their heads clunked on the tile. I heard two thin screeches that died out, as if these dark spirits couldn't get out of there fast enough.

That snake handling deal was pretty darn cool. I'd have to remember that. I had a feeling I'd be running into these guys again.

I ran to the bodies on the floor. Traci Ann looked dead. Pale skin, blue lips, not moving.

"What do we do?" Aaron said.

"Help me get her in the elevator," I said.

We dragged her to the lift and I punched the button.

"We should wait for help," Aaron said.

"There's only one place to go for help that I know of."

"Where?"

It was a good thing all the reporters and gawkers and police cars were assembled on Temple Street. Aaron and I got Traci Ann out the back, in the view of City Hall, now all lit up against the night sky. Aaron helped me get her in Geraldine.

"Where are you taking her?" Aaron said.

"Church," I said. "Will you cover for me?"

"How?"

"I don't know. With the judge maybe. I don't want to get in any more trouble. Will you trust me, Aaron?"

"What is happening here, Mallory? Was that a were-wolf? What do you know about all this?"

I touched his cheek. "Later."

I got to the little church on Selma in twenty minutes. My knowledge of vampires was limited, but the only one I could think of who might have a handle was the white-haired priest.

I left Geraldine at the curb and ran to the door.

Locked.

What? This was supposed to be 24/7. I knocked on the door and waited.

Nothing.

I pounded on the door. Put my ear to it. Still nothing.

Not good. I didn't know how long it took for a vampire to die, or get beyond being revived.

I pulled on the old door handle, wanting to yank it off.

Maybe there was a sleeping quarters somewhere. Priests have got to sleep, right? They could live here, right?

But there was fencing on both sides, and no access to the grounds. The only way in was through . . . St. Peter.

There he was, in the stained-glass window in front.

No, that could not be a good thing. Smashing St. Peter in the front of a church. If I ever got to some pearly gates, he might have that little item marked down on a clipboard.

But there was nowhere else to turn. I wasn't going to go driving around town looking for another church.

And in that moment, I threw all caution to the Hollywood breeze. I looked around for cops. No cruisers in sight. I looked for pedestrians. There was a homeless guy across the street, at least I assumed he was homeless, with a shopping cart piled high with clothes.

I went into my trunk and got to the spare tire and the little tire iron that came with it.

Having a tire iron helped. Instead of smashing, I used the pry end to see if I could loosen old St. Pete without his shattering. I split the difference. Literally. The bottom half of the window came out and landed on the cement, and broke.

Sorry, man. He'd have to get on with no legs for a while. And I'd have to pay for the damages. But that could wait.

I looked in and saw only dim lighting. Candles burning low on the sides made the place seem like a cave with a distant campfire.

But I could see clearly the large crucifix at the altar, with Jesus hanging—

Something else was hanging there.

No, some *body* else.

I shimmied my way up and over the window ledge. Broken jags of glass scratched across my stomach and thighs.

I fell into the church, cursing. Probably not a good idea, but you don't plan these things.

Then I heard a muffled groan.

I got up and hurried down the center aisle.

When I got to the altar I saw who it was. The priest. The old priest himself. He'd been bound and gagged and was upside down, like a Jesuit bat, tied by a rope over a ceiling beam.

He started to twist. His eyes widened when he saw me.

There was a table on the altar with the emblems of the eucharist on top. I got on top of the table so I could reach the priest's face. I untied the gag, a linen scarf.

The friar took in a deep lungful of air.

"Help me," he said.

I said, "Is there a ladder anywhere?"

"In the closet off the vestry."

"Right. What's a vestry again?"

"Go through that door"—he gestured with his head—"and turn right. The first door is the vestry. The door right after that is a closet. There's a ladder in there."

"How about something to cut with?"

"Yes, shears. Garden shears."

"Garden shears?"

"We can't be choosers," he said.

I jumped from the table and went to the door he'd

indicated. I felt around for a light switch and had no luck. So I felt my way down the hall, letting my rods and cones pick up what they could from the sides.

Finally I found the door and flicked on the light inside. The ladder was there and the shears on a shelf, next to a coiled hose.

I took the stuff back to the altar and went up the ladder. I cut the ropes on the priest's hands, and went up a couple of rungs to his feet. I said, "I don't know how to do this delicately. Are you ready to fall?"

"Cut," he said.

I did and he came down like a missile. He crashed into the table of remembrance and sprawled out on the floor.

I clambered down and went to him. He was holding his fuzzy white head.

"You okay?" I asked.

"That's a hard table," he said.

"You have to help us."

"Hm?"

"I have someone in the car. She needs you to do something."

"Me?"

"She's a vampire."

"Vamp . . ."

"And she may be dying or dead or lost."

He tried to sit up. I helped him. "This is a bad night all around," he said. "Where is she?"

He came with me and unlocked the doors of the church. The two of us were able to get Traci Ann inside the church and lock the doors again.

She lay on the floor motionless, pale, as dead looking as anything I'd ever seen. The priest got on his knees, looked her up and down. She had dried blood on her shirt, where the stake had penetrated.

The priest removed a small wooden cross from his frock. He held it over Traci Ann's body. "This will tell us something," he said.

He placed the cross directly atop the wound in Traci Ann's chest. Then withdrew his hand quickly, as if he'd dropped a hand grenade into hole and was waiting for the explosion.

Nothing exploded. Nothing at all happened.

The priest closed his eyes and put his hand over the cross. He began to pray in Latin. I didn't pick up on any of it, except the word *diaboli*. He went on like that for a few minutes, until beads of sweat started breaking out on his forehead.

No movement from Traci Ann.

Finally, the priest's face saddened. He pulled his hand back and slumped, and shook his head.

I was about to issue a scream of frustration that would rise up to heaven, when I heard somebody sigh. And it wasn't me. Or the priest.

Traci Ann opened her eyes. Then her mouth. Her face twisted in agony. She looked like she was issuing a silent scream. Her chest began to heave, her back to arch.

"What's happening?" I said.

"Shh." The priest put his hand up to silence me but kept his gaze on Traci Ann. He said a few more words in Latin, his voice rising.

Traci Ann's body arched more upward, till she was almost taking on a horseshoe shape. The cross on her chest tumbled off and hit the floor with a loud *clack*.

Then she went down, completely. Her eyes closed again. She might have been exactly the same as before, but she was breathing. At least now she was breathing.

The priest placed Traci Ann's hands across her chest. "She must rest now," he said. "The next few hours we must watch over her. The darkness is closing in."

"What's been happening here, Father . . ."

"Clemente," he said. "And what's been happening here is a matter of some importance. I mean biblical importance. Very big stuff."

CHAPTER 34

"Why were you hanging upside down?" I said.

"A warning. They were sent to warn me," Father Clemente said.

"Who was sent?"

"The demons. I don't expect you to understand."

"Give me a shot, Father. I think I just saw two demons try to take down Traci Ann."

He stiffened. "What happened?"

I gave him the story, the hissing, the names, the disappearance.

"Then it is true," he said in response.

"What is?"

"The territorial demons are being gathered. And the most powerful, too. Marduk and Nebo, son of Marduk. These were the chief gods of the ancient Babylonians. They have come here. Or been summoned."

"Whoa now."

"We are the middle of some very dark things. Perhaps the darkest in five thousand years."

"All right, Father, I want you to lay it all out for me. Right now."

He went to a front pew and sat down heavily. "I don't know that you can fully understand. I'm not sure anyone can. Even I."

I parked myself next to him. "Please try."

He said, "From ancient times past, from the pagan authors of old, from the Jewish historians Josephus and Philo, from the early church fathers, Justin Martyr, Irenaeus, and Origen, there is but a single testimony: Demons are the spirits of the wicked dead."

I pondered that. "You mean, bad people die and become devils?"

He shook his head. "The King James version mistranslated the word for *demons* and rendered it *devils*. There is only one devil, and you know his name. Demons are unclean spirits. The Greek noun for demon, *daemon*, is not the same as the word for *devil*. *Daemon* signifies a being between man and God. Plato first set out to define this word. He said demons were the departed spirits of men. Plato got the word *demon* from the one that means *knowing* or *intelligent*. Demons are the knowing ones. What do they know? They know about life, their wicked life, and they know about the spirit world, the life to come. That makes them dangerous, for they know how to influence those of us who are alive."

"So they're wicked dead people?"

"Their spirits, which look for bodies to inhabit."

I took a breath. "How many of these demons are walking around?"

"No one can say. But they obviously know who I am, and who you are, and want something to do with you."

"But why now?"

"That is the question," he said. "I have an idea, but for you to understand it I must take you back, back before the beginning. Back before evil existed, before mankind walked the earth. Back when there was God and the angels and one beautiful angel in particular. His name in Hebrew means the 'shining one.' It has cognates in Akkadian, Ugaritic, and Arabic. The Septuagint, Targum, and the Vulgate translate it as 'Morning Star.' In Latin, he is 'Light Bearer,' or more commonly, Lucifer."

"Satan?"

"The very same. In the beginning God created the heavens and the earth. And the earth became formless and void, a wasteland."

"What do you mean, *became*?"

"The Hebrew is quite clear. The same Hebrew word for *was* may also be translated *became*. That is how the earliest scholars, the Jewish scribes, understood it. You see, the earth was created as a good thing by God, but in Genesis one, verse two, it had become a wasteland. So we must ask, why did the earth *become* that way?"

"I'll bite."

"Because it was cursed by God!"

"What? God cursed his own creation?"

"The second verse of Genesis uses the words *tohu a bohu,* meaning 'without form and void' or 'waste and void.' Those two words together, everywhere else they are used in the Hebrew Scriptures, speak only of a state of affairs that God brought upon persons and places as a punishment for sin."

"Whoa, whoa," I said. "I don't get this. It says God created the heavens and the earth, but you're saying he made it a wasteland?"

"Yes."

"Why?"

"If you look at the next words in Genesis, it says

darkness was upon the face of the deep. Darkness is never good in Hebrew, nor is deep, which also means pit. God, you see, covered his original creation with water, as a curse, just as he would in Noah's day."

"There was another flood?"

"There was."

"Freaky."

"Um, yes. Why do you suppose when Eve went walking over to the tree a serpent was already there?"

"I hadn't thought of that."

"Lucifer was on earth, this was his domain. But from here he rebelled. You see, millions upon millions of years ago—the time is unclear but it's also irrelevant—sometime in the distant past, God created the earth and the angels, and he put in charge of the earth his most beautiful angel, the aforementioned Lucifer. This world was his domain. He was called the guardian cherub of the original Eden. And that was a place full of precious stones and glorious elements. In the Book of Ezekiel we learn that Lucifer was given the highest place in God's creation. He was set upon the holy mountain of God, which in the original language means the government of God. He was made chief prince of this world, and in some ways he still is. He has the power to still roam the world today."

"Why doesn't God just stop him?"

"People have been asking that question for at least four thousand years. That is what the oldest book of our Bible, the Book of Job, is all about. But we are getting ahead of ourselves. Lucifer rebelled. We are told he was perfect from the day he was created until iniquity was found in him. What was the cause or source of this iniquity? According to the prophet Isaiah it was the spontaneous generation of evil in his heart."

Some high school English lit came to me. "I thought his rebellion was in heaven. You know, *Paradise Lost*?"

"Good poem, bad theology," he said. "The purpose of Lucifer's rebellion is found in the Book of Isaiah, wherein it states, 'I will ascend into heaven.' He was going to try to conquer God's own territory. And he was going to launch from the earth."

"Whoa."

"Let me summarize the career of Lucifer. He began on Earth as its prince. He determined to enter Heaven, even into the very throne room of God. He desired to take over the government of God, because he overestimated his own strength on earth. Lucifer declared that he would replace the 'Most High.' Why did Lucifer choose this appellation of God? Why did he not choose, say, the Creator? The Hebrew is *El Elyon*, and it means the one who is the *possessor* of Heaven and Earth. This was a declaration of a coup d'état, a move to take over the whole doggone deal. Lucifer must have planned it for a million years."

"But he didn't win."

"The jury is still out."

"Excuse me?"

"Don't you see? He has been plotting his comeback. Launched from earth once again. And Los Angeles, I greatly fear, is his war headquarters. For five thousand years the world has been focused on the Middle East. The Middle East has been the graveyard of empires, the crucible of conflict. The Persians couldn't solve it. Alexander the Great could only solve it for a season. The Romans couldn't maintain their empire there. The Crusades failed. The Byzantine Empire failed. The British Empire crumbled. And now Israel is there, and everyone is looking at the Middle East still. That's where the focus is, that's what all the prophecy people are writing books about. And all the while, it has just been part of a diversionary plan. The armies of the night are not going to gather against the Middle East in some real battle with horses and spears and arrows and tanks or whatever. No, it has always been a diversion."

"A diversion for what purpose?"

"This is the place from which the last great assault on heaven and earth will begin. We are, in short, in occupied territory. And that is why two chief demons, the ones you met and who hung me upside down, are here now. In Los Angeles. They've left their original territories. That could only mean they've been summoned. By Lucifer. And more must be on the way. And that means something, too."

"What does it mean?" I said.

"It means," he said, "that the worst is yet to come."

CHAPTER 35

We sat in silence for a moment. Then Father Clemente said. "But I wonder, why you? Why have they come after you?"

"Oh, boy," I said.

"You must tell me what you know."

"Oh, boy."

"Why do you keep saying that?"

"Father, I don't want your hair to get any whiter."

"I will allow it," he said.

"I want to. I want to tell someone. I have to. Maybe like a confession."

"I've a handled a few of those in my day."

"Do we have to go into a booth?"

"No, child. You may talk to me right here."

"As long as we agree this is covered by your vow of confidentiality. Because it's going to blow you away."

"Now, now, I have heard many things over the years, so what you tell me will not be a surprise."

"I wouldn't count on that, Father."

"Why don't you let me be the judge of that? Just tell me what is on your heart."

"You want what's on my heart?"

"Yes, I do."

"All right then, listen up. I kill people. I kill people and I eat them. Usually it's their brains that I eat, but I will eat whatever flesh I can if it comes to that. And it scares me, what I am. I don't want to do it, but I have to. How'm I doing so far?"

There was a long pause. I could hear the good father breathing. Or trying to catch his breath. Finally, he said, "Yes, this is a new one on me. But perhaps you'd better explain a little further."

"You know what a zombie is?"

"I was afraid of that."

"So you do know."

"I know that there have been many things happening that are beyond the human, beyond our experience. Happening right here in our city. I feared that this would be one of them. I was in Haiti for many years, so I am not unfamiliar with this aspect of the supernatural. My dear girl, how did this happen?"

"I don't know. That's the thing. I was almost killed once. Well, was killed. Shot. A supposed drive-by shooting. They never caught whoever did it, but I was revived, somehow. They had me in a body bag at the morgue, and I suddenly sat up and said, 'Give me some coffee.' The poor medical examiner fainted. But I was alive again, only I knew something was wrong with me. I could feel it. It was like, I don't know, like my insides were gone, like my heart and soul were gone, and my mind was in suspended animation. I was aware of things, but not able to *do* anything. It was as much like being a robot as I ever felt. And then I heard a Voice. Distant. It was saying, 'Come.' Like, if I were to walk out of the morgue and keep walking, I would walk toward it and eventually find it."

Father Clemente said, "Yes, this is consistent with bringing someone back from the dead, a *bokor*, a controller."

"Yeah, that's it. That's what it was. A controller. I knew that. I knew that's what this voice was. Well, I've never been one who likes to be controlled. So I started to talk back to this Voice, telling it to shut up."

"You talked back?"

"Yeah."

"Astonishing."

"What is?"

"Just what you describe. Always, the zombie is raised and has no will of its own. I find this quite interesting."

"Well, I find it a living hell. Because I soon realized that the only thing that could keep me walking around was human flesh and brain."

"Wait a moment," he said. "That's troubling."

"Yeah, it is."

"What I mean is . . . that the eating of brains seems to have been something invented by popular culture, relating to a zombie virus or some such. But not the type of zombie who is reanimated by a *bokor*."

"All I know is what I am," I said. "And I know I have to stay alive, so to speak, or else I'll end up in flames."

"Why do you know this?"

"Because I had one of those visions. One of those death experiences. It started in white light, but I got dragged down into screaming death, to demons and torture and regret."

Father Clemente placed his hands together, as if to pray. But he said, "You have been given a most wonderful gift."

"Gift? What kind of—"

"A vision of the eternal, of the damned. It is a warning to you, and an open door."

"Warning by who?"

"I can only speculate that it is God Himself."

"All due respect, Father, I kind of expect that answer from you."

"But this is the odd thing," he said. "Your resistance. Your regret at what you are. That tells me you do have at least the remnant of a soul in you. The question is why? Or how?"

"Here's my question: Is there a way out of this? Can I be brought back to real life?"

Traci Ann stirred. Groaned. Then opened her eyes.

"That's a good sign," Father Clemente said.

"Can I talk to her?" I asked.

"That would be a good idea."

I leaned toward her. "Traci Ann?"

No answer, but her eyes swiveled my way.

"Can you hear me?" I said.

Her eyelids went down, then up. "Where am I?" she said, low and faint.

Father Clemente put his hand on my arm. "Let me," he whispered. Then to Traci Ann: "You are in church, my child. Below the cross of our Savior."

He was testing her. The look on his face was one of expectancy, hope.

Traci Ann closed her eyes again, breathed deeply and let it out with slow relief. "Thank God," she said.

Father Clemente smiled as his grip on my arm tightened. "She's back," he said. He crossed himself.

"What now?" I said.

Father Clemente stood and motioned for me to follow. He went a few steps away from Traci Ann, out of her earshot. "Now is the most crucial time of all," he said. "The forces of darkness that brought this upon her will not be pleased. They will come after you, me, and Traci Ann again. She dare not be left alone. This is the most crucial hour." He removed the crucifix on a beaded necklace from around his neck. "Make sure she puts this on and keeps it on, until the danger is passed."

"But what about you?" I asked.

"I'm ready now," he said. "I won't be taken by surprise. Take her to her home and let her sleep. She will probably sleep for twelve hours. As long as the cross is around her neck, the forces of darkness will not be able to touch her. Their attempts will dissipate over time. Do you understand?"

"I do," I said.

"And yourself, you need protection. They will be after you."

"I hope they find me," I said. "I've been wanting to have a little talk with them."

"Do not underestimate them. Even though you are undead, there are hierarchies of strength."

"Father."

"Yes?"

"Is there any hope. For me?" I sounded like a little girl in a dark room. Well, that's how I felt.

He closed his eyes for a moment. "I must tell you, I have not seen a deliverance like this with the walking dead. But that does not mean it is impossible. I believe with God, nothing is impossible."

Which left a sinking feeling in my chest. "I've asked God to help, but He doesn't."

"Only seemingly," he said.

"What's that mean?"

"It simply means we don't know everything that's going on. God's perspective is not limited like ours."

"So how does that help me?"

"You must pray."

"I've tried that."

"Don't stop."

"How about you pray for me?"

"That's a given," he said. "Now take the poor child home."

By the time I pulled up to Traci Ann's, she was dozing peacefully in the passenger seat. She looked entirely different, though the same. Her skin was clear and her body relaxed. Father Clemente's cross rested upon her chest. A good man, the father, a good priest as priests—

Priest. The one who had given Traci Ann her own crucifix that later showed up in a burned-out Charger with a dead cop in it.

Why had I assumed, why had everyone assumed, it was the same crucifix?

I had to wake Traci Ann to get her into the house. I put her arm around my shoulder, the way a sailor might help a drunken shipmate. Traci Ann groaned with exhaustion.

"Just a few more feet," I said, turning over that priest angle in my mind. Why would a man of the cloth do something like that? It was probably just me looking for any thread, even a crazy one like that.

When we got to the front door, it was wide open.

And completely dark inside.

"Etta?"

No answer. I started to fear the worst. A break-in, a robbery, Etta dead on the floor. Traci Ann was almost a dead weight herself now, falling back to sleep. I found my way in the dark to the sofa and got Traci

Ann situated there. Then I went to flick on a light. Found the lamp by the sofa and turned it on.

Etta's walker was in the middle of the living room. With something taped to one of the arms. A piece of paper.

A note.

I grabbed it. It was written in ink by an artistic hand.

Life for life.
As the owl flies.

The first part was evident. They, whoever they were, had taken Etta, taken her because Traci Ann had been taken away from *them.*

The owl reference was something else. Meant for me, like a riddle.

I went to Traci Ann, jostled her.

"Mmm?"

"Traci Ann, listen. I have to go."

"Mm-hm."

"Do you hear me?"

"Mm-hm."

I threw the little sofa blanket over her, locked the door, and left. Then found myself driving like a maniac toward the Hollywood Hills.

Stranger than that, I heard myself praying.

CHAPTER 36

When I got to the driveway at Minerva's place, the night was as dark as any I'd ever seen in L.A. Even the lights of Hollywood seemed to creep halfway up the hill and fall flat in the dirt, as if afraid to show their luminescent tails. A warm wind blew around me as I got out of Geraldine, and I smelled laurel and sage and the faint odor of barbecue. Somebody was cooking meat. But it wasn't human, so it held nothing for me.

I went right up to the intercom on the driveway, but before I pushed the button, the chauffeur whom I'd met the first time stepped out from a shadow. Or maybe he was the shadow.

He said, "We've been waiting for you."

"You? I thought you didn't work here anymore."

"Don't believe everything you hear in court," he said, smiling.

"Bring me Etta Johnson. The cops are on their way, so you better hand her over."

"You didn't call the authorities. You know that wouldn't be wise. Why don't you come on up to the house and we'll discuss things?"

"Why don't you just bring her down here and we'll have our little talk right out in the open?"

"You don't want that poor old woman becoming the undead, now do you? Your bargaining position is very slight. But it's your choice."

"Open the gate."

"Don't try anything," he said. "This time we are prepared for you."

"You're just cute enough to eat," I said. "Open up."

He clicked something and the gate swung open with an eerie *creak*. If Vincent Price himself had been directing this scene, he couldn't have done it any better.

G Dog led me up the hill. Somewhere deep in the valley a girl screamed. It was either laughter or terror. It echoed over us like the cry of an albatross. I wondered if it was going to be the last sound outside these walls I would ever hear. If it was, so be it. I wouldn't go quietly, that was for sure.

G Dog pushed the door open, again with the creak. "A little WD-40 would work wonders for you people," I said.

G Dog said nothing and waited for me to walk past him into the dark house. Which I did. The door slammed behind me. I didn't see if it was the chauffeur, the wind, or one of those horror movie ghosts who did it. Not that it mattered. I was in the belly of the beast now. Alone.

Or maybe not completely. I had this feeling that I wasn't truly by myself. Maybe it was just me hoping. But it was there, and for some reason it gave me courage.

Then the eyeballs came at me.

I was in a dark hallway. Little lights like fireflies appeared in front of me, then started swirling toward me. When they got closer, I saw that they were illuminated eyeballs, floating around in the air in pairs.

I didn't feel afraid. This whole eyeball shtick was intended to shake me up, and had been that way ever since I was a little girl. But I was no more afraid of it than I would've been at something at Disney's Haunted Mansion.

"You can stop with the eyeballs now," I said. "It doesn't do a thing for me. Whoever you are, take your eyes back and keep them to yourself before I go all Moe Howard on you."

The eyeballs still swirled. A couple of sets blinked. One of them came right up to my face. I made a V out of two fingers and jabbed them.

They popped like soap bubbles. I heard some kind of moan. Then all of them disappeared.

"You're going to regret that," G Dog said.

"Get on with it. Where am I going?"

"To hell," he said.

Minerva was sitting on her throne in the middle of the great room. She had her hands spread out on the arms of the great chair.

"And now who is bowing to whom?" she said.

I looked around the chamber, then back at Minerva. "My knees are straight," I said.

"They will not be. Soon, they will not be!"

"Where is she?" I said.

"Not so fast. First you will show your intentions. You will apologize to me for your disrespect."

"We're a long way from that," I said, trying to figure out how to keep her talking. I still had no idea what she had in mind, except that little phrase kept going back and forth in my head: *Life for life.* "Somebody coached you for the trial," I said. "This was a setup from the start. You said you saw Traci Ann turn into a coyote. Since she wasn't there, somebody told you that's what you should say."

"Silence!"

Minerva was unnerved.

"Who was it, Minnie? Who is behind this whole setup? Who put the frame on Traci Ann?"

"This is more outrage from you!" Minerva said. "And you will pay!" She nodded to G Dog. He went out of the room for a moment, then wheeled in Etta Johnson, gagged, tied to a wheelchair. Her eyes were red and wide.

"Okay," I said. "Just let her go. You and I, we'll talk. But let her go."

Minerva pursed her lips and thrust out her hand like a wicked witch, pointing her craggy fingers at me. I half expected little lightning bolts to come flying out, but nothing happened.

What came flying out was an owl. It screeched and flapped its wings and landed on Minerva's throne, just over her right shoulder. Where it stared at me with its ugly face.

Man, I was getting tired of owls. "Is that it?" I said. "Another one of your rat catchers? What is it with you and these flying uglies?"

The owl hissed at me.

Hissing. Demons. With names.

To the owl, I said, "What is your name!"

"No!" Minerva shouted.

"What is your name!" I said again.

The owl puffed up, spread its wings. It actually *expanded*.

Larger, larger, an owl the size of a refrigerator. And from it came the smell of wet feathers and sulfur. Its big eyes were like lemon pies with black Necco Wafers in the middle.

And then those black irises filled the eyes, until all the color was gone. The overspilling black continued beyond the eyes, to the facial disk and then the whole head, down and out to the wings, the body. The whole bird looked as if it had been dipped in tar.

The sulfur smell was overpowering.

The supersized owl hovered a moment, then began to change shape.

Minerva, by this time, was hiding her face. I glanced over at G Dog. He was on his face on the floor.

The shift continued, into the form of a woman. A woman in great shape.

Slowly, color came back to the woman. Features. Long hair, golden. Eyes, luminescent red. Skin, alabaster.

Body, naked.

But not completely. Two big, fat, emerald-scaled snakes slithered across each breast, their tails covering her lower body.

This chick was wearing a serpentine thong.

But it was the eyes most of all that I was drawn to. It was as if the fires of the sun were behind rubies, set in a face of utmost beauty.

And that scared me more than anything. It was a face that could melt you, hold you, mesmerize you.

Control you.

I fought back with my will. But it was like punching a fifty-foot wave as it breaks over you.

"I am Lilith," the snake woman said. "And you are mine."

CHAPTER 37

My undead bones went cold inside me. "You want to run that by me again?" I said, fighting for bravado.

She floated toward me, then around my body as if to observe me from all points. She seemed to be flesh, but also without physical constraint. "You will be my slave," she said as she returned to hovering in front of me. "You will do what I bid you to do. Just like Minerva. She has been my slave for almost forty years."

Minerva groaned.

"Why should I agree to that?" I said.

"You want us to let the grandmother go? No harm will come to her. The cost is you."

"Life for life?"

Lilith nodded.

I looked at Etta. She was shaking her head at me. She was scared to death.

"That's fine talk," I said. "But how can I trust you? What makes me think you won't to go after her another time?"

"You have already seen the girl you took from me, your client. You have protected her, according to the instructions of that vile priest. So long as both of them

wear the icons that I cannot bring myself to mention,
they cannot be touched."

"And all I have to do is . . . what?"

"Of your own free will place yourself in subjection
to me."

I had been fighting subjection for as long as I had
been reanimated. Every day was a struggle. Now
maybe it was time to give in.

I had no idea what this would do to me. But the deal
was saving a life, and maybe I figured that's the best
I could do under the circumstances. Maybe somewhere
somebody would see it and give me a little credit. Or I
could just spend my days trapped in this body and
doing the will of somebody else, maybe forever. That
was what it was, what I hated most. I was giving up my
own will. The one thing that sustained me through all
the darkness and all the doubts and all the attempts to
control me. I would be giving that up once and for all.

But Etta and Traci Ann would be together, and
maybe that was the best thing this zombie could ever
hope to accomplish.

"It's a deal," I said. "As soon as I get her home and
situated, we can complete the transaction."

Lilith puffed herself up. "No lawyer tricks from
you. You will swear your oath now, and then I will let
her go."

"Now hold on," I said. "This contract is conditional.
My oath will not go into effect until Etta is safe at home."

"No," Lilith said.

"Then it's no deal." A bit of bluffing, a bit of swagger. You have to know when to pull those out.

Lilith paused. Her snakes hissed. "Very well. You
now swear fealty to me. You place your will into my
keeping. You'll swear to this."

I took a long breath. "I swear, subject to Etta being placed in my care."

"You have twenty-four hours. Agreed?"

"Agreed."

"You will return here in twenty-four hours and begin your service."

"Anything else?"

Lilith smiled. I could already feel my will draining out of me. I hung on to it with all my might.

"Have a nice night," Lilith said.

Etta cried all the way home.

"I did not want you to do this," she said.

I kept patting her on the shoulder. "No more of that. I'm a big girl. I can take care of myself. You take care of Traci Ann. You keep her covered with the cross, and you, too. As long as you are covered, you're safe."

"But what will happen to you?"

"You promise me. Promise me you'll do as I say."

Etta sobbed.

"Etta? Promise me. If you do that, all will be well."

"I promise," she said.

It was after midnight when I got back to my loft.

I was hungry. I needed to eat.

I didn't do it, though. I didn't go out. I kept Amanda all locked up.

I didn't know how long I could fight it, the hunger, but I was in a fighting mood. I wouldn't be doing much fighting later, once I placed myself in bondage to Lilith.

And I wondered if I'd be wearing snakes. Boas for the well-dressed zombie.

CHAPTER 38

The next morning I was a wreck. My stomach growled as I got to the office. I couldn't concentrate on anything. My whole body was crying out for human flesh. But I didn't want to satisfy it. If I was going to give myself up anyway, why make things worse?

This is what a heroin addict must feel like. I charged outside. Walked down Broadway, maybe for the last time. I wondered if I could make it to tonight without eating. Just go to my doom and that'd be the end of it.

But the fight was on, and it was, I thought, what a raging alcoholic must go through when slapped into treatment.

I kept passing by my lunch.

A Hispanic family—man, woman, child—as a main course.

An Asian skateboarder for dessert.

And then a little girl, only twelve or so, who looked like a scrumptious hors d'oeuvre. That's when I was filled with such self-loathing I didn't care what happened to me. Let it end here, now, on the street somehow.

So when the Voice came, this time I did not resist.
Come! It said.

"Where?" I said.

Long silence. *Are you kidding?*

"Just tell me where, pal," I said.

I am pleased. Keep walking. Keep listening.

I did.

It was way down where Main runs into Olympic
that the Voice guided me. And then into an office and
apartment building that, from the outside, looked
like it dated from the 1930s. There are many of these
downtown, but this was one I couldn't remember
seeing before.

The Voice told me to go in the front and take the
elevator to the top floor. I did. And then upstairs to
the roof.

There was a garden area here, with some white plastic chairs scattered around. The garden consisted of a
few scrubby plants I could not name. It was like an out-
post of the French Foreign Legion in the desert. The
rest of the roof was hot and empty.

From this vantage point I had a good view of lower
downtown. The Eastern Columbia building dominated, with its turquoise art deco exterior and big
clock. Reminded me that time was not only of the
essence, but also running out on me.

Scanning a little more, my gaze fell on the big red
JESUS SAVES sign that used to top the Church of the
Open Door on Hope Street. They demolished the
church years ago, but somebody saved the sign and
there it was, though not as high as it used to be. It was
street level now.

That was somehow fitting. Satan and Jesus duking
it out on the street over the future of L.A.

I saw something flit off to the side, and saw a

humming bird winging toward some sort of trumpet flower in the garden. Somebody had brought a little natural color to this patio, and nature had brought this little bird to get some nourishment. I watched as it inserted its bill into the trumpet. And for one moment I felt something I hadn't in a long time. I don't know what you'd call it. A sense of beauty maybe?

I didn't have time to analyze, because I heard the hard fluttering of wings. Instinctively, I ducked. Predatory birds were becoming a fixture in my life.

Indeed, I was right. Another owl!

The little hummingbird beat it out of there like a bullet. The owl came to rest on the ledge. And I was mad. I didn't hesitate. In one flowing move I grabbed a plastic chair, spun like a discus thrower, and flung chair as hard as I could at the bird.

Almost got it. It would have been a beautiful hit, too. But at the last moment the owl jumped to the side and shouted, "Hey! What is it with you, with the throwing and the flinging? You're like to kill somebody."

The voice sounded oddly ethnic. Sort of Lower East Side Jewish from the 1920s. But I wasn't going to wait around and analyze. I figured this was just another demon so I commanded, "What is your name?"

"Say, what are you pulling that stuff for?" the owl said. "Worries you don't need. Not from Max."

I shook my head. "Max? What kind of a demon name is that?"

"What are you talking, with the *demon*? I'm one of the good guys."

"Good guys?"

If an owl can sigh, this one did. "Listen, kid, you

got your demons, and you got your good guys. You got your wicked dead walking around, and you also got the good ones keeping up with them. The demons, they want to hurt people. It is our assignment to watch and help."

"Are you trying to tell me all this time, you were helping me?"

"Now she gets it! She with the *Hawaii Five-O* music already!"

I looked around to make sure no one was there, listening to me being insane. "I don't know what I get," I said. "You were a human at one time?"

"Lady, not only was I human, I did three shows a night for eighteen straight years. Let me tell you, the Catskills is no picnic. You don't make the people laugh, they don't tip."

"You were a Catskills comedian?"

"Slapsie Maxie Green. One shot on the Sullivan show. 1956. I ate some bad shellfish. Food poisoning right in the middle of my act. Let me tell you, suicide was on the table. But somebody very good got me over it, and I started looking for God. It's a long story after that, but it comes right up to here. Me, looking out for you."

I was still skeptical. "Why should I believe you?"

"I haven't got much time. You want to waste it with credentials?"

"I'm not convinced I need to listen to you yet."

"You want I should tell you about the ravens who tried to kill you the night you were born? In the back of a Ford? And I chased them off? You want I should tell you all the eyeballs I had to keep away all your life? You got demons looking at you all the time. Let me tell you, they don't go easy."

Whoa. Then it was true. Or seemed to be. "Okay," I said. "You're on my side, then tell me what's happening to me. Who killed me? Or re-animated me? If you're my watcher or protector, tell me some of these answers."

"Believe me, kid, I would if I could. But I don't make the rules. There's only so much I can tell you. Mostly, I got to tell you that you have to make some decisions, you have to use what faith you have. That much I am allowed to tell."

"Come on, man! Or owl. Or whatever you are. I'm going through hell here. You must know that."

"That's not far from the fact, kid. But you got friends in high places, and we are all pulling for you."

"Pulling for me? That's all? That's not good enough!"

"But it is. You don't know how much it is. It's the way it's always been, ever since man came along. I can't tell you more about that now."

"I just contracted my life away."

"All I can tell you is to listen real hard, inside. You got a good voice inside you. You're not all dead. You're a lawyer. And you have things to do. Big things. Everything is heating up."

"You mean with Satan and taking over Los Angeles?"

"I can't say any more. But one thing I do want to say." The owl paused and its face seemed to soften into a smile. "I like you, kid. I like you a lot. If I had a daughter, I'd want her to be just like you."

The owl raised its wings.

"Wait!" I said.

"Got to go. Keep listening."

"Will you be in my head?"

"When I can."

"One more question. What did you mean when you kept saying *Miss Uganda*?"

"English you can't understand? Or I should say Yiddish. Not *Miss Uganda. Meshugana.* Look it up!"

And with that Slapsie Maxie the Owl flapped his wings and took off into sky.

I went back to street level in a daze. Nothing made sense. And I was ticked off about the high places Max talked about. If he was talking God, then why wouldn't he tell me that? If he was my protector, why not protect with information? I felt like a pawn in some cosmic game. And maybe that was the way it was, only it was a game to the death.

I turned up Broadway and headed back to my office. I had a contract to keep.

CHAPTER 39

I arrived at Minerva's just past nine at night.

I was dressed as if going to court. In a nice suit, with purse over my shoulder and briefcase under my arm. If this was it for me, I wasn't going to go without a fight.

We gathered again, as if we'd never left. Lilith wore the same snakes, and I wondered if she had a closet full of serpents. I mean, if she felt like summer, could she put on some rattlers? If her mood changed to autumn, would cobras be just the thing?

She was looking smug.

Minerva was seated on her throne again, and I started to get the picture. Lilith was the one in charge, but had ceded a realm of authority to Minerva.

But when they were in the room together there was no doubt who the big kahuna was.

G Dog stood off to the side, to do any heavy lifting. A real team effort they had going.

"You have kept your appointment," Lilith said. "Very good. You will be an excellent servant."

"I aim to please," I said.

"Your tongue will need to be tamed," Lilith said.

"But that will come in time. First things first. You may kneel now and make your pledge. The deal is struck."

I slipped my briefcase out. "There's one little matter to clear up," I said.

Lilith freaked. She made a big heavy wind blow in the room, flapping the curtains on the windows, making Minerva's hair blow out. It even knocked over a chair. The snakes hissed extra loud.

"Nothing to clear up!" she thundered. "Kneel!"

"But there's no deal, no contract," I said calmly, even though I was a swirling mess of fear inside.

"What you speak is a lie. Kneel!"

"Listen up," I said. "We made a contract in the sovereign state of California. But in any common law jurisdiction, a contract is null and void if entered under duress."

I pulled out some of the notes I'd made at the good old county law library earlier that day. "Mental affliction, if used to compel an agreement, negates mutuality. And duress can be derived from the need to protect an innocent party from imminent harm. That is exactly what happened here last night. Sorry, Toots. No deal."

Lilith said nothing. All the air in the room seemed like warm snake breath.

And then she smiled. One of those horror movie smiles, just before you're slapped in the iron maiden, or sealed up behind a wall.

Uh-oh.

Up I went in the grip of something unseen. I got spun around and tipped upside down. Then whirled around the room. My purse hung off my chin by the strap, like the tail of a kite.

The force let me go and I fell into a wingback chair,

headfirst. The chair went over and I did, too. I sprawled on the floor, dizzy, powerless.

It stinks to be powerless. There's nothing a trial lawyer likes less.

I heard Lilith laughing.

Now there's something a trial lawyer likes—overconfidence. When your opponent is basking in some minor victory, that's your moment to look for a weakness.

My head was still spinning, but I managed to turn it. I saw stuff from my purse on the floor. A tube of my special skin cream. Some loose change.

And a tiny bottle.

What? Oh, yeah, the bottle of holy water Father Clemente had given me. I'd forgotten all about it.

But was it worth anything? Did it have any power?

I wasn't exactly full of options here. I reached out, grabbed the little bottle, and got to my feet, staggering like a drunk.

"Now you will bow!" Lilith screeched.

I uncorked the bottle and, with a whipping motion, sent the water toward Lilith.

It wasn't exactly like the witch in *The Wizard of Oz,* but it must have stung something fierce.

First, the snakes started to sizzle. And then they screeched and writhed all over Lilith's body, a jungle dance of pain.

Lilith reacted like somebody who had had an acid bath.

Minerva screamed. "There will be death! There will be blood!"

I didn't know who the heck she was talking to. But then I saw G Dog. I'd forgotten all about him. He was in the main doorway.

Holding a sword.

Now Lilith seemed to be coming back. Like a fighter coming up off the canvas. If I thought I'd landed a knockout blow, I was sorely mistaken.

G Dog raised the sword and started toward me.

Minerva pointed at me.

Lilith got her groove back.

And then, from behind me, I heard someone enter the room.

Nick!

The little fellow had a ferocious look on his face. He jumped in front of me and shouted, *"Non semper Saturnalia erunt!"*

That did it. The whole place exploded.

At least it seemed to. A flashing of light, a swirling of papers, a wind blowing through the place with gale force.

Nick grabbed my hand and started me for the door. "She's gonna blow!"

I went with him.

Outside, down the driveway.

"Did you follow me here?" I said.

"I am a barometer," he said. "Also, a good investigator maybe, huh?"

We got down to the street. I hopped in Geraldine. Nick drives a Honda. I told him to meet back at the office.

As I was driving away I looked up at Minerva's house.

It was glowing, as if the whole thing was on fire inside.

Against the window I saw the outline of a figure. Minerva. Her hands were on the panes of glass. As if she was trying to escape.

Then the entire roof blew off.

A stream of luminescence shot up into the sky,

black smoke trailing, and such an intense shriek that I had to cover my ears.

I told Geraldine to burn rubber, and she did.

It was almost ten when we got there. In my office, Nick said, "I know about you now. You are one of the walking dead."

"So what? Right now all I want—"

"I must tell you. I am something, too."

"Don't say barometer."

He slid himself into my client chair. "Do you know the Kallikantzari?"

"It sounds like a desert in Africa."

"No!" Nick said. "This is not a matter for which to laugh!"

"I'm not laughing now," I said.

"I was born, in Greece, during the ides of Saturnalia. You do know that Saturnalia was a pagan festival, yes?"

"Explain."

"To mollify the people. To let them soak in foolishness. A curse was placed upon the children of Greece. Any child born was in danger of becoming Kallikantzari. The time of my birth was in the center of the time, so I am what I am. The people think we steal children, but that is not what I do!"

"What is it you do, Nick?"

"I have been brought here to Los Angeles, to be a . . ."

"Barometer?"

"I did not want to say."

"I'll give you a pass. Nick."

"But will you give me a job?"

"I'll think about it, Nick. Tell me what happened back there?"

"We made the demons angry," he said. "That is a good thing. They are irrational that way and we made our escape. But they will not forget. They will come again."

I sighed. "All right, Nick. You and me. We'll take 'em on together."

He jumped around like a kid on Christmas.

"You will see!" he said.

I finally went home. I wondered about all that Nick had said. About demons and not forgetting. About what my father had said, about me maybe being singled out for this.

But all I wanted to do was rest.

I prayed. I asked God for sleep. I think I actually told him to toss me a bone.

Whatever it was, I slept. And did not dream.

Thankfully, I did not dream.

CHAPTER 40

The next day I went out to see Traci Ann. The sun was starting to set on L.A. She was in the backyard, on her knees, weeding a flower garden. A flower garden that had seen better days.

She heard me come up and didn't stop what she was doing. Almost like she'd been expecting me.

"I never thought I'd like flowers again," Traci Ann said. "It's good to get back to it."

"We need to talk," I said.

"I'm doing so well. I can be outside again, smell the roses."

"Look at me, Traci Ann."

Traci Ann said nothing, and continued to poke her spade in the dirt.

"You lied to me," I said. "You've not been up front with me from the start. You've been hiding something and I need to know what it is."

Traci Ann froze a moment. Then she stuck the spade in the ground and turned to me. "I'm sorry," she said.

"Not good enough."

"I can't."

"Why not?"

"I'm afraid."

I sat down in the dirt with her. "You can't exist in fear, Traci Ann. There are things bigger than both of us here. They want to destroy you. They will destroy you."

She was silent. And that's when I noticed she wasn't wearing something.

"Where is your crucifix?" I said.

Traci Ann looked at the ground.

"Why aren't you wearing it?" I said. "Look at me."

She did. In the dying light I could see fear on her face. She looked like she wanted to speak, but something was holding her back.

Behind me Etta said, "What's the matter, dear ones?"

She was hobbling toward us with her walker.

"It's all right, Grandma," Traci Ann said. "Ms. Caine wanted to talk to me."

"Oh?" Etta said. "Can I get you something to drink. Hot cocoa perhaps?"

"I was just telling Traci Ann to put on her crucifix," I said. "And you, too, Etta. You must wear them. Believe me."

"I'm sorry, dear," Etta said. "I've been so upset."

"I understand, of course," I said.

"Maybe we should, Grandma," Traci Ann said.

Etta nodded, and sighed deeply.

Then she lifted her walker and threw it over my head, and kicked me in the face.

I thudded back into the flowerbed. Little roman candles exploded behind my eyes.

I heard Traci Ann scream.

Forcing myself up, I saw Etta, or something in the form of Etta, biting into Traci Ann's neck.

With all the strength I could muster I got up and

grabbed the Etta-thing by the house dress and pulled it off Traci Ann.

Then it was a street fight.

The Etta-thing bared its fangs and hissed.

"What's your name?" I said.

The Etta thing laughed. And flew at me with fists.

I spun, doing a Krav Maga pirouette, and elbowed the Etta-thing in the face. I felt hard teeth under my skin.

"Get your crucifix!" I yelled at Traci Ann. "Now!"

Etta-thing shot out its fist, ramming my chest. It was strong, and knocked me back about ten feet.

It took off after Traci Ann, who was almost to the house.

I got up and charged, having the angle. I got there just before Etta-thing and tackled it. It growled and hit me with the back of its hand.

Once more I sprawled.

It rushed through the door of the house.

I got up and followed. "Traci Ann!"

I heard a scream.

Only it wasn't a scream of fear. It was a scream of outrage.

In the living room I saw what it was. Traci Ann was wearing the crucifix and holding it out toward the Etta-thing, which had turned away from the cross.

And was now looking at me.

"You'll pay," Etta-thing said.

"Get out," I said.

It hissed at me. Then turned into a bat and flew at my head.

I smacked the flying rat, right in the snout.

Then it zipped out of the room and out the back door.

CHAPTER 41

We found Etta, the real Etta, lying on the floor of her bedroom. She was out. Looking dead. Except her chest was going up and down. Barely.

I had Traci Ann bring a wet washcloth. I dabbed Etta's head until she started to groan.

"Etta," I said. "Can you hear me?"

"Mmmmm."

"It's Mallory Caine."

"I'm . . ."

"Easy."

". . . sorry."

We helped her up to a sitting position, then onto the bed. She wore no cross. I told Traci Ann to get the other one and put it on her grandmother.

As soon as she did, Etta got a little more peaceful. "I'm so sorry," she said. "He looked nice."

"Who did?" I said.

"The man at the door. I let him in."

"What did he look like?"

"Handsome," she said.

"Anything else?"

"Dark and handsome. Dressed nice."

That wouldn't help.

"You rest now," I said. "Traci Ann, come with me."

I put Traci Ann in a chair in the living room and said, "Now tell me what you're hiding."

"They said they'd kill me," Traci Ann said.

"They can't hurt you if you do what I say. I'm getting to know these guys now. So talk, and trust me."

"I'm sorry I lied," she said.

"Forget it."

"It's like this, Ms. Caine. I got picked up in Hollywood one night. By that big black car, remember I was telling you? What I didn't tell you was that I thought the big black car had somebody else in it. Somebody who was seeing me on the side as a regular thing. Somebody who didn't want anyone to know."

"An actor?" That was a good guess in this town.

Traci Ann shook her head. "He said if I told anybody about us I'd be, you know, taken out. I didn't care. I wasn't going to tell. The money was good. Real good. At the start. Then it dried up and he expected it for free."

"Who was it?"

"He said he was in love with me and he was going to leave his wife, but he needed to make something of me. You know, a makeover."

"Like Eliza Doolittle."

"Who?'

"Never mind. Who was it?"

"You mean, who is it. He's still out there and I'm still afraid of him."

"You don't have to be," I said. "First of all, I'm your lawyer and this is all confidential. But even so, I've learned these people bank on fear."

Traci Ann's face grew tight, and she didn't speak.

"Listen," I said. "There's a lot going on here I don't quite get yet, but know that there are forces that want to hurt good people. And I've learned about bullies. The only way to handle 'em is to stand up to 'em. If you're willing to take that chance, I'll be right there with you. You don't have to be in this alone. None of us does."

She took in a deep breath. "Okay, Ms. Caine. I'll tell you. It was the mayor."

"Garza?"

Traci Ann nodded. This news did not come as a shock to me. Nothing that happens here can shock me anymore. Besides, it just seemed to fit.

"So who was the other guy in the car?" I asked.

"I never saw him before. But he bit me and as I was fading out, thinking I was dying, he said I would do whatever he willed, whenever he willed it."

I sat back and processed that information. Pieces of this puzzle started to lock in. A few of them I may have had to force, but still a picture was emerging.

I said, "The man who became a wolf, who attacked you in court. Did you recognize him?"

She shook her head. "He smelled, though."

"Like what? All I smelled on him was fur."

"Sort of like stinky eggs."

Sulfury. The stink of hell.

CHAPTER 42

Downtown, next morning. In the tallest building. I went through the reception area without stopping. The woman at the desk squeaked a protest. I kept right on going, down the corridor, and right through the heavy oak door of Charles Beaumont Manyon's office.

He was at his desk, leaning back in his chair with his hands behind his head.

"Been expecting you," he said.

The harried receptionist came in behind me, spouting apologies to Manyon. He waved at her. "It's all right, Jen. Just close the door for us, will you?"

Jen gave me a hard look, then left us.

Manyon said, "Now why don't you tell me what's going on in that fevered undead brain of yours?"

The smell of his cologne was strong, like the first time I met him. I wondered if he did that on purpose, to make his opponents sick.

I said, "You're the mayor's lawyer, aren't you?"

"I told you as much the first time we met."

"How much do you know about the mayor's extra-curricular activities?"

Manyon's friendly, avuncular face became hard. I could see in his eyes the cold-blooded killer he must be in court. "Whatever do you mean by that, Ms. Caine?"

"He was seeing my client, Traci Ann Johnson, on the side. And he's threatened her. I'm here to deliver a message. Back off. Will you tell the mayor I said so?"

"Ms. Caine, I find your tone a bit odd and aggressive."

I caught another whiff of his cologne. But this time mixed with another scent. Not a pleasant one. What was he covering? Massive B.O.?

I said, "What do you know about the mayor's rise to power?"

Manyon said, "I don't think I owe you any information about my client, Ms. Caine. I think I'll ask you to leave."

He was getting heated. And as he did, the bad smell got stronger. Sulfurous.

Rotten eggy.

"Wait a second," I said. "You don't come from Oklahoma at all, do you?"

"Excuse me?"

"You. You have a connection with the devil, don't you?"

Manyon stood behind his desk.

"Let me see if I get this right," I said. "Los Angeles has a mayor that the forces of darkness control, because they put him there. This mayor sold his soul some time ago, in exchange for power. But then he got to be a problem. Started to believe his own press notices maybe. Wouldn't take orders like he used to. Something like that. How'm I doing?"

"You're on thin ice," Manyon said.

"So one night they take the mayor's mistress, a young hooker, and turn her to their will. They make her a vampire. And they hold this over the mayor's head. He either gets back in line, or they will use her to bring him into submission."

Manyon's teeth began to bare.

"You didn't want to just kill him," I said, "or bite him into submission. You wanted to make an example of him. Because you have a whole bunch of people getting into positions of authority, and what you want is their *willing* submission. That's the key to the whole thing, isn't it?"

"My stars," Manyon said.

"So you were the one who turned Traci Ann into a vampire. You were the one who showed up last night in the form of Etta Johnson. You are a lawyer and a vampire and can shift your shape."

"Should that be news? Aren't we all bloodsuckers from the start? Why not revel in it? Why not glory in it? Don't you see, Ms. Caine, that's why I want you to come work with me."

"And submit?"

"I call it partnership, Ms. Caine."

"'And the devil showed him all the kingdoms of the world, in a moment of time, and said, "All this I will give you, if you will only worship me."'"

Manyon nodded. "That's a very good deal, Ms. Caine. Jesus was a chump for not taking it. We are the winning side. But it's even better than that! We're the underdogs, the ones they've always said would lose in the end. But have you seen the world lately? Which side is on the upswing? Don't you want to be part of that?"

"I choose what I want to be part of."

"Do you?" He got up and came out from behind his desk. "You think you have any free choice? You're undead and headed for hell. You can't do anything about that. It's over for you. All over. You need to embrace it now. Squeeze as much juice as you can from it. Rule, while it's still possible."

"And if I don't?"

He smiled under his bushy moustache. "Slavery. Disaster. Forced submission. You don't want that, do you?"

I looked at that face, the one they said could hold a jury mesmerized. And for just a moment I thought I saw something there. A small pinprick of uncertainty, maybe even fear.

Or maybe it was just my imagination, as fevered as it was. But now I'd come around from where I was. I wanted to keep going. I wanted to find out more.

"You're not as fearsome as you think you are," I said.

"Don't allow yourself to think that," he said.

"If you could have stopped me, you would have by now."

He sighed. "This is your last chance."

"Then I have only one thing to say," I said. *"Non semper Saturnalia erunt."*

I started out of the office.

"Don't think that this is over, Ms. Caine!"

I opened the big fat door.

"Don't think you can be protected forever. You hear me!"

I slammed the door shut and made my way to the elevator, then out to the street. The air in L.A. seemed fresh for a change, even downtown. Across the street, the central branch of the L.A. library glistened in the sun.

And right on the library ledge, looking at me, was an owl.

I think it was Max.

CHAPTER 43

I met Aaron at the top of Angels Flight. We looked down at the splendid L.A. afternoon. City Hall was looking normal again, against blue sky. For a moment it seemed like the world was back to what it should be—even though I knew it would never be the same again.

"Now that we've determined that the evidence was planted," Aaron said, "we won't be refiling on Traci Ann Johnson."

"A wise move," I said.

"But somebody killed that cop. Horribly."

"He was dirty, Aaron. I suggest you look deeper."

"Do you know something?"

"I know many things." I bobbed my eyebrows at him. "I know that you are also going to drop the case against Harry Clovis."

"Why would I do that?"

I faced him. "Because Bracamonte was another dirty cop, and he was a zombie when Harry cut his head off. Self-defense, Aaron."

Aaron said nothing.

I went on. "And I know Bracamonte was out digging up dirt on the opponents of the mayor."

"How do you know that?"

"Aaron, it's me, Mallory."

"And it's me, Aaron. I still call it murder. And there's a little matter of a judge who lost his head in the same way. I wonder if you know anything about that?"

"I wonder if you wonder."

He smiled and shook his head. "I don't wonder about us needing to be together."

"Aaron, I have to tell you something about me. . . ." Was I going to do it? Tell him what I was? I wanted to. I wanted him to know.

"Okay," he said. "Tell me."

"I . . ."

"Yes?"

"Have trouble with commitment."

Aaron laughed. "This isn't over, Mallory. I'm a persistent guy."

"I'm sort of counting on that," I said.

Aaron left to go prosecute some poor slob. I stayed up there another half hour or so, then went to see my father at the men's jail.

As a deputy shackled him to the interview table, I looked at my father's eyes. They were red with dark circles underneath, setting suns dropping into black seas.

"Hey, Harry," I said. "You hanging in there?"

He nodded. Slowly.

"We'll fight this thing," I said. "Don't give up hope."

The thin wisp of a smile moved his whiskers upward. "Can I tell you something?" he asked.

"Sure."

"I just wanted to say, I think you turned out to be a

really good person. I'm glad you're my daughter, even though I tried to kill you."

"That's okay, Dad," I said. "Family misunderstanding."

"You called me *Dad*."

"Yeah, I guess I did."

He jangled his shackles, as if he had wanted to reach out toward me. "We can get you healed. We can save you from this fate."

I sighed, wanting to believe him, but not knowing what to believe.

Then I did something very unlawyerlike. I reached over the table separator and touched his hand. And wonder of wonders, hope of hopes, I realized I did not have the slightest urge to eat him.

You have no idea how much that meant to me.

That evening, back at the office, Nick and I popped a bottle of champagne to celebrate our new partnership—Mallory Caine, attorney-at-law, and Nick Papadoukis, private investigator.

At one point Nick went back to his office to fetch his *bouzouki*. I was standing at the window looking out at the city I love and saw, not the lights this time, but the darkness between the lights. Encroaching, as if it were an oil spill heading toward the beach at Santa Monica.

And I felt a helplessness of my own. Out there were people I had been fated to kill and eat. Why me?

Because also out there was someone who had tried to murder me, and someone who had raised me from the dead.

And demons. And vampires and werewolves and tourists.

And owls. Please, if I never see another owl . . .

And me in the middle of it. Between forces of good and evil, both trying to have their way.

Nick came back and started playing Greek folk songs. I sat in my chair, leaned back, and just listened. The little guy can't sing worth a lick, but it was sweet somehow. And that was enough.

For one brief moment in this hellacious existence of mine, I was happy.